Raven: a conspiracy

by

Rachel McJury

conFAB Books
Scotland

Printed in Scotland

First Printing, 2020

ISBN: 978-1-8382052-0-1

conFAB Books
Glasgow, Scotland

Cover Design by: Danielle Banks
www.daniellebanks.co.uk

Printed by: Mixam, Watford, WD25 7GS UK

www.confab.org.uk

Grateful acknowledgement to
Dee, Mary and Alison

Part One

Chapter One

I don't remember the first time. Why would I? Why would I remember something so easy, so part of myself? And it was easy then, when my own form was not fixed so. My grandmother, I call her grandmother as she was all the immediate family I ever knew. She was sister, brother, mother, father, grandmother all in one compact frame and form. I wanted for nothing.

I was really tiny, just a few weeks old. She had put me down next to the cabbages that were just coming into bloom. I had been contented, gurgling and chirping to myself, when suddenly there was silence, only the gentle murmur of the bees to break the peace and that was when she said she knew. She dropped her trowel and peered into the basket, seeing what she knew she would see, nothing. She said at that moment she felt such pride, such joy she had not felt before tempered by as much fear. Fear for the present – what if she was too late and there was no getting me back? Fear for the future, and all that it promised. But mostly she felt love. Love that she had been waiting for all her life; love she had always believed in; love that had come to her in the dead of night with a timid knock and a basket left on the stoop of her door. Before she had even met me she had felt me, believed in me and loved me. She said the details had been vague. They always are, and it is always the detail that matters the most. But still she had been waiting. All of that in an instant and then she knew to follow the bees.

They were making a lot of noise, excited. I was enjoying the freedom of my new-found wings. I could move so fast and the world was a blur of colour and scent so strong and heady it was glorious. At least that's how it's been since so it must have been then because I cannot remember. She says she did not know how to find me. Would I be bigger than the rest? Smaller? Or worse, was my talent such I was no different? What if the other bees detected an invader and turned their sting to attack me? What if I fought back? What if my venom mixed with them and a new hybrid of human bee was born? But she said a smile soon filled her being. She followed the sound of the bees, their excited buzzing, and she saw them rise up and down, circling. She says she heard them laugh and knew everything was as it should be.

A tear of peace and joy rolled down her check as she watched the bees teach me their wisdom, saw the way they were ready to catch me if I fell, guided me if I flew too high, the way they laughed with love when I stumbled on an air current and spun in circles, out of control. I learnt how to fly before most other things, walking, talking and the like. But then how would she get me back? Should she get me back? But inside her she had seen a long future together, in human form, not with a resident bumble bee. She did not need to be afeard for soon I grew tired, came to rest on a dandelion, then soon came to flatten the dandelion as I regained my human form, my default. The bees danced around my head like a halo or a crown and went upon their way as I fell into a deep and peaceful slumber. She says she gathered me up back into my swaddling, placed me in my basket, took me inside, put me down on the table, took a draft of ale for herself and sat.

She sat looking at my peaceful repose, feeling the joy inside my soul, falling deeper in love and wondering what to do. What to do between now and when words would make sense to me and she could say 'No shifting today.' But how to cope till then when any number of beasts I would encounter. Creepy crawlies, four legs, two legs, wings, and what of other humans? Did my gift travel that far? How could she protect me from myself? Shifting was already a gift we were not supposed to possess. We were already a secret, denied our freedom for no good reason. What reason can there be to deny another's freedom, to deny their right to be? And as she sat there, watching, falling, loving so, all the beasts she feared would take me from her came and sat with her. Mother Spider walked across her palm. Brother Fly sang in her ear. Her cat sat next to my basket, grooming and purring. The cow and pig danced and sang in the yard. The brook gurgled, the sun shone through the window and the breeze carried the scent of Mother Earth. It was then that my grandmother knew she was not alone in her task, knew I was child of the Earth and that would be enough. I do not know if she ever asked about my birth parents, if she sought their names or how they knew. For when I asked all she would ever say was I was child of the Earth – what more did I, could I, know?

After that, she said, there was no stopping me, but always she was present, always attentive, her friends, the beasts of the earth, and my guides, made sure of it. By the time I can remember I had woven webs, dug burrows as a home, chased hares in the dusk light, chewed grass into curd, stolen cream from the top of the milk and curled up to sleep in front of the fire. I was strong and fluid, but to keep it a secret must have been so hard. We lived in a cottage just enough on the outskirts of town to be independent but not isolated - not for fear of loneliness but for fear of attention. There is no person so well observed as a recluse whose every move is known by all folk around. My grandmother understood that being a face in the crowd was the only way to be a true recluse.

We had a small patch of land that served us well but all beasts need other beasts and so it was with us. There was not a person in the shire who did not turn to my grandmother when a malady could not be cured, be it of the heart or of the flesh. Discretion was part of my grandmother's valour and we were largely left alone and protected. There were not many families or lovers in the shire that had not had use of her services with the unwanted fruits of their desires. My grandmother was a keeper of the shire's shames and her silence was in everyone's interest. Most who received her assistance were also appreciative and understood the value of her knowledge so sought no harm to her, to us. Although they would never say out loud, they knew her wisdom would always be needed, no matter what the scholars and politicians and men of God decreed. When we brought flour, we got more than we paid for. When we ordered two draughts of ale we were only charged for one. We were comfortable and protected, our place in the community understood, but for how long, we did not know. For as with all beings, our lives were fragile, dependant on a fine, tenuous balance.

I was not the only baby left on my grandmother's stoop but I was the only one she kept. Some were gifted and some ungifted. The gifted, of course, were hard to place. Their homes had to be sought through the intricate and secret connections of our kind. The ideas that man used to master man had changed but we had not. The ungifted could be placed more freely, but even then, secrecy played a part. Up and down the country my grandmother placed these lost souls with labourers, husband men, lawyers, and even gentry. Her connections were vast and spanned the length and breadth of the country. My grandmother navigated the dark waters of people's shame to unite souls and find homes for love. And she was cautious, she listened closely until she found the right match, even if that match did not lead to peace but a pain that must be trod all the same. She was known as Grandmother Iris across the land from the richest to the poorest but you would never hear her name spoke, certainly never in good company and only with due respect in bad. But I was the one she kept, the one she had been waiting for, her very own foundling.

It was a spring morning in 1500, she says, when she opened the door to let in the fresh clean air and fill her lungs and heart with joy. I was not a surprise. It is hard to surprise one who listens to the earth so acutely. She had heard the basket gently placed on the stoop, felt the pain, the fear of my birth mother as whoever left me turned and hurried away. She waited a discreet amount of time before opening the door. She already knew what I looked like, a bundle of flesh, thick dark hair and blue eyes. She already recognised my smell. She knew the sound I made when she picked me up and held me in her arms. I looked into her eyes and I was home, bound by love and something much deeper, more than love, something I will know but not understand for many ages to come. All around me was life, happy open life. Life at peace with living. My new home was humble, but we were wealthy beyond imagining. My grandmother had a round open face, her hair, long since grey, tucked away under her bonnet, her eyes a pale blue, almost misty, and wise. Her smile enfolded me in comfort, her smell an afternoon of baking and roasting in a cosy kitchen. We smiled and the Earth sighed. 'You'll do,' she said. She knew my name was Raven but would not call it until I had chosen it.

I do not remember any pain. Mostly I remember joy and wonderment. We lived quietly, the two of us. The townsfolk knew of me. There must have been great speculation as to why I had been kept. It must have been a concern; was my grandmother now setting up an orphanage to challenge the monks? Would the shire's secrets be paraded about town. But I only vaguely remember the pausing in conversations when we went to the local stores or the curious looks as we went about our business. It did not feel hostile, just nosey; we were a harmless topic of conversation and gossip. I think now I must have had questions of my own, but they did not seem important enough to ask. We had all and more than we needed but now I wish I had had more curiosity.

The first time I remember shifting, I was standing at the medicine table. Ours was a modern cottage with a fireplace, chairs and a bench in front. Reeds covered our floor and made a comfortable bed in front of the fire. We had a wooden sink in front of the only window, a raised area in the rafters for storage, hiding and sleeping. Our cottage was perched on a bank leading down to a brook that led into the town, the castle and the local river; to our left was a woodland that became a forest and two deer parks cradled us. We were surrounded by a bounty that overflowed the medicine table with remedies.

The rest of the table was covered in pots, pestles and mortar, earthenware vases and boxes, herbs and plants, valued parts of beings, some that had taken their seller a lifetime to collect with dangers overcome, storms at sea survived, bribes given, paths through jungles and deserts trodden to return battered but triumphant with a small priceless bounty. All to cure a malady for someone far, far away. My grandmother said it was bigger than that. That all things are connected and we are to help each other out. I stood in front of the table, looking at the jars and pots and plants; my grandmother had not told me their names or their uses or their properties, I had not been told how to use them, but standing in front of them I felt a deep connection with them. They lost physical form and appeared to me vibrant, radiating energy, their colours shifting and shimmering. I saw their form, their matter, but it was not that that spoke to me. I sensed their purpose.

Later my grandmother calls this intuition, says we are all born with it but most loose connection to it. But with me she encourages, develops it, tests it. I can sense what the substances inside the bottles do because I am part of them and they part of me. It is comforting, peaceful to be surrounded by the jars, remedies, herbs, like being inside myself. My thick dark hair is tied back in a ponytail, kept short. Sometimes Grandmother uses my hair in remedies which is good - I don't want my hair long. I wear trousers – how can you climb a tree in a dress? I am young enough, and we have started young so no one will be the wiser.

Standing in this peace next to the table I look down and my right hand has changed. My body feels fluid, nothing is fixed. It flows, is connected and unfixed. Green scales spread across my hand. I sense everything, my sense of smell is acute. I can feel the hairs on my body as they react to the air, the energy about me. I watch the scales spread up my arm. I think I should be scared but they are so beautiful, the colours shimmering and dancing. I concentrate and discover I can control the spread of the scales, let them progress or make them retreat. Inside I laugh; this is fun. I let the scales spread till I am covered. I change size and shape. I move differently. I can do things, feel things, sense things differently. I see through different eyes but still I am present. I am a little clumsy in this new body. I smash and knock things over, yet I can move so fast. If this new body could I'd be squealing with joy. Grandmother stands in the doorway, tells me to stop, to come back, her tone is calm but firm. I do not argue and, somehow, I know how to come back. The scales recede from my body and I sense the same fluidity I did before and then it is like coming into land, like I drop back into myself. She sits down by the fire and sits me on her lap.

'I had hoped for more time, but we are here so must proceed. Your gift is great, and you must treat it with great respect as with it comes great responsibility,' she says.

'What creature was I?' I ask.

'A dragon lizard.' she replies.

'What's a lizard?' I ask.

'Well, apparently you know very well what a lizard is...'

'But...'

'You must tell no one of this gift, do you understand?'

I nod.

'Good, tell no one. Now off you go.' I climb down from her knee, out into the yard to climb my favourite tree, full of awe and joy at knowing I can do this wonderous thing. Not caring that I don't know why I can do this or for what purpose. It does not matter then that my gift is a secret.

Chapter Two

Of course, after that I experiment. Grandmother said not to tell anyone, not to not shift. Why would I not practice? At first it seems to happen at its own will. I am playing or doing a chore in the garden or around the house and suddenly I am growing fur and a tail. I feel timid but sharp and totally alert, my body is light and my paws tiny but the perfect size to grasp a nut or an oat. At first, I think my grandmother doesn't know. We are a house of secrets, so it seems natural to hide things. She did say tell no one. But she observes as I learn. I learn that at first the shifting happens because I am near the beast that I shift into, that I am drawn to the beast and it triggers this reaction in me.

I am in the garden tending the vegetables and I see a large fat earthworm and I decide to see if I can stop the shifting. I feel the tingle in my toes and look down to see my feet shrinking out of their boots. I feel my insides become fluid and I tell myself to stop. I fight with all my might. I struggle and wrestle with all the energy I can muster, hoping that the shifting hasn't already taken. It's like a huge storm is raging inside me. Every part of my body is torn in different directions; the pain is unbearable. Every part of me is confused. I fall to the ground, rolling in the mud, flattening and destroying what should grow to feed us for weeks. I have no sense of where I am. I am lost in darkness. I feel I am tiny, torn apart fragments all pulling in different directions. I am terrified. Then I hear her voice and my grandmother is singing. I do not recognise the words; they form shapes I have not heard before and yet I seem to know them and, together with the tune, they are calling, as if the Earth is singing, calling to me. Her voice gets louder, stronger, and my fear begins to abate. All the shattered fragments are drawn together and slide into place like a puzzle. I feel the earth under my feet. I have feet. I look down and the darkness lifts and I am in one piece, my grandmother's arms are around me and her voice singing in my ear. I surrender to her embrace and we sink to the ground, held by the earth as she sings me to sleep.

I awake on a bed of reeds and blankets by the fire. I feel shaky inside. Everything is vibrating but the dull ache of confusion in my head makes me feel weighted and heavy. Grandmother hands me a bowl of pottage and some bread. Food has never tasted so good and soon the internal shakes subside yet the throbbing in my head remains. I am filled with a sense of horror. I feel I have betrayed myself. Grandmother comes and sits by the fire, chewing an arrowroot. We sit in silence, as we often do, but I do not feel the usual peace. Eventually, I can bear it no longer; I am filled with questions that have no answers, filled with questions I am not sure I want the answers to. I turn to look at Grandmother; she knows my question without its asking.

'The intention was right, but the method confused,' she says. I do not understand, this again she senses. 'To harness your gift is essential, to work in partnership so your gift is your aid, of benefit to you, of benefit to the earth and all beasts within. But fighting your gift will never do.'

'But if my gift is my gift why does it not do my will?'

'Your will will only get you so far.' Before I can protest, she says, 'Now the sun is setting, and you have just enough light to clear up the mess in the garden.' She looks at me with kind but sure eyes. I know that look and know there is no argument. I stand, feeling the weight of my mistake. It is the first time I ever feel uncomfortable in my body.

Outside the air is fresh and clear which helps a fraction. The vegetables look broken but on closer inspection I am able to restore much. To feel the earth between my fingers is good and soon my work is complete. I sit and, as the first moon's rays grace the garden, an earthworm creeps out of the mud. It curls its tail and looks at me. I am filled with an overwhelming sense of humility and for some reason it feels like a release and I know then what I will do when next I shift.

I do not waste time the very next day. I know I must try. Grandmother has been called to assist a birth and may be gone for many hours. I take this opportunity to take a break from my duties. It won't take long. I sit in front of our cat Bronwyn and will myself to shift. Bronwyn is curled up by the fire in Grandmother's favourite spot. She is choosing to ignore me. She knows I am there but is persistent in her sleep. I try again, try to focus everything on Bronwyn, willing my body to change, but nothing happens. I don't understand. Before it has been so easy. I haven't wanted it to happen and it has; now when I do, nothing. I poke Bronwyn; maybe she has to be awake for it to work. She frowns at me and tucks her head under her paw.

I try again – nothing. It does not occur to me to seek a different animal or a different place. Why would that make a difference? I do not think how it has been before. How I have been before. It had just been there and now it's not. I do not understand. I try again, almost bursting with effort, red checks and frowning face. If I'd have known how to curse I would have. I do not know this feeling but it's a power within me, a force that feels it is being denied and I try again. But nothing happens. Then I open my mouth and scream. Bronwyn is on her feet and gone before I have finished. A fire consumes my body. I grab reeds from the floor and toss them where ever they go, throw them into the fire. Anything I can grab I throw and smash. The chair is snapped into kindling, the medicine table swept clear, bottles and jars sent any which way, not caring what is lost, what is broken. It takes but a few moments to wreck and spoil almost all we have. I beat my fists upon the now bare boards of the table and howl in confusion and frustration and fear. I feel betrayed, by what, I am not sure. Confused as to why I have this, so called, gift. Frightened I have lost it. Tears roll down my checks. I crawl into a corner and hide, curled into a ball, resting my head on my knees and wait for the tears to stop. I have no sensation in my body at all.

As they do I feel the heat in my body leave and it is as if I have come back into myself. Bronwyn returns; slowly she walks around the room, sniffing the debris, stepping around broken earthenware. She walks up to me. I turn my head away towards the wall and curl up tighter. She sits down by my side and gently mews. I refuse to respond. She tries again, louder. I turn away, as much as I can. Why should I respond when she wouldn't let me shift. But she gently places her paw on my knee and quietly but surely insists I pay attention. Reluctantly I turn my gaze towards her. She withdraws her paw and turns to look about the room. I cannot help but follow her gaze. I feel a new sensation; it's unpleasant and I chose not to name it. A choice later, I will regret. I look at the devastation I have caused. I do not know what to do. Bronwyn sits down and begins to calmly wash, licking her paws and sweeping her ears and checks. Then I know.

Slowly I crawl out of my corner. I wipe my eyes and face and come to stand. I adjust my linen, my doublet and hose, and set about repairing what I can. I return what is not broken to the medicine table, carefully putting everything in its usual place. There are a few gaps. I gather up what contents I can from the broken pots and gather up the broken pieces. They will be useful in the garden for soil drainage, at least. I lay down what reeds I can and then lay new ones. I have never sewn before but studying my grandmother has served a purpose and I repair what I can of what I have torn apart. I build up the fire and rescue what I can of the pottage. All this supervised by the watchful eye of Bronwyn. It takes some time but eventually a semblance of order and restoration to what was before has been achieved. I am behind on my chores and the animals need tending so I do not have time to ponder my actions. I work fast and diligently and dare not think of what has suffered because of me. To work is a relief, a distraction from myself; it is the first time it has felt thus.

It is late by the time I am done and a clear moon, a day away from full, fills the night sky. It's beauty almost an affront. I am exhausted, my bones throb and my brain is heavy, full of static energy. When I step inside the cottage I find Grandmother sitting by the fire, Bronwyn curled up at her feet, a tankard of ale at her side. I stand in the doorway unsure.

'It has been a long day. You must be tired,' she says, without turning her gaze from the fire. I do not know how to respond so do nothing. 'You'll need to rest,' she says and indicates with the tankard the blankets she has set out for me by the fire. I say nothing but remove my boots, my doublet and crawl inside the blankets. 'I see we need some more bog-myrtle. Tomorrow when the moon is full you may go and collect more.' I look up at her, ready with apologises, but she raises her hand to silence me, she bids me goodnight and wishes me gentle dreams.

Chapter Three

The next day is as usual; we rise with the sun, tend the animals, the garden, the cottage. We breakfast then it's my turn to do the laundry. Grandmother spends all day working at the medicine table, repairing and restoring, but there is no recrimination; we are easy and at peace with one another. I want her to be angry though. Why does she not hate me for my stupidity and selfishness? How can she forgive me so easily? I pick up the bag of laundry and head for the door.

'It is easy to love when life is easy, but love is of greatest value when it is needed,' she says, answering the question I dared not ask her. How did she do that? I want to say so much, to thank her, to apologise, tell her how much I love her. How I was scared, frightened. How I didn't understand, still don't understand. But all I say is, 'Sorry.'

'Accepted,' she says, 'now on with your work. You have a long night ahead.' I don't know what she means, collecting bog-myrtle is an easy task, one I could do in my sleep, and really doesn't take long when you know where to look. This time doing the laundry makes sense, for the first time as I use the beating of the cloth against the stone as release for these confused, conflicting energies that burn inside me.

After dinner we sit watching the flames in the fire. I feel nervous and expectant, but I don't know why. I am stalling, and my grandmother knows it. She lets the heat of the fire settle in my bones and then says, 'Bog-myrtle is an accommodating plant, but it still needs encouragement to make its way on to our table.' She smiles, and her kindness and love wash over me. There is nothing I would not do for her. I get to my feet. I want to tell her how much I love her but instead I say, 'Madame, excuse me for as convivial as your company is I have a great task afore me.'

'Why, kind sir,' she re-joins, 'of course you must fulfil your calling. May your journey be fruitful.'

I bow a sweeping bow, grab my cloak and hanging bag and step out into the cool night air.

The moon is bright and the sky cloudless, I'll not need a flame. I head into the woodland. After many years of our tramping, a clear path leads towards the forest. Under the trees it is dark, but the moon's light breaks through the gaps, creating a pattern of silver on the earth. It's great fun to dance between the patterns, in and out of the light. Before I get to the forest I take a left through a less travelled path towards the meadows which is actually a bog land that gets flooded in the winter. No trees grow there and, from a distance, in the summer, it looks like a lush green meadow in the heart of the woodland until one steps there and sinks down. The meadows will be rich in bog-myrtle at this time of year. Collecting herbs and plants for Grandmother is one of my favourite things to do, not least because of the wandering, the exploring for a purpose. Night gathering is a thrill as the world comes to life with different beasts. I reach the meadows; they glisten in the moonlight, an island of possibility.

I can see the bog-myrtle, its eager, hungry heads. I take my knife from my bag, bend down and address the plant.

'Bog-myrtle, thank you for your gift.' Gently I ease the plant from its moorings and, with care, place it inside my bag. Bog-myrtle is a powerful but temperamental plant and will work best when cosseted. I take several plants in this manner then I spot it, catching the moon's rays; it's beautiful. The Moon Flower, so called because during the day it closes up, looks plain and dull in sunlight, but by night it blossoms and opens. Rather than taking in light it seems to radiate light, an echo of the moon. This will make up for all my wrong doings. Grandmother will surely be proud and grateful.

It is away in the middle of the bog. Some would be afeared for sinking mud; there is many a tale told, and ballad sung of weary travellers falling prey to a bog on a moonless light. But I am not afeared of sinking; mud has never worried me, and the moon is bright. I take one jump on to a patch of ground and then another. I am close now, just one more jump but it's far. I survey the situation. There is one possible route, but it will be a big leap. The challenge exhilarates me. I can do this. Have I not leapt many, many times afore? Is it not one of my favourite games? Without much hesitation I spring up, but as I do the ground beneath me gives way, crumbling into the bog. But it's too late; I am committed and fling all of myself towards the Moon Flower. I am just a tiny fraction out - my feet do not find the ground and I fall into the bog. I scramble, confused to find nothing solid. Somehow, I right myself with my head facing towards the sky and my feet sinking further into the ground. I wriggle, sinking more.

It is not how I expected but exactly how it looks. If I move there is nothing solid and I sink deeper, faster. If I am still I am held and sink slower. I look about; solid ground is far from reach and in this light I can see no branch to grasp hold of. I can already feel the wetness seep into my body through my garments. I will soon be cold. I am not sure how long I can stay here and what is worse, I have let my grandmother down again. Tears begin to flow down my checks. I want to writhe, to twist, but know I cannot. I look about me; the beauty and peace of the moonlit night seems a cruel joke at my expense. Never before have I felt this about the earth. I think soon my grandmother will know something is wrong and come to look for me. Does she not know everything? If I stay still surely she will come and find me. Then, without moving at all, I suddenly drop a little further into the mud. I am truly scared. Surely I am too young to die, my life too short lived. I feel helpless. This fear goes deep and beyond panic. It is a stone cold, sober fear that grips every part of my being. Then I hear it, cutting through the stillness of the night. Raven calls my name. I look up and I can see it sitting calmly on a branch of a nearby oak tree. I look into its eyes and it gives a long, slow blink. Then I understand, it is within me, it is within me to do so. I can escape this plight. I can escape any plight. I look to the raven. My mouth is almost too dry to speak but I mange somehow.

'Raven, thank you for your gifts.' And I feel it, the fluidity in my body, the melting and reforming. I feel my body shrink away from my clothing. The wings sprout from my flesh and, before the mud can fold around me, I am in the air, sweeping above the tree tops. It is the best feeling ever, the air through my wings, the space after confinement. I sweep back down to the bog, to the tree, and the raven launches from its perch and joins me in flight. We dance and circle around, playing. The raven welcomes me to its world - we are different but the same. Eventually my companion needs to eat so we part company and I take to the skies. I have to explore, not just the night time sky but what it is to be me. The night sky welcomes me and guides me through its wonders, cutting through the darkness.

When I can fly no more I make my way home; I think to surprise her, to impress her, but why do I think this? I expect to have to tap on the door, to caw for her attention. But as I approach our cottage she is standing by the door, scanning the sky. She sees me approach, waves and, majestically, I sweep up to her and hover in front of her before I tell myself, 'Raven you are released,' and slowly I fall back into my human form. I stand before her naked. Her eyes are filled with love and something more than pride, something like conformation.

'You'd better come inside afore you catch a chill,' she says and holds me so close to her. Inside the cottage my clothes and bag are rinsed and drying by the fire, the bog-myrtle bundled on the table. Grandmother hands me my first tankard of ale. 'Welcome home, Raven,' she says as we clink glasses.

After that I can't help but practice. I find I cannot shift without purpose. My gift is not a plaything but something much more. I find the animal I shift into matches the purpose, the different animal's qualities and talents fitted to the need. The animals are so generous, loving, caring creatures each and every one from spider to the sheep. I learn each animal kills in the kindest way they can. That to fight, to defend their territory, their kind is essential. But above all I discover inside myself a deep connection to a consciousness inside everything. It is very reassuring. And so, I grow with the earth, part of the earth and all in it, my grandmother, our home and the earth to explore. I do not know I want for anything else.

Chapter Four

I crouch in my dark hole, holding my knees to my chest. I can sense and feel the earth full of life around me, but I fear no intrusion from that life. It feels safe, like a womb. In the darkness I see with my senses. I've been here a while, but I am not bored. It's fun, a game, I am hiding. This is my space, I have found it, I enjoy it.

I hear the men come out of our cottage. They mount their horses, they say something to my grandmother, but their tone is soft, and I cannot hear. Her smile is the reassurance they need, and they turn and canter away. Grandmother watches them leave, looks to the bank, looks in my direction, my signal, afore she turns back into the cottage. I creep out of my hole, loving the feeling of space and movement after such a long confinement. I dance about, enjoying the change as I head towards the cottage. Inside the visitors have left a gift. It is precious marchpane in the shape of an owl.

'Here,' says Grandmother, 'don't eat it all at once.' I had never seen the like before. It's too beautiful to eat, I think, and simply stare in wonderment, too feared to pick it up even. 'Start with the head,' she advises. 'I do.'

I look at her.

'No?' she asks, picks up the owl and opens her mouth and I snatch the owl away from her and bite its head off before anyone else can. She smiles and then cannot help but laugh as she watches my expression. I have tasted nothing like this ever before. Honey has been a staple, but this explosion of sugar and almond takes me to a place I have never been before. I am completely lost in the sensation and do not wish to be found. Then it's over, it's gone. Part of me is bereft, the other sublime.

'It's late, let us rest,' Grandmother says, but rest is the last thing I want to do. I lie in the blankets jingling; it is not unpleasant.

'Grandmother?' I ask.

'Hum?' she replies, sleepy and reluctant to chat.

'Will your guests come again?'

'Hum,' she replies.

'Will they bring sweets again?'

'Next time you can ask them yourself. Now go to sleep.'

That night my dreams are full of places and people I have never seen before, all witnessed through a sugary haze. And that is how it is. We have few social guests, but my grandmother has the best of ways with folk. Most of our visitors arrive in some state of distress, some in the dead of night, and within a very short while Grandmother has taken the sting out of their jangled nerves and embraced them in a peace they never knew existed. Sometimes when we have guests, I am sent to the rafters out of sight. I watch and learn; how Grandmother puts people at their ease, draws out their troubles, administers potions or enacts upon them a treatment. Sometimes I am sent to my hiding hole and then I know it's serious and important. For a long time it's clear Grandmother knows everything, and with simple instruction and gentle guidance, I am encouraged to explore all I am. I listen to plants, sing along with trees, shift into all manner of beasts, for life is fun. In time I am trusted with running small errands.

Grandmother calls me in from the yard where I have been clearing out muck from the barn. 'Get cleaned up,' she says. 'I need you to deliver this remedy.' I pump water from the well and clean hands and face. I use the coarse hoarse hair brush to get most of the mud from my clothes. Grandmother says when I was but a babe in arms she tried to put me in a gown as is fitting of my sex. She said I let out such a loud and fearful screeching, no matter what she did she could not quiet me. In the end she was worried the sheriff would come and detain her and she would be hung for maltreatment and abuse. She took off the gown and my screaming ceased, instantly. She said that is when she knew, and I have been dressed as a boy ever since, so that all but my grandmother know me as a boy.

I present myself to her.

'You'll do,' she says, after a brief examination. I pick up the package and ask where it is to go. She says it's written on the box and it is then we both realise my studies to date have not included reading. I am well versed in the ways of the earth but know nothing of pages. There is a school, but it is not for the likes of us. It is for the sons of husbandmen, lawyers and the like, and while in my doublet and hose I'd fit right in, there is no conceivable way that the "good" men and women of the town would allow the foundling of the local healer to attend their school and mix with such honourable offspring. My doublet and hose are excused and tolerated because of Grandmother not because they fit our station. Besides, discretion is the key to my grandmother's business. Who would trust that a young spit of a boy would keep secrets? Of course, Grandmother could teach me herself, but how would we get everything done and have time for lessons? She tells me the address I am to go to and sends me on my way. Instantly all thoughts of school and reading leave my mind as I embark on my errand, eager for the sights and sounds that await.

It is a few weeks later, and Grandmother calls me in from the yard where I have made a game of cleaning out the chickens by shifting in and out of chicken - a game the chickens love. Reluctantly I go inside, stamping the last of the chicken waste from my boots before I do. She sits me down at the medicine table, so I know it's serious.

'I have found you a tutor,' she says. 'She is sympathetic to our ways and will not fill your head full of nonsense. Be sure to mind what she says and show her respect. It is a great gift that she should give her time to you; make sure you honour it.'

I do not know what to say. I am surprised and intrigued but also unsure. Do I get a choice?

'You need to learn to read and write. When I am…in the future you will need these skills and Grace, Widow Buchan to you, will serve you well.'

'What if I don't want to?' I ask.

'Want has nothing to do with this, this is about need.'

From the look in her eyes I know there is no argument to be made and anyway, I have grown curious of other folk, how they might be.

'Now folk will need a story, and this is it. Grace, Widow Buchan, needs help around the house as she is a widow with no husband. You are to go every afternoon for two hours, except Sundays. If asked that is what you say, understand?' I nod. Another story, why folk need so many and turn from the truth I do not know. 'Here, take this lavender oil with you and be gone.' I snatch up the gallipot and head out into the afternoon sun.

Widow Buchan lives in the centre of the town in a two-storey house with glass windows. My visits will be known by all. But I care little of this as I breathe in the scent of summer. The trees, the flowers, the grass, are all bursting with life, greedy for light and warmth. The sun provides them with both and it is such joy. I follow the brook into the town, enjoying its song; the walk alone will be a daily joy.

In the town it is market day and everywhere is bursting with life. Stalls of all manner of things could drive one crazy with wanting but I want for nothing so am able to enjoy the spectacle without yearning. In the centre of the town, a minstrel has collected a crowd of all the regular townsfolk; the butcher stands apart whilst Mother Lovell, her husband, and Ben, her son, take, as expected, the front row seats. I find I am unable to resist the minstrel's song. I drop unseen into the crush. It is a long ballad of true love and bitter broken hearts, as always, but the minstrel has a way about him that draws all into him, as if he is singing to each and every one of us. I am entranced. If there is to be yearning then it's for this, to have a voice that melts hearts so. At the end of the song, Mother Lovell's eyes are the only dry ones in the crowd. As the cheers die down and the hat is passed round, the sound of Goodman Lovell's tears drown out the idle chatter; all turn to see Goodman Lovell and his son standing lost in the moment, helplessly weeping. The hat reaches Goodman Lovell. He is ready with a shilling but before he can drop it into the hat, Mother Lovell, known throughout the town as a virago force never to be crossed, snatches the coin away from him and clips her son, with a thud that is clearly heard, about the head.

'Saint's preserve us, are you soft in the head as well!" she exclaims, without any sign that she has just witnessed the song that has entranced us all so. 'Come away with you both. There is no end of work to be done.' And she pushes them away. Goodman Lovell follows her lead; he glances back at the minstrel and the crowd with an apology. When he turns back, the looks he gives his wife's proceeding back chills me to the core. I have not seen such an expression before and I hope never to again. Ashamed I have no coppers to offer, I shrink away, worried I have dawdled too long already.

Widow Buchan's house is a little off the main square and I step into the calm from the activity. I have never met Widow Buchan before. I have heard tell of her story, how hers was a true love, how they could not be parted, how they had met on his travels, how she had travelled with him, wed and settled in our town. How he was a wealthy merchant, travelled far and wide. How he lost his life – some said a storm at sea, some said a duel to defend an innocent maiden's honour, some said a drunken brawl that got out of hand. Since then she has kept herself to herself, as is expected. She sold most of her husband's businesses but kept a small import and export concern. All said she could have lived as a queen but, as modesty demands, she lives simply. Her presence is felt at all the festivals and she is a regular at church, donating appropriate sums for repairs to the roof and sustenance for the poor. I have learnt all this from the idle talk of my grandmother's visitors, so I think I knew what to expect, think I knew how it will be.

I tap on the front door. Her housekeeper, an older woman with a face that needs to be reminded how to smile, answers. She takes a long, hard look at me from top to toe and says, 'Round the back for you, my lad,' and slams the door shut in my face. I feel humiliated, disappointed in myself; where was my discretion? I have delivered remedies to any number of houses now and never had need to be told to go to the back door. My sense of secrecy is so attuned, yet today it fails me. I step into the darkness between the houses and welcome this momentarily respite. I do not need to tap the door, it swings open as I approach, and standing in the doorway to greet me is Grace. Her smile is such that I feel as if every trouble I may have ever had or will have is dissolved into nothingness and I am held. Her eyes are a piercing, clear blue that seems to sparkle, drawing in and reflecting back light.

'Master Raven, how pleased I am to meet you at last.' She holds out her hand. I am dumbfounded, unable to move or speak. I simply gaze into her eyes, my own wide and open. I hope she is merciful, as right now I am an open door. Still holding out her hand she says, 'I'm so sorry, do excuse me. I am Widow Buchan, but you may call me Grace.' And she offers her hand once more. Still lost in her eyes, I dip my knees and take her hand. A rush of energy surges through my body. I have never felt such a thing and would drop the hand in fright and wonder if I did not hear Grandmother's voice in my head schooling me on manners.

'At your service, madam,' I manage just in time and my voice sounds funny as if I have heard how it sounds to others for the first time.

'Call me Grace, please,' and she smiles, dipping her head slightly. She knows she has my heart and has received it graciously. She steps aside and gestures for me to enter. I have delivered many packages to houses all manner of sizes, but never before have I been inside. I stamp my boots before I enter.

The kitchen is the size of our entire cottage. It has two fireplaces, a huge table; there even seems to be a pump for water inside the house, a thing I could never have imagined.

'You have already met Mother Gray, my housekeeper.' Mother Gray stands in the doorway that leads to the rest of the house and nods acknowledgement.

'Ma'am.' I dip my head in a respectful bow. I am trying not to show it, but I can't help looking around; the walls are lined with copper pots and pans, all manner of knives and utensils, earthenware and glass jars. I have never seen such opulence, never even considered it a possibility. I have never wanted for anything and we have a fraction of this. I am at once stunned by the beauty and perplexed by it. Why do they need so much?

'Cat got your tongue?' asks Mother Gray and the two women glance at each other, warmly.

'Pleased to meet you,' I say and remember the jar of lavender oil. 'A small token.' I place it on the table. 'Lavender oil.'

'That is most kind, thank you,' says Grace. 'Now we should get to work.' She indicates towards the doorway Mother Gray occupies. 'Mother Gray, a tumbler of milk for our guest and a small glass of wine for myself, if you'd be so kind.' Mother Gray steps aside as we step into a cool dark passageway.

'I think the living chamber has the best light for our task,' Grace says, and we go up a narrow, dark staircase and on to a landing. The doors to the other rooms are closed so it again is dark. She opens the door on the far end of the hall facing towards the street and light floods the landing. We step inside, another treasure trove. A tapestry depicting land rich in fauna and beasts fills the near wall, another opposite, of intricate design from another land. The floor is covered with a rug, again from a land I do not yet know. By the fireplace are two grand chairs that look like you would never want to stand again if you sat in them. Either side of the mantle are two ornate candle holders that look too grand for their task. In front of the window is a table and two chairs. On the table is an ink well, a quill pen, parchment and a book of some kind. The hustle and bustle of the street outside feels a long way away but echoes around the walls. I want to study the tapestries and try out the chairs but have manners that say not to. 'Please, take a seat,' she says and gestures towards the table.

'Thank you,' I say and clumsily sit on the chair nearest. She sits down next to me, close enough for me to breathe her in, she smells like comfort, like I want always to be enfolded in her arms. I have never felt this way afore. It is wonderous but terrifying.

'I have this old primer which I thought would be a good start but before we do I thought it would be a good idea if we got to know each other a little. Do you not think?' I am unable to speak but manage an enthusiastic nod.

'Good,' she says. 'I thought a little game would be in order. Do you like games?'

I have never played a game in my life, spinning tops, tug-o-war or football.

'I don't know,' I respond, not sure if it's the right answer. She looks concerned and I am bereft that I have caused her distress.

'Now that is something we shall remedy,' she says. 'Let's start right now. We shall call this game the reciprocity dance. We each get one question a lesson. I get to ask you a question and you have to answer. Then you get to ask me a question and I have to answer, does that seem fair?' I nod enthusiastically. I have so many questions. 'Good. Now, Raven, I shall ask the most important question I can think of to ask you, is that agreeable?' I nod. 'A simple yes would suffice,' she says and waits until I realise.

'Yes.'

'Good, now what is your favourite sweet?'

'Marchpane,' I say with some certainty and confidence that it is no secret to hide. Again, she looks disappointed, then says,

'A fine choice, young sir. I shall make a note of it. Now your turn.'

I want to ask so much but all of my questions seem silly. In the end I choose what I think is a question she will like, and I think is safe.

'The tapestries are so fine. Where are they from?'

She laughs 'What a fine question. A land far from here, home to the Bedouin. The design is traditional to the Bedouin people. The tapestry tells the story of their people and what they believe.'

'So everyone knows?' I ask.

'Indeed, so they can tell their story to their people. Yet not everyone will be able to read the story from the pictures.'

'Like they have a secret?'

'Exactly, to some they are pretty patterns and pictures and to some they tell a very important story.'

This I understand, I have never felt more at home away from my own home before.

'Do you like them?' she asks.

'Very much,' I say, and we smile together and at each other. It is as if we are held in a glowing, golden light and I know I will do anything she asks of me ever.

'Now lets us become friends with the ABCs,' she instructs, and opens the book.

On the way home, my head swirls. I pass through the market place and do not notice the smells, the people, the games. I walk back beside the brook and do not hear its song. A multitude of feelings, ideas and sensations crash around my brain, losing shape, making new shapes in a dance all of their own. As soon as I see our cottage I race towards it. Grandmother opens the door and I rush into her arms; they have never felt so safe. She takes me inside and we sit by the fire. She has prepared a calming infusion and as we drink I tell her of my great adventure. I have climbed the tallest tree in the forest, sought out herbs and plants from the remotest places, but this has been the biggest challenge yet. People, I discover, are the hardest adventure. Yet each time I tell my grandmother about another new emotion, she asks me what the earth would do, what the beasts would do, what the trees and plants would sing and I find bit by bit I know the answers. I know I have fallen in love for the first time and nothing will ever be the same again.

Chapter Five

The next day the lesson cannot come soon enough. I race there, enjoying the brook, the trees, the flowers, but not lingering. I weave through the streets of the town, taking back routes to avoid conversation and prying eyes. I knock loudly on the kitchen door and can barely wait for it to be opened. Mother Gray answers and it is all I can do to be polite before I take the stairs two at a time up to her. She opens the door as I am about to knock, and we laugh. I have never known such joy before. Our lesson takes the same form as before. We share a secret at the start and look at letters that swirl and float and make no sense. But she is kind and patient. I am not sure if they are supposed to dance about the page but as long as they bring me here I will tolerate them.

At the end of our lesson she escorts me down to the kitchen. There on the table is a wooden box. She asks me to turn the key in the box. I am a little nervous. What can be inside and why does she need me to see it?

'Are you afeared of a wooden box?' goads Mother Gray. I stare at her and boldly and deliberately turn the key. The lock is smooth, well used; I lift up the lid and it folds backwards on hinges. My eyes almost explode; inside is one perfectly formed egg-shaped piece of marchpane. I look at Grace and she indicates for me to take it.

'And what do you say?' asks Mother Gray

'Thank you,' I mumble between mouthfuls of delight.

'That's better. Now time you were on your way. Your grandmother will be fretting.' I do not want to leave but I'm too excited to stay. I quickly hug Grace, then I catch Mother Gray unawares. 'Away with you,' she says as I dash out of the door. If lessons are like this, why not learn?

And so it goes on. The days are a dream to me; mornings for work, afternoon lessons. The letters never seem to stick from one day to the next, still they swirl, but this seems such a minor point to me. Numbers are fine; I have needed to count long before now, so we do not fuss with them. Each day my grandmother greets me, and we seek wisdom from our friends the beasts and plants. I am careful when swapping secrets not to mention our business or that I am a girl dressed as a boy or that I can change my shape as the need requires and she does not ask.

Then one morning I am working up a sweat chopping wood, resisting shifting to beaver to make the job easier, when Grace walks out of the woods and up to our cottage. I drop the axe, run to the well and pump water over my head and face and dry them on my linens. I throw on my doublet and go to greet her, full of excitement and ignoring the feeling of dread nagging at the back of my senses. She smiles when she sees me; it's like a sun shining in my heart. I want to ask why she is here, what emergency has brought her thus, but she seems as calm and peaceful as ever. I want to show her around all the secret places I know, show her how everything works and how I know how everything works but Grandmother soon joins us. She tells me we are short of meadowsweet, asks me if I'd be so kind as to collect some now. If I say no, what will Grace think of me? If I say yes I cannot be with Grace. It's a cruel choice. Grace releases me. She is impressed I know to do such foraging, is looking forward to hearing my secret tips for collecting at that afternoon's lesson. Reluctantly I head towards the meadows by the brook as they head inside the cottage.

Grace has left by the time I get back. I place the meadowsweet on the table. Grandmother is quiet on my return and I do not know why. She offers me my dinner but it's not easy between us. We do not share our usual ease and comfort. I have not seen her this way before and do not know how to be with her. Eventually I ask, 'What is it that ails?' She sighs and looks at me.

'We must be close you and I,' she says. I am confused. When have we not been close? I would lay down my life for her without a moment's hesitation.

'I did not know we are not.'

'And yet you do not share your struggles with words with me?'

I am at a loss; what struggle have I?

'I have no issue with words,' I say. 'I love their dance.'

'Their dance?' she asks.

'Yes, the way they dance about the page.'

'Words do not dance,' she says.

'I do not understand. Is Grace displeased with me?' I am bereft; our lessons have been nothing but joy to me. How can I have displeased her?

'No, you have not displeased her.' I do not believe her. 'You have not displeased me.' I do not believe her. I stare into the flames.

'Raven, my love for you is as deep as the earth and as high as the sky.' I look at her. 'Can I ask of you one small thing?' I nod. 'Can you look more at the words than at Grace?' I don't understand why I would do that. I frown. 'It is a small ask, is it not?' Reluctantly I nod. I am not sure what she means or why she asks it. 'And you will try your best?'

'I will try,' I say, and I will, but words on a page make no sense and Grace does. What is it that I have done that is so wrong? I do not understand why words should not dance.

It's time for my lesson. I am not sure I want to go but my grandmother cheers me along. She reassures me all is well and reminds me to work hard at the words on the page. Yet a doubt has taken residence in my heart, and when I pass the brook its song sounds like a laugh at my expense, the trees do not welcome me and the flowers with their joy mock me. For the first time I hesitate to knock at the door but Mother Gray is ready to open anyway. 'What is it that has detained you?' I do not speak but step inside. 'Today you are on time which is late in your case.' I shrug my shoulders and skulk towards the stairs.

Grace too greets me, her smile warm and gracious as ever. I do not look at her, cannot look at her. What have I done? What is it about me that has caused such action? She does not speak but stands aside so I can enter. She closes the door behind me. I sit in my usual place and stare at the floor. The bright patterns of the rug torment me with their joy. She sits down next to me. Her smell, always so comforting before, feels like a betrayal. 'When first I came to words on a page,' she says, 'I did not want to. I wanted wide open spaces and there was so much to see and do in the world. I saw no need of books.' Still I do not look at her but turn and open the primer. 'I have shared a secret with you, now it's your turn.' I begin to sound out the alphabet. Before I had enjoyed the dance of the words. It was part of the joy of our time together. Now our intimacy has been exposed and there is no such joy, just a muddle and confusion. I get half way through my recitation and I stumble, the letters do not come, and I cannot find them. Fire fills my belly and fury blinds my eyes and, despite myself, tears well. I stand and turn and begin to move towards the door. I am just in front of the tapestry of beasts when she calls my name.

'Raven.' It is my name she has called but her command is to stop. I am so taken by surprise, never before has she shown such strength. I stop with my back to her. I do not want to hear what she has to say so I stare hard at the tapestry. I do not hear her words, but her tone is kind yet firm.

As I stand there not listening, refusing to hear, refusing to cry, refusing to feel my own despair, a despair I did not have till this day, I notice a small, almost imperceptible, movement in the tapestry. I blink. It must be the tears confusing my eyes, but it is there again. I look closer, willing the tears to clear from my eyes without my wiping them so I can see better. A small spider woven deep into the fabric, so is not the first beast you see, unravel itself from the threads of the textile. Then it begins to weave a beautiful silver thread. I look closer, wiping my eyes now, not caring if she sees, and there the spider has woven the letter I lost when reciting the alphabet, the letter O. Suddenly it is clear, and I begin again from the start, cutting through her lecture. ABC...it flows, and I follow the silver thread and each letter follows on from the next and a connection is there that wasn't before. I reach the end and we both laugh. This is the first time I have been able to do this. I turn to her and we smile. I turn back to the spider, I feel she is smiling too. I go to the desk, pick up the primer. The words still dance but now I can follow their thread. I know now that I can call on Spider to weave words into meaning and understanding. It is the key to a whole new universe that will take lifetimes to explore. Words will always dance for me but now I have a way to follow their pattern. On the way out I stop to look at the tapestry, but spirit spider has returned to thread.

'It is beautiful,' Grace says as she comes to stand behind me. I know she wants to ask what it was I saw in the tapestry, but she knows I will not tell her. That day the marchpane tastes especially sweet.

That night Grandmother and I hold a simple ceremony in honour of Spider; as I spin, she weaves. This is a new sort of joy and I am not afraid of it. After that, lessons are easier, and we fall into an easy pattern. It's always a challenge, but always worth it.

Chapter Six

It is a fine spring day, the perfect day to collect Yellow Archangel. It requires a warm wet environment and can be found deep in the forest. My grandmother has important visitors so this is a fine opportunity for adventure. I am sent off with a satchel, mostly empty apart from the bread and meat Grandmother has packed for me; water I can find along the way – fresh flowing from spring or brook so safe to drink. I will have to travel deep into the forest so set off early as the sun lightly kisses the earth. Song fills my heart as I step lightly down the lane, inwardly acknowledging my friends the trees and beasts as I go. After a short distance I pass the neighbouring farm.

Farmer Harrington's children are playing in the yard. I wave and they run over to greet me at the gate. Mary, the oldest, takes a shy glance at me; do I wish to join their game? I assure her I do but have important work to do so cannot. She scuffs the earth in response as the two smaller children stare in silence. I have never had time for children's games. I am acquainted with all of the local children, and many of their parents, but I have never needed of more than that. Once I tried to join a game, I was curious to see how it would feel. The boys were playing in a corner of the market place one afternoon on the way to lessons. I watched as they marched up and down, fired make-believe arrows and make-believe pistols and fought with stick swords. It looked fun. They saw me looking asked if I wished to join them. So astonished and flattered was I that they would think me worthy of their game, I did not hesitate. But soon my joy turned to disappointment. The leader of the group, Ben Lovell, was mean and cruel. He bossed us all about, would not let us choose our own battle. He hit the smallest and youngest for no reason other than he could. I said I was late for my work and got away. It was the first and last time I tried to join a game with my peers.

With no brothers or sister of my own, I had spent little time with other children and it seemed to me they were ruthless in a way I had never known possible. No beast I knew was ever so. I do not miss my peers but there is something that I feel I do not have. It is no hardship not to play chase with my neighbours. Although, as I turn away and walk on, I feel an uneasy emptiness I cannot describe. I have had this feeling before but never understood it. Yet soon I am distracted by the spring flowers and the cherry blossom and I forget this yearning.

Inside the forest it is damp and cool, a perpetual dusk light filters in through the branches above. A stillness fills the air even though life is rich and abundant. Walking is hard off the paths. Underfoot is unsteady with fallen branches, sprouting trees, moss and fungi. If you know what you are looking for a feast is at your feet. I take the path as long as I can until I can sense the Yellow Archangel. It is the only way to find what you are looking for. Follow the signs and your knowledge but soon both will run out and all you have is feeling and intuition. You have to feel the pull, the direction. It so happens the feeling takes me through rough ground. The going is slow and tough. By a waterfall I take a break, drinking from the cool fresh water and greedily eating some of my bread and meat; it is all I can do to save a little for later.

Restored, I get to my feet again. I can tell I am not far now, although I am in a part of the forest I have never been in before and have travelled much deeper than before. It's but a little distance further and I spot the Yellow Archangel, its bright colours standing out clearly in the black of the forest. It smells so sweet as I bend down to pick it. I have filled half of my satchel when I hear it, the breath, the laboured, heavy breath. I would be frightened but the sound, I know, is of a beast in distress. I turn to the spot. All senses alive, there is not a part of my body that isn't listening, that isn't ready to respond. I look round but cannot find the source. Then I smell it, smell the blood. Then I am on the trail and it is seconds before I trace the source.

She is lying at the edge of her hide, badly wounded from a careless arrow. Her eyes say she would like to pounce but her body asks for help. I approach with gentle easy caution and then I understand her concern. A tiny yelping comes from under her paw and I see her cub not more than a few weeks old, hungry and confused. I do not have a moment to spare. I move as quickly as I can without causing alarm. I gather blood moss to quell the bleeding and approach Mother Wolf with humility. She tries to rise, to protect, but I offer her the little meat I have left. She does not take it but pushes it towards her cub who, once released, bounds over without fear to eat from my hand. As she chews on some gristle, I quickly scoop her up and into my satchel. Her cries for help are muffled but Mother tries to stand anyway, but she does not have the strength and falls back down. In her moment of weakness I move in and pack her wound with the moss. Frantically I try to think of a beast that can help me now. Is there not one that will help? I have not met a beast, other than mankind, that can stand on two legs and carry a heavy weight. I could shift and fly for help but it would take hours to return and we do not have that time. I cut a vine from a nearby tree and tie a tourniquet around her wound. I am a good size for my age, but she is as big as me. I do not think I can do it, but she lets out a low grumble of pain and she is in my arms and I am making my way through the rich, dense forest floor before I know what I am doing.

I pass by the stream and wonder if I should stop and give her some water, but I must get to Grandmother - only she will know what to do. I press on, not feeling the pain, not caring for other dangers. Each step feels like an eternity. I cannot move my limbs fast enough. Yet it feels like what has taken the best part of a day for me to idly find my way to is now taking just a few short hours to retrace.

I reach the edge of the forest at dusk. I stop to catch my breath and for the first time I feel the pain race throughout my body. Yet I dare not set her down for fear I'll not be able to pick her up again. The cub fidgets and yelps in my satchel and Mother Wolf raises her head, manages a tiny yelp in return and I set off again. I cannot be seen with a wolf and definitely cannot be seen to be saving an injured one, such is the law of the land that seeks to wipe out all wolves. I cannot take the road. I have only travelled it once before but if I can remember the path over the hill, while it will be harder, if I don't get lost, it is a more direct route.

As it grows darker I call upon Raven and feel my eyes turn round, and bright and I can see as if it's day. I have no time to think. Every part of my being is focused on taking the next steps but somehow the steps are in the right direction. I have no sense of how long it takes but eventually the cottage is in sight. I fight every instinct in my body that wants to stop and fall to the ground when I see it. I push hard until I reach the yard; I master my breath and call, 'Grandmother.' She opens the door as I stagger in.

'By the fire,' she orders and with the little life I have left in me I gently lay Mother Wolf down in the rushes. I kneel beside her, reaching for breath. Grandmother gets busy examining Mother Wolf. She strokes the wolf's head and she is at ease. Is there no one my grandmother cannot put at their ease? She makes the wolf comfortable, unpacks the moss and applies soothing ointment. I sit back and watch, pulsing as energy continues to surge round my body even though I am so tired I cannot move. Then we hear it, a tiny yelp that would tear open the coldest of hearts. I reach inside my satchel and pull her out. She cries instinctively, wide-eyed and unsure of where it is she has come to. I place her by her mother's head and her mother nestles and licks her. They rest together, at peace and as one. My grandmother has loosened the tourniquet, cleaned the wound and administered another ointment but she does nothing else. I look at her, expectant of good news but she gently shakes her head. An involuntary tear rolls down my check and I wipe it away with contempt.

To have carried her so far, to have tried so hard. I turn away. 'You did all you could,' my grandmother says. 'It is her time.' I stare at her; it seems such an insufficient answer.

'It is the way of things – like it or not,' she says.

'How long?' I ask.

'It is done,' and she nods towards the mother wolf. I look again and see it is more than sleep, her pup resting by her side unawares. This time tears flow down my checks, silent tears falling as if from an endless stream.

'She went held in love and at peace.' I try to wipe away my tears but they just keep falling. 'You gave her that,' she says. I look down at mother and cub and she does indeed look at peace, much different from the frightened creature I found in the forest. I take some comfort from that.

'It's a little before we might have planned but it seems you are to learn what motherhood is.' I look at her quizzically. She studies me back. 'Or maybe fatherhood.'

I am still confused, and she nods towards the pup. I look at the cub and the love that fills my being is beyond imagining. I look back at my grandmother. Can this really be so?

She smiles. 'This is not an easy calling but called you have been.' I look back at the pup. If my first taste of love has been Grace, this is my first taste of devotion. Every part of me feels connected to the pup and life is already unimaginable without her.

'She'll be awake soon. You'd best be prepared.' She goes over to the earthenware crook and takes out a piece of salted venison. She washes it clean and hands it to me. I look at her. I am to feast on raw venison to help my pup?

'What would wolf do?' she asks.

'Am I to shift?' I ask.

'Just ask,' she says, and I close my eyes.

In the vast dark stillness I ask and instantly I am answered. I take the raw venison, cut off a mouth-sized piece with my dagger and begin to chew. The taste of blood and salt fills my mouth. I resist swallowing and continue to chew until the meat is a fine, broken-down pulp. I spit it into my hand and place it on the table. I cut another chunk of meat and repeat. As the second mouthful is ready, the pup wakens and begins to yelp, nudging her mother and confused at getting no response.

Instantly I am by her side, kneeling on all fours, my hands full of chewed up meat. I stuff my mouth with a handful of meat and offer my face to the pup. She smells the meat and eagerly licks my face. Gently I spit out the meat and she eats, eats as if she has never eaten before. I fear two handfuls will not be enough but by the end of the second she is full and fat. I hold her, curled up into a tight ball ready for rest. I hold her close to my heart. Her scent is like coming home, as if I have always known it. Soon we are both asleep curled up by the fire. From that moment on we are never apart.

Chapter Seven

When I awake, my grandmother has lifted Wolf Mother on to the medicine table and covered her in an oil skin. She has placed a saucer of milk beside us. 'Your dreams were sweet,' she says and it's true. I am not sure I have ever slept so deeply before. The pup awakes and begins to cry. Grandmother hands me a piece of meat to chew. I chew fast; to meet my pups needs is my only desire. She feeds and then we play. She is still unsteady on her paws, but she is so much joy. When she is sleeping again, my grandmother and I have breakfast.

'Your lessons for the next few weeks will be the care of your pup,' Grandmother says. 'I'll let Grace know when I go into town later but now we must harvest.' I am afeared to cut apart Mother Wolf while her pup sleeps so near, but Grandmother says it is best this way, best for the mother's spirit to be released when the pup is present.

We strip her skin, scrap her bones, pick out the organs and bowels that shall serve in potions and ointments, then gift the crows with what we do not need - to honour her life no part shall be wasted. I stop regularly to feed and play with pup, who shows no curiosity in what we do but seems content to explore her new surrounds. She is not shy at all. In the afternoon, my grandmother takes to the town and I stretch out Wolf Mother's skin to dry. Then I prepare for that nights naming ceremony. I build a fire outside, set seats beside it. I lay out gifts for offerings – one front paw of Mother Wolf, the other I shall keep for pup – bread and meat and ale and a selection of fruits and plants. I have never felt so contented.

Grandmother returns at dusk, her bag heavy with venison. We have a hungry mouth to feed. We take supper as we wait for the clear full moon to rise. Then we go outside. I tuck the pup inside my doublet for ease and comfort. In silence we light the fire and build our offering. On a flat piece of wood we place our gifts, at the centre Wolf Mother's paw and then, taking turns, we each place an offering of bread or meat or fruit. When we have a beautiful pile we place it in the centre of the fire. I take the pup out of my doublet and hold her out to the fire.

'To the East, to the West, to the North, to the South, to the Sky, to the Earth, please accept our gifts. Pease accept our gratitude, please accept our love,' says Grandmother. 'Tonight we call on you to name this new arrival to our family and grant us grace to serve her as she needs.' I hold the pup up to the moon; she wriggles but my grip is firm.

'How are we to know this precious gift?' I ask, and the answer is clear and quick. I cannot tell if it's only in my head or spoken out loud, but the voice is without hesitation.

'Sassaba,' it says and I know the voice is from a distant land.

'Sassaba,' I repeat and Sassaba yelps in response; she has claimed her name. 'Thank you,' I say to the Universe.

Grandmother allows me a small tankard of ale and herself a large one as we sit by the fire and sing to Sassaba songs we are no longer meant to know.

We are inseparable. I wake in the night to feed her, give up my portion of milk for her. She is with me when I do my chores, causing mischief and joyful relief. I have never seen Grandmother laugh so much, it is as if Sabby's joy of life has released our own or invigorated it, at the very least. It is as if she has filled a need we did not know we had. I know my grandmother has fallen in love too, but she lets me lead, advising and guiding where necessary. - We have treated and softened her mother's skin and laid it as rug in front of the fire, and when she is tired Sabby takes the paw and sleeps on the rug. Usually she sleeps with me or near me if I am not sleeping. When she sleeps on the rug she makes the tiniest yelping sounds in her dreams, as if she is crying. I have never wanted for anything. My grandmother's love has always been undoubted, her care of me a lesson in love.

Yet when I hear Sabby crying her quiet, gentle tears, I feel a stirring deep inside that speaks to a pain I did not know I had. I do not understand this pain. I cannot name it. I feel it a discomfort in my being I have never felt before. I try my best to ignore it, ignore this unwelcome sensation. The third time Sabby goes to sleep this way we have been playing in the yard and we have been having the best time. I have shifted to mouse to help her learn to hunt, to dog to chase her and teach her how to flee from danger. I have teased her as bee. It has been so much joy. Yet when our game is at a close, she seeks her mother's paw. I am filled with frustration. Why can I not be enough? Then I think the answer is simple. She needs her mother and I have the power to give her that. I know exactly what her mother looked like, and, with such a vivid connection, the shift should be simple. Gently and quietly, I approach the rug and the sleeping Sabby. I crouch on all fours, set my intention and wait.

Yet nothing happens. I think I am not connecting enough and try harder. Yet still nothing. I think maybe I need a physical connection so place my hands on the rug, nothing. I am cross, frustrated and confused. What use this gift, that costs so much, if I cannot use it at will to ease the pain of a loved one That is a purpose. Hot, angry tears begin to flow down my face. I cannot help Sabby, cannot provide the comfort she seeks. Instantly she becomes the villain. To ask of me what I cannot give. In rage I raise my fist, ready to bring it down hard on Sabby, for it must be her fault I cannot shift. My grandmother catches my fist. How is it that she is always at the right place at the right time?

'You cannot be that for her.' I stare at her and try to pull my arm free, but she holds tight. 'If I release, can I trust you?' Shame fills me. How could I have wanted to hurt what I love so much? I soften, bow my head and nod. She lets go of my arm and I curl up into a tight ball. She crouches down next to me. 'Come now, what use your tears? What purpose? Do you not hold the life of another in your hands?'

Her words seem harsh and cruel when clearly, I am of no use at all. I look at her accusingly. Should she not provide me the comfort I seek?

'You cannot be her mother, but you can be yourself.' I frown. What does she mean? 'Wolf and Raven are all time companions,' is all she says, then she pats me on the shoulder and goes back to work at the medicine table. I turn back to look at Sabby; she yelps her tiny cry and I almost think I see a tear on her check. Before I know what I am doing I have shifted into Raven. Gently I approach Sabby's head. I find a spot to sit and in her sleep she curls her body around me; her yelps stop and I feel a deep peace settle over us as I close my eyes and rest.

Chapter Eight

Weeks pass and Sabby grows bigger each day, as does our companionship. We learn each other's ways, our likes and dislikes. Our games expand as Sabby does and soon we are rolling and chasing; play fighting is our favourite. I could shift to any manner of beast, dog or bear, but I have discovered I enjoy the game much more as human. I work hard to get chores done so we have more time to play. Usually Sabby helps or at least helps by waiting patiently. Yet today we have had to hide in the hidey hole because my grandmother has received her first guests since Sabby.

It is late afternoon before we can begin the chores, before we can sweep the yard. Sabby is impatient and begins to chase the broom, yet today it's not funny. I am grumpy that the day has been lost. We could have gone for an adventure in the woods instead of the hidey hole, but Grandmother says it isn't safe for us. That if it is discovered we have a wolf cub we will not have a wolf cub for long. I cannot believe anyone could be so stupid or that mean to see Sabby and not love her. Wolves, I have learnt, know the depths of love. Yet Sabby does not know all this and wants to play. She pounces on the brush, I shake her off. She thinks it is part of the game and pounces again. I shake her off, this time angry. She goes to pounce again but I swing the broom out of the way. It looks like I have swung it to hit and instantly Sabby changes. She hunches down and growls.

Suddenly we are fighting but there is no play in it. I charge at her and we roll around the yard. I push her biting jaws away, but she shifts her head slightly and I feel her teeth sink into my hand. I let go of her and we stare at each other, her teeth in my hand, our bodies separate. Eventually I bow my head and she releases. We sit in silence back to back. I hold my hand; she has not bitten so hard as to tear apart my flesh, but the teeth marks are deep and lasting. Already my hand is swelling and changing colour. We sit some time in silence.

Eventually my grandmother, drawn by the silence, comes out into the yard to investigate. She sees us sitting, examines my hand and tells us both to go inside; we do not argue. Sabby lies by the fire, she lies flat, squashed down like she is trying not to be there. My Grandmother tends to my hand, washes it and applies an ointment to ease the swelling and bruising. I look at Sabby; I want to hold her, to say sorry, to explain nothing was meant, to say how much I love her, but I do not know how. Grandmother places a large chunk of salted venison on the table. 'Here, it's time you two made your peace,' she says. I quickly wash off the venison at the pump in the yard and begin to chew. When I go back in Sabby is already waiting and our nightly ritual is restored. After she has eaten I lie as close to her as I can. I never want for us to quarrel again.

The next morning Grandmother leaves the cottage early, before we have begun our morning tasks. We work fast so by the time she returns we have completed our duties, milked the cow, cleaned the chickens, swept the yard, tended the vegetables. I have even prepared the breakfast, a berry infusion to go with the pottage. We have arranged seats outside, so we may take in the morning air as we eat. When she returns we offer her a seat, serve her food and she receives it as the apology it is intended to be. We finish eating and take a moment to enjoy the heat of the sun.

'Tonight at dusk you must take Sabby to the West Deer Park. There you can teach her to hunt.' Our eyes pop open wide. I am exhilarated. To hunt, to be trusted on our own at dusk in a deer park we hardly know. Just as quickly I am filled with dread; how can I teach Sabby something I don't know? 'Raven and Wolf have been forever companions. Trust your intuition and together you will feel the calling and know the way.' We look at her with eyes that don't believe. 'But you must take great care never to be seen, never leave your kill. You must leave no trace. We risk ours and others lives if we do.' We nod. 'Promise me this is understood?'

Sabby barks and I say, 'I understand, Grandmother, thank you.' She sends us to the river to do the laundry but really we are too excited to do anything much very well.

That night, as dusk draws near, we stand in the yard ready to go. 'It's time, if you leave it any later it will be too late,'

Grandmother says. Sabby and I look at each other, unsure of how to start. 'Raven and Wolf,' Grandmother says, 'off you go,' and that is all the prompt I need. My feathers begin to grow, and I am in the air. I circle the yard and call Sabby and we are off. It is clear the connection between us is strong, if not stronger like this. We can communicate clearly without any obstruction. I lead the way, flying ahead, sensing and seeing the direction we need to go in.

Grandmother is right - our companionship is almost palpable as we work as one slick hunting team. I do not know the West Deer Park. I have only been allowed to venture inside on the odd occasion in search of plants that can only be found growing along the brook that cuts through the park, but with Raven's eyes it's clear what routes to take. Sabby is nowhere near full grown so we do not go so far and set our sights on smaller prey. Soon we reach a clearing, a wide open, grassy bank enclosed by low bushes. I perch on a tree and call Sabby. I watch as she hides in the trees, waiting for the moment. We do not wait long. The rabbits are plentiful and bold; this is their territory and they do not expect wolf. So many wolves have been killed by man, a 'nuisance' for the sheep and cows. Sabby does not waste time though; she is lightning fast with single focused attention on her prey, and in seconds she is holding a fat, ageing rabbit in her mouth and we are speeding out of the park. When we reach home Sabby drops the rabbit at my grandmother's feet, who graciously receives it. She gives the head and limbs to Sabby and the rest is added to the pottage which has never tasted so good as that night.

It is weeks since my last lesson with Grace and with words. I know not what Grandmother has told her but know it will be discreet. I have not missed the words but, at small moments, when Sabby has been sleeping, I have caught myself with a feeling of missing followed by guilt at not having missed Grace more. But Sabby has needed and taken all my attention and for that I do not apologise. Yet Sabby is growing bigger by the day and I know Grandmother will soon say it is time for lessons once more. I know she will say I must leave Sabby at home, but I know I will not. So when she says at breakfast one morning I am to take up my lessons I am not surprised. I say I am happy to return to my lessons with Sabby at my side.

'You know it's not safe,' she says. 'You know if she is seen as wolf she will be killed.'

'We cannot hide her forever.'

Grandmother sighs long and deep. 'What is your plan?' she asks.

'We shall say she is mixed,' I reply. I have thought long and hard about this; when Sabby is full grown she will need a lot of meat - we can't hide that. Grandmother does not respond but stares deep into the flames.

'If we introduce her now and they see her good nature, get to know her now, as she grows, their affection will grow with her.' Still she does not respond but I can tell she is listening. 'What better way to hide something than in full view of all?' She turns to me and smiles and I know she is proud of me.

'How you have grown,' she says. 'We will try it your way.' I cannot help but grin from ear to ear. 'If she is to stay with us, if that is the calling, then you and she will have to work. How else shall we feed her?' This could not have gone better. Sabby forever at my side, part of our family and we shall go to work. How I have grown, indeed.

That afternoon Sabby walks proudly to heel as we strut into town. We are stared at by all we pass. Yet we are proud and happy and they smile more often than frown. When we get to the market square, we see a group of children playing a chasing game. They run and squeal between stalls and feet, their laughter their saviour from a clip round the ear from an irritated adult. It's not long before we are spotted and soon we are surrounded by a circle of silent, curious children. Ben Lovell is the first to speak. 'If that's a wolf it won't be for much longer. Not when my mother finds out.' His band of cronies snigger. Mary and her siblings help make up the crowd and I notice she stares at the ground.

I say, 'Gentlemen, let me introduce Sassaba, most part dog, least part wolf.' Nobody moves. 'Who shall be the first to pet her?' I ask. 'Her fur is soft and her welcome warm.' Sabby barks in happy agreement. Still no one moves. I look around the faces with a sweet welcoming smile. No one. I look Ben in the eyes. 'Goodman Lovell, will you be the first?'

Ben shrugs. 'I'm no fool,' he says, and his cronies pump up their chests. While they congratulate themselves on their wisdom, Mary quietly steps forward and Sabby goes to meet her. In seconds they are all licks and smiles and tickles. Mary strokes her head and stops to look at me.

'I did say soft,' I say and she smiles, even manages a small laugh, and then all the rest, bar Ben, pile in. Sabby has never known such attention and loves every minute. I see her pack instinct come to the fore and a pang of pain shoots through my heart - I cannot give her that. She rolls on her back and her tummy is tickled, she play pounces when invited by game. She is at one with the children and the game.

'That's no wolf,' says Ben. 'You cannot pet a wolf.' He spits in bitter disgust. He turns and whistles through his teeth and his gang stop their game and hurry after him.

'Sabby, we must go too,' I say, and she stops her game immediately and is by my side. The smaller children complain but I reassure them they can see and pet her the next day. I look Mary in the eyes. 'Thank you,' I say, and she smiles shyly and looks at the dirt, kicking it with her foot.

'She's a beautiful dog,' she says and looks me straight in the eyes with a sly glint.

I smile. 'That she is,' I say, 'and we'd best be on our way.' I nod to her and call Sabby and head towards Grace's house. We are already late.

I check we look our finest and then knock on the kitchen door.

Mother Gray opens it. 'Oh goodness,' she exclaims, then looking round quickly, adds, 'Quick, get inside.' We do and once she has closed the door I try to calm her.

'It is all well, she has been introduced and taken for dog.' Mother Gray looks at me in disbelief. 'Mother Gray meet Sassaba, Sabby to friends.' Mother Gray does not move but looks at both of us with suspicion. Sabby sinks her front legs and head down, bowing to show there is no need of fear.

'Oh, away with the pair of you,' she says, regaining her usual composure. 'Mistress is awaiting you. You are late and for your first lesson back,' and she shoos us out of the room and up the stairs.

Again, I check our appearance before knocking on the door.

'Come in,' Grace says, and I realise how much I have missed the sound of her voice. I push the door open and stand in the doorway.

'May we enter?' I say, and I see her face light up, first at me and then at Sabby. Grace is on her feet and Sabby has gone to meet her before I can say anything more. It's as if they have always known each other. The bond is instant and unchallengeable. I feel a heat flash through my body and remind this jealousy that it's a good thing they like each other. Eventually I take my usual seat, take up the last book we were reading and begin to read out loud.

'Raven, it is so good to see you,' Grace says. 'Come, let me greet you.' And she pulls me to my feet and engulfs me in the sweetest embrace so that I never want to be released. But release me she does.

'Let me look at you,' she says and scrutinizes me up and down. 'Now I see you had such a good cause I can forgive your absence.' Sabby barks in agreement.

'Come, sit and tell me of your adventures.'

Once I start I cannot stop. I tell her all that is safe to tell. How Sabby was found, but not how the moon told us her name - there are many things that are secret even from Grace. I tell of how Sabby has played her part so well with the townsfolk. Grace encourages and enjoys the stories. At the end she thanks me for such a beautiful tale and says she has found us a story that she thinks we shall appreciate. Although I have not seen words on pages for weeks now, she asks me to read out loud and I find I am confident and sure. I read:

Wolf and Raven Forever Friends

Once upon a time the Earth invited the beasts to come and stay. She offered them light and warmth and rain. All things grew, both plant and beast, fast and full and fat. They grew happy to enjoy the gifts of the Earth. Yet the Earth turned and grew tired and as the Earth turned the seasons turned and soon the beasts met snow for the first time. At first the beasts welcomed the beautiful blanket, welcomed winter as a game, a toy to play with, but the snow did not pass. Days, weeks, months passed. The plants hid, and the tall trees shed their leaves and slept. Soon other beasts followed - surely the snow would have passed by the time they awoke. Others withered away as their short time on earth passed. Yet other wandering souls found no shelter, found their bellies empty, found their searches endless. They roamed the snow-covered earth, lost and confused.

One night the sky was so clear and lit up by so many stars, the moon so round and so bright that it looked a much more welcoming home than Earth. Wolf, who had grown thick fur to keep warm, still felt the hunger in his belly gnaw at his soul and he let out a howl to the moon. If only he could travel there and escape this Earth. On and on he howled, nothing could make him stop. Finally Raven, perched high in the leafless tree, huddled up against the cold wind, cried out, 'What ails you, Wolf? What causes this noise?'

'Oh, Raven, my belly is so empty, it pains me so. I howl to the moon for maybe life there would not be so hard.'

'What? Why is life hard for you? Why is your belly empty?' asked Raven.

'How can you ask? I have travelled all this land and find only snow,' barked Wolf. Raven perched high in the tree could see a long distance in all directions. He could see where the prey the wolf sought was wandering.

'But I see your prey and it is plentiful.'

'How can this be true?' cried Wolf. 'Please help me, for I shall not live long without.'

'And if I find you prey, do you eat alone?' asked Raven

'If together we hunt, together we feast,' replied Wolf, certain the Raven was playing a trick.

'Then follow me,' cried Raven and he set off from the top of the tree. But Wolf was tired and uncertain; at first he did not follow.

Raven soared ahead then circled back, singing, 'Follow me, follow me, follow me,' but Wolf considered dropping to the ground and letting the snow take him - he was so hungry and it would be so easy, yet Raven was so certain. What had he to lose? Either way could lead to death. With one last cry from Raven, Wolf summoned the last of his strength and began to follow.

It was not long before Raven led them beyond the forest to an open plane where a herd of red deer roamed. Wolf did not stop to think or thank, and within seconds the oldest, weakest and slowest hind was firmly clasped between his jaws. Raven screeched, Wolf howled, this time with joy, and so happy was Wolf that he honoured his agreement and soon the two feasted. Since then Wolf and Raven have been forever friends, hunting and feasting together, and on a cloudless night Wolf can still be heard singing to the moon in honour of the time when Wolf and Raven became forever companions.

When our lesson is ended she says, 'This lesson has been one big secret sharing.' I nod. 'You must make sure to keep it so.'

'Of course,' I say. What is another secret to me?

'Good,' she replies. In the box are two pieces of egg-shaped marchpane. I remember how much I have missed these gifts too. It turns out Sabby also enjoys the taste.

After Ben Lovell spreads the word that Sabby is nothing but a soppy "dog", she soon becomes everyone's pet. We cannot make it thought the market place without every stall holder wanting to pet her or treat her. It gets so we have to leave earlier for lessons to arrive on time. I try to keep in the background, not used to such attention. I find it overwhelming at first but Sabby enjoys every minute; she feels part of a pack and I cannot deny her that. Grandmother says it's no bad thing I am known to the townsfolk, as I said myself what better way to hide something than right in front of folk. She encourages me to make connections with Sabby's admirers, be on friendly terms.

It is not easy; most of my childhood it has been my grandmother, beasts and me. My friends have been the tress, the earth, the river. It is strange for me to think of people in this way. You need words for communication, instead of an unspoken meeting of consciousness, and it's hard to fathom what people are actually saying with their words. The meaning of the words they use bear little resemblance to what they really mean. I do not understand this roundabout route and prefer the straightforward speech of the trees who seem to not know subterfuge at all. Still, over time I come to see the kindness at the heart of people, even though most try to hide it or silence it, which I do not understand. Sabby does not have such hesitation; she seems unafraid and I follow her lead.

Soon we are a fixture, a local legend that travellers from far and wide hope to encounter on their first visit. As Sabby grows so does the love for her. She is fine and handsome, her coat a mottled grey and brown which looks like pink. She is at ease in her body and her charm is unsurpassed. I learn a lot from her. Yet her size requires feeding. She needs meat and a lot of it. Our hunting trips for rabbits must come to an end. A rabbit is no longer sufficient and to hunt deer an impossibility that would lead to both our deaths. How would we explain the loss in numbers of his herd to the gamekeeper? It is time for me to go to work. My first job comes from an unexpected source.

Chapter Nine

My lessons have progressed well. I can now read and write with ease and confidence. We arrive at Grace's as usual. We have finished the primer and read some simple books full of instructions on how to tend house, things that I already know, things that confuse me. Why write in a book what is already known? Grace says not everyone is as wise as me and I could afford to be more generous. But I do not understand what she means.

We sit down at the desk. I am excited and nervous. What direction will our lessons take now? For a moment I am filled with dread. What if the lessons will come to an end? But there has been no indication that this will be so. I quickly dismiss the thought from my mind. Yet the quill and ink are not set on the table and there is no paper or book. I look at Sabby for reassurance and guidance. She seems calm although also expectant. After welcoming us, Grace has left us alone. Again unusual. I take the opportunity to take a closer look at the tapestries. I find the spider that helped me and wonder at the life of the beasts woven into cloth. The patterns on the opposite tapestry are dazzling, as if they vibrate and shimmer. It's easy to get lost in the sensation they create - a sense of being truly wide awake and alive.

Grace comes in carrying a candle and I quickly go back to my seat.

She laughs. 'It's not a crime to appreciate art,' she says and comes and sits down next to me, placing the lit candle out of sight of the window. She turns to face me and indicates I am to do the same. She looks at me earnestly and openly in the eyes.

'You have studied well,' she says, and my earlier fear that this is the last lesson resurfaces. 'You can now read and write. You have worked hard and faced your challenges.' Sabby barks in agreement. 'And it has been worthwhile - a whole universe to explore is now at your fingertips.' Books are expensive, and we have none at home, but I appreciate the principle. 'What I am to show you now you must not tell another living soul. Can you do that?' I am confused, she knows I am good with secrets; they have been a constant in my life. 'Your grandmother already knows and will not need an account.' I am more and more confused but also excited. I am being trusted with something, I can sense, is of great import. 'Are you ready?' she asks, and I nod.

'Of course,' I reply, and she smiles.

She gets up and walks over to the right side of the mantelpiece. I think it is light enough, why light more candles? Expense may not be an issue but why waste the work of bees? But she does not light the candle in the ornate candle holder, instead she slides her hand around where the frame attaches to the mantle. There is a click and the multi-coloured tapestry swings on its pole away from the wall. I laugh with surprise and glee. I have never seen such a thing. She steps over to the other candle holder and, as before, slides her hand around the frame. This time there is a click followed by a clink as a door opens up behind the tapestry. Now I am astonished and slightly scared.

I look at Grace, who smiles warmly. 'Do not fear, it is not a dungeon I take you to,' and she comes over to the table and picks up the lighted candle. 'Come see our hidden treasure,' she says and walks over to the door. She swings the tapestry further out of the way and pushes the door open wide. It is pitch dark inside and I cannot see anything. She goes inside; she must be lighting other candles because soon a warm glow issues from the room. She comes to the doorway having put down her candle.

'Welcome,' she says and gestures with her arm for us to enter. Sabby does not hesitate and eagerly goes ahead, tail wagging. She is drawn by the smell, a fusty but somehow welcoming and comforting scent. Sabby's ease reassures me a little but I have been taught to trust no one fully and still I fear my vulnerability. Yet I approach slowly, trying to look calm and hiding my curiosity which tears at my insides so it's all I can do to stop myself from running full speed at the door. Grace turns, I can see she is smiling to herself, and walks into the room, confident I will follow.

I reach the doorway and am stopped in my tracks. It's a small, square room, with no windows, and from top to bottom on all sides are shelves full of books. Books of all different shapes and sizes, some of them printed, some of them new and printed on a press but most handwritten, some simple, some beautifully illustrated. In the centre of the room is a small table and chair. Most of the table is covered with candles for illumination but an intricately-carved, leather-covered book lying next to a book stand, lays claim to the rest. I am speechless. I have never seen so many books, never imagined there could be so many books. Who can possibly have written them all?

'The treasure you see before you is worth more than any gold,' Grace says and she runs her fingers along the spines of the books on the shelves. I feel a pang of jealousy as I realise the love she has for these words on pages is deeper and more than she will ever feel for me, more than she will feel for any one person. I both want to destroy each and every single one of them and at the same time I want to be part of this love. I want to share this love with her. I think then that these books will never mean the same to me but if I can at least acquire a taste then I will get a chance to be closer to her and the books.

'Come take a seat,' she says and offers the chair to me. I am at once humbled and honoured. I walk over, gazing at all the books as I do, and slowly I sit down. Sabby barks approval and comes to lie at my feet, panting contentedly. Grace pushes my chair into the desk, so I am facing the book stand and despite everything I know and understand about myself, it feels like home, as if I have never felt quite so comfortable in my life before. This feeling does not make sense to me, but before I can protest Grace places the leather-bound book on the stand. It's not a big book, the print is small and the pages thin, like delicate butterfly wings.

'This will be a place to start,' she says and indicates for me to open the cover. It is much heavier than I imagined, dense with an intricate lace-like pattern on the dark green cover. All the books have been carefully crafted with love and this love fills the room.

'Welcome to my library,' she says. 'Each book is a priceless treasure, each one rescued or salvaged or discovered. Most are the only copy created or remaining. It does not need to be said that these are forbidden books whose knowledge and wisdom is no longer welcomed. These books are a connection to wisdoms that reach deep into the past and connect us with our earliest ancestors. They are a history that others seek to deny and destroy. It has been my life's work and secret passion to gather these jewels together.' Again she caresses the covers. It feels so good to have been welcomed into this secret. I want to express my gratitude but can find no useful words to say.

'They are beautiful,' I manage and feel nothing but inadequate. She smiles, hopeful she has found another enthusiast.

'I am expectant for many contented hours together with these books. Just you and I and the books,' she says, and we smile. It feels like we are conspirators in a fabulous adventure. 'Not all the books are in English, but I will help with the ones that are not,' she says in a more business-like tone. 'But today is your first day at work.' She gestures for me to turn the pages of the book.

I can feel something under the pages, just a little way in. I flick past the first few, only glancing at the brightly coloured illustrations. There, at the start of the first chapter, is a paper, sealed with wax, a letter, on it an address. I know the place, it's on the outskirts of town, but the other side to my grandmother's. I look up at Grace with a question in my eye.

'You know the place?' she asks. I nod. It is not easy to get to but as Raven I have flown far and wide across the shire and there is not a place I do not know or not know how to get to. 'Then go quick and direct. Tomorrow we shall begin this work,' and she strokes the open pages of the book. Hesitantly I rise to my feet, but she nods encouragingly. Sabby is already at the door to the library. 'Do not tell anyone your destination or why.'

'Of course,' I say.

'I seek no response but make sure you deliver in person. Go directly home afterwards and we shall rendezvous as usual tomorrow.' I nod and tuck the letter deep into my doublet, out of sight.

We head out as Grace takes a seat at the library table. That day Mother Gray gifts us two books made of marchpane and we almost can't eat them so precious the shape has become to us.

Our delivery is in the opposite direction to our home, but we chose to leave the town as usual; to do otherwise would raise questions and I know by now that is the last thing anyone wants. Once safely outside the town walls we cut through the woods. It's much longer that way but by now it's growing dusk and we will be unnoticed amongst the leaves and bushes.

I have never been to this house. It is well known and often spoken of but always tales of fear. The occupant is a ghost, a devil not of human form who eats babies and small children given half the chance. He is a wizard who casts spells against all who offend him. He has a withered arm and hand and a hunch upon his back. The house is possessed. The truth is no one has ever really spoken to him. He has only been into town himself a handful of times and then mostly passing through on route to elsewhere. His manservants attend in his place, of which there seems a steady changing procession, but never anyone local. The house is simple and the grounds ample but not excessive. Yet he never seems wanting of anything. He is a mystery the townsfolk would like to solve, would like not to be, would like to dispose of but have not yet found the means by which to do so. I do not know his name but his outsider status I recognise and feel a kinship to. I am not afraid to approach this recluse and, anyway, I have Sabby at my side. We decide to be direct and not get swayed by the woodland at dusk. If a rabbit is found and caught on our way home, then what harm is it to anyone? On our way there it would be a different thing.

The house itself is hidden, surrounded by tress on all sides, the garden and grounds behind high stone walls but free of trees. The path to the front door is faint but we find it. For some reason I look around before we approach. All seems quiet and Sabby is at ease, which stills the small but nagging doubts in my mind. Sabby fearlessly goes ahead to the door and I follow, not wanting to be left alone. I expect to find it dirty, unkempt, overgrown with moss and cobwebs, but it's a simple wooden door in perfect condition with an iron door knocker in the shape of a wolf which both Sabby and I appreciate.

I raise the handle to knock but the door is opened before I can bring it down. It is dark inside, and I see little and no one but the door is opened barely more than a crack. I go to speak but a hand appears out of the darkness, open and expectant. I look at Sabby. She is sniffing the air, alert but not frightened. I reach inside my doublet and pull out the letter. The hand grabs it from me.

'Wait,' instructs a dry, cracked voice, one that is not used to talking, and the hand disappears behind the door, only to re-emerge moments later holding an oilskin wrapped around something large and quite heavy.

'I request no answer,' I say.

'For your time,' replies the voice and pushes the oilskin at me so if I do not take it, it will fall to the ground. Then the door is shut firmly in my face. Sabby shows great interest in the oilskin and a small peek inside reveals large cuts of venison, raw and fresh and thick with juices. So this is how it is to be. I take us into the woods and, at the first hidden, safe spot, I open the oilskin and using the small whittle tang knife I carry, hidden at my back where my hose meets my doublet, I cut a chunk of meat for Sabby. If I do not I fear we shall not make it home at all. Slightly satisfied she agrees to wait until home for the rest. We go as quickly as we can and waiting at the door as we arrive home is Grandmother; her smile tells of her pride in us. That night we all feast. Sabby may never know the joy of the hunt and the kill, but she will never go hungry either.

Chapter Ten

And so it goes that what started out as lending a hand to my grandmother becomes our profession. We have our chores around the house, our lessons and our delivery service. At first it is just Grace and my grandmother but my discretion when delivering Grandmother's remedies – whatever they are for and to whoever needs them – is our recommendation and soon our services are required far and wide. Priority is always with Grandmother and Grace but it's not long till I am known as the messenger boy. Despite our infamy no one ever knows how or when we deliver but the recipients. Sabby grows healthy and quick to full size on her diet of the best, fresh meat. The butcher grows fat on Sabby and always passes us the best titbits of the leftovers when we pass by. I grow too, long and thin, my hair a thick black mane, which Grandmother tames regularly, my eyes a piercing blue which get brighter and more vivid every day. I feel strong and love the power of my body as it grows. Our lessons go well, and we are of service to Grandmother, Grace and our community. We have a community to which we feel now an accepted part. There is much subterfuge in our world, but it has ever been so for me; I know no different and it has always served me. All is well with our world.

Shifting has always been natural, easy. I feared as I got older I would lose it, not be able to do what always felt right, but it simply grows with me. Grandmother says as I have shifted since I was born, my bones and flesh will never truly set, that I am Shifter, and nothing can change that. And I do not want it to, why would I want it to? I do not understand why I have to keep it secret even. Surely folk would flock from far and wide to see such a rarity. If we wanted wealth surely it would be easy to secure. Yet we do not, and Grandmother is so certain that I would not live the day out if someone found out, that even though it has taken all my will not to, I have never let my secret out. Until it is contained no more.

We have been working our way through the books in the secret library. The collection so far has focused on remedies, herbs and potions, things I already know but did not know had been written down. Occasionally I discover a subtlety that I did not know before but mostly it's just reading practice. Gradually the books get harder, more complex and the subjects varied. Sometimes the books are in a language I am not familiar with and Grace helps me with the sense. Big tomes of words on Fairy Law and creatures of other worlds. These are my favourite so far and we linger over the descriptions, the illustrations. I know this is forbidden law, that fairies and the like are fiction for most folk, that the law says it is so, but we know different. Fairies have always been a part of my life. Others would read these books as fiction but to me it's simple fact, although I believe many of the beings to be now extinct; until I turn a page and find myself - on the page. A whole chapter on Shifters.

At first, I am thrilled; this is the first time I see myself reflected back to me. The idea there are others like me in the world has never occurred to me and it is as if I have received all my birthdays in one. Yet the book is antiquated, hand-written and teaches of the wrongs these fairies and other creatures are. It teaches of how best to destroy and "remedy" the world of such terrors, and here I am amongst them. I do not need to read the words, the illustrations are enough - pictures of torture and the slowest, most painful deaths. How we are to be spotted and how we are the vilest of all because we can so easily disguise who and what we are. I cannot help it. The joy of recognition so brutally changed to horror and despair.

Now I understand my grandmother, now the secrecy makes sense. The tears cannot be held but fall from my eyes. Grace moves the book away, so they do not spoil the pages. I cannot help but feel shame and fear. To be hated so. How is it possible that I can be so rejected, so misunderstood, and with each new horror that I think, I shrink a little. I am so distraught that I do not even notice I am changing until I find myself a shivering dormouse in the corner of the room. Sabby is distraught, standing over me, growling and barking, ready to take on anybody or anything that comes near me. I look at the pile of clothes, what will Grace be thinking? Is she running scared? Has she gone to fetch the sheriff, the townsfolk, to chase me out to torture or to kill me? I think I'll turn to Bear should they try to catch me; I shall rip and tear at their beings till they are nothing but scraps of flesh and bone. I will not let them take Sabby either; I will defend her to the death as she will defend me.

But Grace does not run, she does not scream, she does not cry. She does not jump on the table at the sight of a mouse. Rather she approaches Sabby with gentle but certain caution, offers her open hands as a demonstration of her good intentions, her voice is calm.

'Sassaba, still, Sassaba, quiet, Sassaba, sit,' she instructs and Sabby softens, pulls her fangs back into her mouth and stills her growls. She sits but close to me. Grace reaches out her hand and Sabby lets her touch the top of her head. Then Grace crouches down to me.

'Raven, do not fear, you are amongst friends here.' I am not sure and edge a little closer towards Sabby. 'Come, you know my love of you is true. Not a mother but a sister.' And something inside me bursts and melts as if I have been carrying around a heavy sack of putrid puss which I have now put down.

Then it is easy, as I relax, I shift back. Sabby is ecstatic and races around the table several times and I stand naked before Grace. It is a disadvantage of shifting that I have not yet found an answer for.

'Sister,' she says, and holds me to her and I have never felt so open, so honest. I did not know it was possible to feel so. Tears of relief fall from my eyes as easy as breathing. 'Come, fear not,' she says and hands me a kerchief. I have never seen a naked man. I know the difference between male and female but not the specifics. Instinctively I go to cover the small bumps that are forming on my chest. She considers me for a moment and then says, 'Wait here.' I hold Sabby close, her heat and the feel of her fur against my skin is all the comfort I need. By the time Grace returns some of my usual cheek has recovered.

'Here,' she says and places a steaming hot mulled wine on the table. 'For your nerves and for your looks.' She holds up a long thin sheet of linen.

'Come,' she instructs, 'arms up.' I stand with my arms in the air as she tenderly binds my breasts, wrapping the linen around, just tight enough to flatten my form but lose enough so I can breathe and move easily.

'There,' she says as she fastens with a pin. 'It matters not so much now but this is a lifelong habit for you.' I look down at my now flattened chest and know this is my life. 'Don't catch a chill,' she says, indicating the rest of my clothes. 'When you are ready, join me next door.' She leaves me and Sabby alone. I hold Sabby near; I do not fully understand but feel my life from now on will not be the same again.

I dress quickly as I begin to feel the chill; I take my wine and step into the chamber. Grace is sitting by the fire, lost in its flames. I sit the other side of the fire and Sabby settles in front of me. We sit in quiet stillness for a while.

I am not sure what to do so in the end I manage, 'Thank you.' It feels inadequate. It is as if I have disturbed her from a distant land; as she returns she smiles at me, then a troubled frown forms across her forehead.

'I have been fortunate,' she says 'in finance and have never wanted for money. I have spent much of my life collecting the library. Collecting all I can of my people, our ways, our wisdom. I do not need to tell you those books are dangerous.' She looks at me hard and I nod reassurance.

'They tell our story and they tell of how we are now forbidden too.' It's as if a cloud is lifting from my brain. There are more folk like me; we are forbidden and we all live in secrecy.

'We are not alone, it's true,' she says, 'and we are all connected.' More clouds lift; the visitors to my grandmother's when we have to hide in the hidey hole, the messages we have carried.

'Yes,' she says, 'it's true, you have always played a part in keeping our medicine alive.' I feel a strange mixture of pride and doubt. 'Our family reaches across the world. Know that you are part of a large, connected, beautiful, worldwide family.' I have spent so much of my life as an almost recluse I cannot even imagine what that means, but my gut knows it's true and I feel a surge of power sweep through my being.

'Now is not our time to live freely and openly. Mankind is lost in its own importance, has lost touch with its humanity, but a time will come when we are once again celebrated and not feared for our gifts.' I have so many questions but before I can ask she says, 'Until then we continue to progress, continue our connection, continue our truth, out of sight, out of sound, out of the minds of those who seek to conquer and dominate.' There is pain in all she says and yet a peace is birthed inside me as if a million doubts have left me.

'And you?' I ask, 'if I be Shifter you be...?'

'It is late,' she says, 'your grandmother will be concerned.' She is soft in her tone but I know she is resolute and do not ask again. She holds me tight before we leave and squeezes Sabby close. There is a bond now that cannot be broken.

'Tomorrow, sister,' I say as we leave; she smiles and nods. I know that later she will shed a tear of joy when she remembers. In the kitchen as we are about to leave, Mother Gray calls us back.

'Here, today you should not leave without these,' she says and hands us two heart-shaped pieces of marchpane.

'They are beautiful,' I say. We do not eat them but rather I place them in my doublet close to my own heart.

'Safe home,' Mother Gray says as we step out into the clear moonlight night.

'Thank you,' I say and Sabby and I look at each other; can Mother Gray be one of us?

We take our time on the way home, dawdling along the brook, watching the moonlight dance with the water, listening to the water's song of reassurance. My head is heavy with information but my body alive with possibilities. I have never felt a loss or known that I felt a lack but now I know there are others like me I want to meet each and every one, or at the very least one other. I feel as if a need in me that has been safely stored has been released and I feel more comfortable inside myself for it. Sabby is by my side and I know we shall go on this journey together. I am not alone. When we reach home, Grandmother has brewed a calming infusion and made up my bed. I have hardly taken a few sips before I fall into a deep sleep curled around Sabby.

Chapter Eleven

In the morning after chores and breakfast, Grandmother tells of a past time when our ways of the Earth where celebrated and honoured, when our wisdom was wisdom, before man invented evil and used it as a way to treat others as less and themselves as more. I belong to a vast and beautiful family of healers, guides, all manner of gods and creatures with all manner of gifts to share with the world.

Yet we are strong, so strong, how have we not been able to stop this dominance? How have we not stopped our own extinction? Grandmother cannot answer. It seems a mystery how all that was once understood, all that once served mankind, has now to be forbidden. She says what she does know is that no matter how hard they try to eradicate us they will never succeed. How can anyone or anything stop what is? She says our persecution has been gradual, bit by bit our place in the world eroded. But ever since the first word was spoken against us we have protected all that we are. Across the world we have made connections and, as all happy families, we look after our own. We do not seek to overthrow, merely to be who we are in peace and safety. And we shall find ways to be so.

She tells of a time a long way in the future when we will be free to practice what we believe. Says our duty, in the meantime, is to be custodians of our wisdom until the time we can practice openly and freely once more. I want to do all I can for my people and she reassures me I am, that I have been. My grandmother has been active in this underworld ever since and as I grow, so shall I, if I want to, but it must be my choice. For me there is no choice, no question, my right to life will never be in doubt or my allegiance to my family.

'This life will not be an easy path,' she says.

'This path will be my life,' I reply.

'So, it's agreed,' she says.

She stands and goes over to the medicine table; she takes the two marchpane hearts given to us the night before and hands them to me. I kiss each heart, bend and let Sabby lick both. I breath in their smell then cast them into the flames;

our fates are sealed. We watch the marchpane melt, bubble and spit. Grandmother and I turn, face each other and embrace, a deep, long hold. We all know now there is no way back. When we break we are back to the every day.

'Be careful your binding is not too tight,' Grandmother says as I straighten my doublet in readiness for my classes. It is the first time she has acknowledged the changes in my body.

Now my lessons take on new meanings; words on pages no longer seem an idle pleasure but the quenching of a demanding thirst. I want to know all. I want to read each and every book in the library, yet there are so many. I am in turns exhilarated by the opportunity and devastated by the enormity of the task. I can never thank Spider enough for the key she gave me. Everything has changed now; when I walk through the town I understand my subterfuge and work my charm to my advantage.

It's Grace that gives me my next messenger job. It is to the old recluse again, so I think little of it. We do as before, leave the lesson taking our usual route out of town then doubling back through the woods as before. This time we knock on the door and it opens wider than before and a soft quiet voice from inside calls, 'Come.' We hesitate.

'You are welcome.' Sabby hesitates no more, she is inside before I can stop her. I am more cautious; I peer into the darkness. I see nothing and sense nothing. Then I see Sabby; she is sitting comfortably, and I can just see a pale hand stroking her head. I step inside. It takes a few moments, but my eyes begin to adjust. I can make out the smiling open features of an older man, thin wrinkles that tell a thousand tales. He holds out his hand and steps towards me.

'Cerano,' he offers.

'Raven,' I say, and we shake hands.

I reach into my doublet and hand him the letter.

'No reply sought,' I say.

He takes the note and nods his head. He reaches into the darkness and brings out the oilskin.

'Thank you,' I say. He nods again.

'Sabby,' I call, and we turn and head out of the door. I turn back to say goodbye, but the door has already been silently shut behind us. It's not until we get home that I notice that tucked inside the oilskin is a note. At first, I am annoyed we have just returned home to go out again and to have to go out again and at this hour, but on closer inspection I see it is addressed to me.

The penmanship is beautiful, clean and crisp and precise yet flowing and natural. He has a well-practiced hand. I take the paper and sit by the fire. Sabby sits close and I unfold the paper. The border is beautifully illustrated with trees and flowers all common to our shire. Oaks and snowdrops, the occasional poppy, daisies, how did he know my favourites? In the middle of the papers is a poem.

Sister So You Seek

In the silence You shall hear
In the darkness You shall see
In the pain You shall heal
In the losing You shall find
In the dying You shall birth
Sister so You seek what
Has always been within

Grandmother has joined us, and I hand her the paper. The poem is beautiful, but its meaning escapes me. It is a riddle and it is not a riddle, I am not aware of seeking anything. Grandmother sighs deeply when she has finished reading and hands me back the sheet. I look to the fire, then my grandmother.

'Should I?' I say, and she sees how much it would pain me to do so.

'One day,' she says, 'for now make sure no one will find it.' I think of a place to house it but of all the nooks and crannies I can think of no such place. I am unsure of hiding it in the cottage for fear of endangering Grandmother.

'Would between the planks of our loft keep it out of sight?' she asks. I nod; it's such an obvious place in plain view.

That night my dreams are laced with his words; it is both comforting and disturbing.

The next day it arrives. I had not thought about it, not planned for it, not anticipated it. I had forgotten about it. My breasts have proved little issue, they have not grown so big and are easily hidden with some binding and a doublet. I do not have a battle with my body – it is people who have a battle with my body in clothes they think it should not be in. I do not understand why the law concerns itself with the cloth on people's backs, do not see what concern it is of others what feels comfortable to me. Yet it seems for some there is a rule, it seems for some there is a law for everything. It seems odd to invent so many when there are ample laws in nature that cannot be made or destroyed. Why do we need more? It seems that mankind must make itself busy in one form or other.

After a dream-filled night, I awaken to a pain in my womb and my lower back. I can smell it but still I reach under the covers, my fingers return covered in blood. Now my menses have arrived, how will I hide these from the freedom of the hose? I am not shocked. It would be hard to live so close with beasts, to see their yearly cycle, and not understand how life is created and birthed. Not to mention the amount of fertility remedies and ceremonies we trade, they are education enough. Yet somehow, I never really expected it to happen to me.

Grandmother stirs and in her stirring I see her sniff. She smells it too. Her eyes open and we look at each other. I may have forgotten but my grandmother has not. She rises from her bed, opens the linen draw in our chest and takes out a fresh pair of linens for me and several tightly rolled, short pieces of wool. The linens have been soaked in deer musk and have a heavy smell not altogether pleasant, but it will hide my very feminine smell with a very masculine one. I do not need to be told the woollen tubes, the pessaries, go inside.

I feel nothing, neither joy nor regret. It's a part of my growing and I accept it as such, that is all. But when Grandmother hands me the linens and the pessaries I can tell it's so much more for her. She does not show it but when she turns away I catch her smile; it is one of great joy and satisfaction. When I return from my toilet I wash away the blood. I do not need to be shown how to insert the pessary but it's good to know there is help at hand should it be required. When I am dressed and becoming accustomed to my new scent, Grandmother hands me an envelope. For the first time after lessons I am to deliver to the inn and await a reply. Now this does inspire an excitement in me.

I love my lessons. I love that each day I learn a little more about who I am, who my ancestors are, what our ways are, how we view the world. It's entering dimensions I understand, that understand me, where subterfuge and secrecy are not necessary. Yet today I cannot wait for them to pass, such is my excitement at visiting the inn. The inn is on the main road through the town, just to the edge of the square. I have often had cause to pass by and often wondered about the raucous noises from within, the singing, the fighting. It has rooms above and many a traveller takes a night's lodgings there. For that reason it is somehow apart from the rest of the town. I am sure Grandmother will have made many deliveries there, but this is the first time I have been trusted and I am determined it will be some of my best work. I do not let on even to Grace or Mother Gray my task.

We leave the lesson as usual but soon slip out of sight down the lanes and behind the houses and shops. We dart from shadow to shadow. It's getting dusk which we use to our advantage. We make our way to the back of the inn. It's busy, the livery attached to the inn has regular comings and goings. The kitchen is at the back and the cook seems in a constant rage, the kitchen hands constantly afeard for their lives, ducking knives that fly through the air with piercing accuracy always just missing their target. The confusion will work to our advantage; it will be easy to slip into the corridor and back passages of the inn unnoticed, just another boy on an errand.

We wait in the shadows until the livery boy is busy feeding the beasts and the cook is tearing strips off the kitchen hands. We stroll easily across the yard, following our principle that it's easier to be invisible in clear view. I take a subtle glance behind to check we have not been seen. I turn back to see

Sabby disappearing into the shadows by the back door. Someone is coming but it's too late and I bump full body into Mary.

'Mary,' I say.

I would like to apologise but we are both too startled by each other to speak and for what feels like the longest time we stare into each other's eyes. It's like we have entered another world. There is a loud crash from the kitchen and suddenly we are back in the yard of the inn. I look down and see Mary is carrying two heavy buckets, one in each hand; they are covered so must be slops of some kind. It seems we are both gainfully employed.

'I'm sorry,' I say, eventually. 'May I be of assistance?' I go to take the pails but she holds fast and shakes her head.

'More than it's worth,' she says, and nods her head towards the kitchen.

'Ahh,' I say.

'Up the back stairs along the passage and on the right,' she says. I start to protest but she says,

'I've seen nothing and no one,' and she pushes past me on her way towards the pit. For a moment I watch her go. I am full of questions but Sabby is out of the shadows and through the door before I can stop her, and I follow in fast pursuit.

The passageway is empty and dark. It is not far to the stairs and we move silently as shadows themselves. There is only one floor and all the rooms are closed, so finding the last door on the right is simple. I knock loud and clear once, then knock again more gently in a pattern that should be known and understood. To my surprise the door is flung open and standing in front of me is a bold young man a few years older than me. He smiles a broad open smile.

'Welcome my friend,' he says, 'pray enter, I hope the news is good.'

He stands aside from the doorway and gestures us inside. Sabby trots in confidently but I am not so sure. I want to turn and run in the opposite direction but don't understand why. Yet I bow my head a little and step inside. He quickly checks there is no one else in the passageway and almost slams the door shut. I jump a little. I am used to hushed tones and lowered eyes, but this gentleman is the opposite to all that.

The bright glare of the room is startling after the darkness of the passage. Sabby has taken a prized spot in front of the fire. The windows catch the glint of the setting sun and candles abound.

'Come, please take a seat,' he instructs, and I find I am powerless to argue. He pours us both full tankards of ale and slides one towards me.

'Thank you,' I say

'To all that is dear,' he says and clinks my tankard. I sip hesitantly, could this be some kind of trap? Has my real recipient been dispatched and this imposter set in his place?

He is a fit but slight built man of some means if the fine leather saddle bags are much to go by. He is clean and clean shaven with a little shadow and his clothes the finest weave. He has little luggage save the saddle bags, a fine fur-lined cloak and an oilskin. He watches me trying to pretend not to scan the room.

'Fine beast you have,' he says, then, 'I'm sorry, Constantine,' and he offers his hand to shake. I offer the letter from my grandmother. It is my intention to be gone as soon as possible.

'I await a reply,' I say as he takes the paper from my hand.

He says nothing and is business-like at once. He studies me as he unfolds the paper and then turns his full attention to the words. His face remains expressionless as he reads. It is the first time I have witnessed the receiver of the message read the message. I begin to think Constantine has learnt that hiding is best done in the open too. When he has finished reading he folds the paper back up, stands, goes over to the fire and drops the letter in. We all watch it burn.

Once it has turned to ashes he turns to me. 'Raven, brother, come,' he commands. I stand; is this the reply?

'Come,' he says again. I take a tentative step in his direction. Sabby is watching with interest but still seems at ease which confuses me as I am not.

'Brother,' Constantine says and comes to me and embraces me with an unexpected warmth and familiarity.

I would break away, but I do not think I could escape his clasp. He relinquishes slightly, and smiles. He takes his right hand, still holding me fast with his left, spits on the fingers of his right hand and smears his hand down his right cheek. His beard shadow smudges clean away. My eyes jump from their sockets; can this be? Is standing afore me another like me? Constantine laughs and releases me.

'Yes, it's true,' he says and hands me my ale. I take the tankard and sit back down.

'Welcome to the family,' he says and clinks my tankard again; this time he sips and I down my drink in one. A few months ago, the only family I knew was my grandmother, Sabby and our beasts; now it seems I have no end of families.

'So, let's begin at the beginning,' he says.

That night is a huge initiation. First, he checks my binding and shows me how to tie it to the most effect but without causing harm. He shows me how to have stubble from the burnt end of a cork.

'Now,' he says, 'thus far you have got away with it but soon not so.' I am confused now as to what he is referring.

'If you are to pass then every move you make, in public at least, must have a masculine flavour.' Why had I not thought of any of this before?

'Why?' I ask. 'Why must all this be so, just so I can wear hose and doublet and not be confined by skirts and petty coats?' He sits down and drinks from his ale.

'The sense is to keep us all in a place, most often a place not of our choosing, so it is the law of the land.'

'What use a law that protects a few and traps the many?' I ask.

'I think you need to ask the few,' he says and laughs.

'I do not seek to be man. I am not afraid to be woman,' I say.

'But what a woman is in this time is not how you feel?' he suggests.

'Yes,' I say and it's the first-time feelings that have waged a silent war inside me are expressed and so simply put.

'You are not the first to feel this and you shall not be the last,' he says.

'How does that help me?' I spit. I feel overwhelmed and my first instinct is to run. I stand. Sabby lifts one lazy eyelid; it's clear we are not to leave just yet. I stomp over to the window.

Night has fallen, and the town is busy making haste for home. Torches and candles create a festive feel to the end of yet another day. I see Mary standing with her father outside the inn. It's clear they are arguing, despite their efforts to hide it. She tries to return to the inn and he grabs her by the arm. I feel myself contract, tensing my muscles, ready to pounce. How dare he? But she spits in his face and stamps on his foot. He cannot help but to release her as he hops from foot to foot, wiping his face. She throws some coins at him and walks back into the inn as he scrabbles on the ground for the pennies.

'But it's more than just clothes?' he says. I had been so engrossed I had not realised he has come to stand behind me, to look over my shoulder.

'What?' I ask, what is this that he means?

'Many cultures, many peoples have a name for people like you and me. Sometimes we are considered to have great insight and spiritual powers. Here we have been written out of existence.' I am still confused, he has not answered my question.

'Ask Grace, she will show you the books you need to read.' He knows Grace. 'The girl, Mary, is it? You have loved her long?' he asks

'Mary?' I ask, what can he mean now? I have heard people talk of love, know it's on the horizon for some but it is not an option I had ever considered for myself.

'Ah too much, I go too far,' he says, 'for now let us prepare you for what lies ahead.'

He reaches inside his hose and pulls out a tight roll of linen. I have only seen a naked man once before through the reeds at the riverside and then in books Grace has shown me, but I do not need to be told what it is. 'The easiest way to walk like a man is to ape what is between his thighs.'

At last something makes sense. I want to ask why I cannot just shift into man when he says, 'This is shifting,' and then I understand.

He shows me how to make my own, where to place it, how to walk and sit. The hardest part is the voice, how to speak with my lower register without sounding ridiculous. He says to practice long before I speak in public, tells me not to worry, it will come naturally when I apply my shifting skills.

To help our labours we drink much ale and although my head swims with new information and experience he is a playful tutor and we laugh a lot. It feels more like a game than lessons that later in life I will depend upon.

When I am fitted and comfortable with this new form he pulls the cord for more ale. There is a firm but polite tap at the door which interrupts our play. He pushes me forward, my first public test. Full of the confidence of the Dutch I fling open the door. Mary is standing there, holding a large jug. I beam, stupidly, at her; she shyly smiles and looks away. I can do nothing but stare. Eventually he steps in.

'Mary, my pretty, thank you so much. Please add it to my tab.'

He swaps the empty jug for the full. She bobs a curtsey and throws me a smile before turning and hastening down the passage. He closes the door gently. I do not know how much I am feeling or how much of it is ale, but my legs feel decidedly wobbly and my head floats away from my body. He guides me to a chair by the fire.

Chapter Twelve

The next thing I remember is Sabby's warm, wet tongue on my face waking me up from slumber on the soft rushes of my grandmother's house. My mouth is dry, and I feel shaky inside as if my bones have turned to jelly. I look down and find I am in my linens, my doublet and hose folded neatly to the side.

'When I sent you to be initiated this isn't quite what I had in mind,' Grandmother says and hands me a large cup of fresh, clean water. I drink it down greedily and then I remember my pack. I reach down; it's not there. I reach for my hose, then the horror hits me; has Grandmother, but she interrupts my thoughts.

'Constantine laid you to sleep,' she says, 'the pair of you singing the whole way home. We're lucky none of the neighbours bothered to come after you, as you will have surely raised them from their slumbers.'

I groan as flashes of memory return. I remember feeling like a king riding bareback on Constantine's horse, him at the reins, me at the rear. We were singing to woo the moon and believing we were doing a fine job.

'Still there will be no doubt now, if there was before, you will have proved yourself a true man to all the town,' Grandmother says and hands me three raw eggs in a cup mixed with spices and herbs.

'Drink this,' she says with a look that does not allow for dispute. I close my eyes and down it in one. It is no wonder she has such a prosperous business.

'Get yourself washed and pressed, with fresh linens mind. Constantine will be here soon, and you'd best be ready when he arrives.' I am thrilled to see him again, what fortune, but it is quickly followed by dread.

What exactly had happened last night? As the cold water from the pump hits my head, snatched memories return, fragments of stories, Constantine sailing with pirates, of Bedouin women with jet black hair, piercing blue eyes and olive skin, of the winning and losing of fortunes, of life at sea and expeditions on land. I remember dancing badly and falling over. I remember none of it hurting.

The shaking in my bones has ceased and the fresh air and water have cleared my head. I dress and place my pack. I call Sabby and we walk down to the brook; it seems we have a holiday from chores today, as we wait for Constantine. We sit in our favourite spot and I hold Sabby close; she does not complain but nestles into me and I find tears where I expected peace. She lets my tears flow into her coat, sometimes I feel she is constantly and patiently waiting for me to catch up, as if she has always known we would be here now with my tears. Walking with the pack came easy enough and I can feel it change every movement in my body. It is doing its job and I am reciprocating but I cannot help feeling it does not fit, that it will never fit. Why is it that no matter where, I do not fit?

My tears have dried and we are still if not peaceful. Suddenly we hear the breath and snort of a horse. We turn. Constantine is behind, astride his beautiful white mare. How have they arrived without us hearing? I must ask for tips on his silent approach.

'Grandmother said you were worse for wear,' he teases. I shrug and turn back to the brook. Sabby has already gone to greet them. Constantine jumps off his horse, Blossom, with a hefty but playful thump and comes and sits beside me. For a few moments we sit in a companionable silence.

'This is all very pretty but we do have work to do,' he says. I turn and look at him with a question in my eyes.

'You do not think I just happened into town just when you started your menses? Just at your hour of need, did you?'

'Course not,' I grumble and turn back to the brook. Whatever this work is, I'd rather laundry duties.

'I suppose then it's of no interest to you, the part you could play to help your sisters and brothers, your new family?'

I shrug my shoulders.

'Shame, because your new duties could take you far and wide.'

I shrug again, determined to be unimpressed.

'I had my eye on a beautiful young colt who I think would be perfect for you. Still if you are not going to be a messenger then you won't need him.' At that I leap to my feet and Sabby and I are at Blossom's side before Constantine can blink.

'What?' I ask as Constantine stifles a smile.

'Too easy,' he says as he mounts Blossom. He reaches down his hand and pulls me up. I sit astride, too proud, too confident to clasp his waist. He gives Blossom a gentle squeeze and we are off at a brisk canter, weaving through the woods, Sabby at our side. It is as if we move as one being.

I am so enchanted I do not pause to think how we shall explain to the townsfolk how I have a horse or why or how we will feed it. How I will know how to ride it. I just know inside me it has to be. It is the first thing to make sense these last few months. We go further than we have been before, take turns I have never taken, paths I do not know. Soon we have reached a wide-open grass land, a plain not yet claimed by humans. The way through would be long and arduous but Blossom knows the way and we come to stop at a high point in the middle of the plain. The forest blocks the view back to the town and ahead there is only space. What are we doing here? I had expected a horse fair or a farm at least.

'Are you going to sit there all day?' asks Constantine.

'Here?' I reply, incredulous

'Here,' he says and from his tone I know it is so. I jump down and wince as the blood returns to my feet. Sabby is sitting, panting happily. I look around, but the grass is almost up to my chest. The sun is high now and a stillness fills the air; only the most determined of insects is at work.

Constantine stays mounted. He cups his hands around his mouth and in unison with Blossom lets out a high-pitched whinny that bursts out in flowing waves across the plain. Three times they cry. Then we wait in silence. At first there is nothing, just the lazy summer haze. Then in the distance it can be heard, a rumbling like a cacophony of drums beating in the distance, then louder and more distinct, becoming hoofs hitting the ground heard far in advance of sight. Then the smell - a rich, happy sent of horse sweeps across the plain. Then the dust is the first sighting, a huge bellowing cloud of earth. Then as they approach, individual shapes, forms come into view. It is the most beautiful thing I have ever witnessed. At least twenty-five, different in ages, different in colours, different in size but together as a whole. Another family, I think.

They are soon upon us and come to a gentle co-ordinated stop. They settle and the leader steps forward. Constantine and Blossom approach and bow, Constantine bending forward as Blossom lowers her front legs and head. The lead mare reciprocates and then all three whinny in agreement. Constantine and Blossom retreat to the raised area where Sabby is standing, alert and focused. The lead mare looks at me and we both bow our heads.

Then she turns and walks away; gradually one by one she is followed by the other horses until finally there is only one horse left, the beautiful, black colt. He is nervous, almost shy, but does not turn, does not leave with the rest but waits patiently. I look towards Sabby who gives an encouraging yelp. I do not need to be told. I feel the connection so strong it almost hurts. I walk calmly and with certainty towards the colt. I can feel everything around me, the heat of the sun, the dust on my boots, the scent of the wild flowers, but it's as if everything is suspended, as if everything is waiting. I want to run up to him, to clasp him around the neck and hold him tight but know this is for another time. I expect him to run, to turn on the spot at the last moment. So I stop a few feet away from him. We look at each other and it is as if we have always known each other.

Together we walk into no man's land and meet each other. Our breath mingles and becomes woven. There is no question, no hesitation. I walk to his shoulder, clasp the base of his mane and swing up onto his back. I have never had charge of a horse before, barely even been on the back of one, but on him I am home. My legs know how to fold around his sides. I can feel him, and he can feel me. We do not look back but trot easily over to Constantine and Blossom. Blossom greets him with a gentle knowing whinny. He lowers his head. Sabby greets him with soft but eager licks and Constantine a dip of the head. We do not look back but we both know the other horses have gone and he has joined our family as I have joined his. I beam at Constantine; how could I have ever doubted? He gives me a cheeky wink. Blossom turns almost on the spot and we are fast through the forest. That night I know we shall learn his name.

Grandmother has prepared a feast for the colt on return. Hay and oats abound. We shall not fence him in or tie him up. He will know his home and we shall trust that he does. Sabby is on watch if anyone decides the colt should be theirs but I would like to see them try and catch him. I already know I am a guest and not a master. It is his will as much as ours that he is joined with us. I am so humbled and honoured to have such friends and confidants. That night we set the fire outside and call the moon to reveal the colt's name. As with Sabby once it is heard it seems so obvious. Jet is so fitting and such an easy choice, I wonder that we had not known it all along. Sitting around the fire we sing Jet's name into life. We know it has been claimed when Jet rises up on his hind legs and whinnies to the moon. That night we tumble to our beds drunk on magik rather than ale.

Chapter Thirteen

At first light Sabby and I are at Jet's side. All we want is for us to be together. The three of us stand in communion, me at Jet's shoulder, Sabby at Jet's front hoofs. We could stand there happily for hours. Constantine arrives just before breakfast; he has business with Grandmother so leaves us undisturbed and joined by Blossom. Eventually Sabby and I are called for breakfast.

Constantine is a fine conversationalist and can bring forth words and wisdom from the shyest souls. Breakfast in our cottage has never been so lively, the food never tasted so good. It feels like a party and not the first meal of the day. I wonder if all of life feels like a party to Constantine. I would like my own to feel as such and wonder how it will ever be so. 'Now, young master,' Constantine turns to me, 'it's time for us to visit the tannery.' Before I can protest, he says, 'It will not do to ride bareback.' But the thought of binding Jet up in leather and iron is too painful and we do not need it; a simple tug on his mane and a squeeze of leg is enough. 'You cannot be in disguise if you do not wear one,' he says and to that I cannot argue. I have received such gifts, we must offer reciprocity. I go to tell Jet the news but find him standing at ease with Blossom and I know he understands.

The tannery is some ride out the other side of the town. Constantine says we should ride proudly through the town so as to blind folk with apparent honesty. I am more than happy to show Jet off, why would I not be? It takes some time to make our way through the town, everyone wants to pat and admire. Jet is a paragon of patience, not startled or frightened by the attention, rather soaking it up as if it was his rightful gift. Jet, it seems, is no stranger to adoration. Constantine has to pick up something from the inn and we wait patiently outside as he goes in. A small crowd soon gathers and at the very back I see Mary. I blush. What must she think of me after the other night.

Pushing to the front of the crowd is Ben Lovell, followed by his cronies. He takes his time to study Jet, walks round examining haunches and fetlocks. I feel the heat of his jealousy from where I sit. Jet does not take to him. He begins to step on the spot, ready for flight.

'Careful, he's a handful for such an inexperienced rider as yourself,' sneers Ben and his gang snigger.

'All the better for me to learn then,' I say. 'He has a good nature, and is a perfect judge of character and situation, so I fear not.' I would encourage Ben to pet him but it's clear this would be a mistake. The crowd begin to disperse as Jet becomes more agitated. Soon the only people left are Ben, his gang and Mary.

Ben laughs. 'You have a nervous one there. It's a shame; he is fine looking, but it will be no use to you.' Before I can respond Mary approaches and as she does I feel Jet begin to settle. Ben sticks out his arm, blocking her path to Jet.

'Watch your toes,' he says. Mary stops and takes her time to look Ben in the eyes.

'Thank you, Ben, your chivalry is appreciated but unwarranted.' She holds his gaze until he slowly drops his arm. She approaches Jet and instantly he is calmed. She strokes his nose and he snorts a gentle approval. Ben is saved further humiliation by the humiliation of being called to heel by Mother Lovell.

'The best of luck to you,' he says as he and his crew turn away. As he walks off he calls over his shoulder, 'You'll need it,' and his gang titter. I look to Mary and the four of us enjoy a quiet laugh. She strokes Jet's neck, breathing in his sent. She is comfortable with him and I would like her to be as comfortable with me.

'Want to take a turn?' I ask and offer my hand for her to join me.

'Not now and not here,' she says under her breath and heat rushes through my body as I realise I have transgressed. I am saved from my humiliation by Constantine's return. He gives me a sly wink as he mounts Blossom. A yell from the innkeeper calls Mary indoors, but we both turn and look back at the same time as we go our separate ways.

The route to the tannery follows the brook and is well-trod with much trade back and forth. We leave the bustle of the town behind, and the closer to the tannery we get the stiller and more eerie it becomes. The skins spread out to dry keep all manner of beasts away so there is a stillness, an emptiness that surrounds the place. To fill the void, Constantine begins to whistle and, within a few steps more, small children, speckled with dirt and mucus, run to greet us and I realise the tune was more than a distraction. We give backies to the children as Constantine whistles us past the drying hides and hung carcasses. The smell is overpowering, and I wish to join the beasts that stay away. As we approach the cottage, whitewashed, a heavy plume of smoke coming from the chimney, the tanner and his wife come smiling from the door, red-faced, round bodies and a warm welcome. Sabby and Jet are taut, their bodies tight, not frightened or aggressive, rather oppressed by the carcasses and hides and the smell. I feel the same and do not quite understand how the tanner family can live so happily surrounded by such manifestation of death. Blossom and Constantine seem as buoyant as ever. I am not sure if it's an act, but it helps to soften the nerves anyway.

'Good day, good day and welcome,' says Master Tanner. We dismount, and the older children take the reins and mane and lead our horses to shelter and sustenance. Constantine is shaking hands; it seems they are old friends long since met. 'No need to guess what brings you, come, this way,' and Master Tanner leads us towards the barn.

I expect sheep and pigs, maybe a cow. Yet when we step inside my eyes are affronted by leather straps, harnesses, reins, saddles, bags, rugs, soft plied leather ready to be moulded to whatever purpose is required. This smell is intoxicating and heady and somehow reassuring. The workmanship and craft is undeniable and then I understand their joy, to spend your days transforming the discarded waste of one beast into such useful beauty is satisfaction indeed. I wander amongst the display; some bridles and saddles are inlaid with silver and gem stones, some with feathers, some plain and simple but stunning in their simplicity. The others watch from the door.

'Take your time,' says Master Tanner. 'You will feel when it's right.'

Everything seems to speak so loudly to me that I can't imagine how I will ever make a choice. No one has mentioned cost and I do not know how to. Yet it's much easier than I think and as Master Tanner said. In the far corner laid out is the finest leather but simple cut and sewn with no ostentation but light and thin; it almost looks fragile. The bridle bit is equally light and soft-looking, the saddle different from the others, barely more than a thin layer of leather, strong in its flexibility. It calls to me as if a thread is connecting us.

'These,' I say, and everyone sighs and nods in happy agreement, as if they had been expecting it all along.

I go to pick them up, feel them and be introduced but Constantine stays my hand.

'Later,' he says, and I realise that the family have departed and it's just the three of us. 'You have a long time to become acquainted but now we have other introductions to make.'

The tanner goes over to the opposite corner of the barn. He pulls on a hook that holds an ostentatious head piece and the entire wall sighs in relief as it swings slightly ajar, just enough for a man to slip through. It is stunning and genius - an entire wall, not just a door. Master Tanner steps inside.

'After you,' offers Constantine. I let Sabby go first; she sniffs intently, shoulders hunched. She steps with caution, ready for fight or flight in an instant. Tentatively, I follow.

Inside is a good-sized room, ceilings high as the barn. It is largely dark, windowless and empty but in the centre is a table lit brightly with candles. Around the table is a group of men; some of them I know instantly from the visits to my grandmother when we are required to hide in the hidey hole. Constantine follows us in, and with a pull on a lever to our left shuts the wall to.

'Come on in now, no need to stand on ceremony,' Master Tanner instructs as he takes his place at the head of the table. Constantine, with his hand on my shoulder, leads me to the table. Sabby stays close and I am reassured by her presence. We take the two remaining seats.

'Good,' says Master Tanner. 'Some refreshments, gentlemen?' A jug of wine and some marchpane is passed our way. I am unsure of the wine, my body still in full remembrance of the night before last, but the marchpane is too good to resist. Yet I am unsure of the custom and wait to see Constantine's choice. He takes the jug and pours us both some wine, raises his glass.

'Your good health, gentleman,' he says and drinks, so I do too.

It's the first time I have tasted wine and it is nothing as I expected. Fruity, yes, but sour in a way I had not anticipated. I quickly take some marchpane to take away the taste and I do not care about the subtle smiles that pass around the room. I ignore their disdain as I pass Sabby some too.

To the right of Master Tanner is a tall thin man, finely dressed, by his side a long-haired greyhound sitting peacefully panting by him. Sabby is not concerned and the two beasts seem happy to keep a respectful distance.

'Welcome, Raven, to this, your first meeting with the Society of Historical Spiritual Studies. Should anyone ask you, we are a society of amateur historical scholars who seek to preserve for prosperity a record of ideas, thoughts, practices and philosophies before the Lord God saved us all. Lord Affrington at your service.' He raises his glass as then we all do. The second taste is not so bad. 'But you may call me by my found name, Astral.'

'It is an honour,' I reply.

'Our society reaches across the known lands,' says the man sitting opposite Astral. He is a large, square and squat man with hands that look like they could crush bones. 'Captain Langan, but Captain will suffice.'

'In truth we are a disparate group,' says the man next to Astral, a soft, fine-boned man with a shy, gentle smile. 'All joined by a common thread. It would be my great pleasure if you could address me as Philip.'

'Philip,' I repeat and smile and nod.

'Our work is one less of record keeping,' says the man next to the captain, 'and more practice. Master Farthingale but I am known as Theron,' and he gives a broad grin and a wink of the eye and I find I giggle like a girl, so surprised I am when his appearance is so elegant, his clothes of the finest silk, finely woven wool and his demeanour so contained.

'For sure we are a happy creed,' says the man next to Philip. 'No matter what measures are taken they can only silence our truth for a while. They cannot take it away. I am known as Fergus by all, be they the high and mighty or the low and humble.' He smiles and it feels like more of a warning than a welcome. He sits a little way away from the table and I cannot help but notice the calf skin shoes he has.

'We seek no conflict, it is not our want to rule. We seek merely to practice the ways of the Earth in peace,' says the man opposite Fergus. 'Robin, pleased to meet you.' We all drink more wine.

'Very well then,' says Master Tanner. 'You know Constantine and we all know you, so on to business.'

My head is soft and sluggish from the wine and it's easy to lose track of the conversation. Mostly it seems dull reports of what was said by whom and when. I cannot tell the significance of all that is said. Stories of rape and murder and the slaughtering of cats are not uncommon. It is clear that the family to which I belong lives in secrecy and each day a little of our right to be erodes. I wonder how long this meeting will last. I am unaccustomed to sitting still so long and can barely keep my seat on my seat. I would shift into ant to escape but the wall door is sealed, and I see no other gap built into the side of the hill as this room is. Besides, it's an honour to be here, even if it does not feel so. Yet how can a life so full of magik be made so dull?

'Master Raven,' Master Tanner says at last, 'we thank you for your services to date. We are dependent on secure and effective correspondence; you are a vital link in that chain.'

'It is an honour,' I mumble, slightly slurred. Whilst they have talked I have drunk. Constantine subtly slides my cup away and the marchpane closer. I pick a heart-shaped piece and place all of it in my mouth in one go. I bite down and hit something hard inside. I almost gag. I think I have been unobserved but when I look up all eyes are on me. I swallow as much as I can, cover my mouth and cough a round material object out of my mouth.

'Sew the gold coin into your doublet so it may always be at your service if you need it,' instructs Astral.

'It may save your life one day,' adds Philip and they beam at me with expectant faces.

'It is a great pleasure for me to serve my kind,' I say. 'I would want nothing more from my life.'

'Good, then gentlemen,' says Master Tanner, 'pray excuse us whilst we provide the tack this man and his horse require.' All stand. There are no formal goodbyes, rather hugs and back slaps and handshakes. Before I know it, I am blinking in the sunlight streaming in through the barn doors and there is no indication that behind a wall the future of an entire people and way of living is being planned.

Out in the yard Jet has been saddled up. He looks at me with patience and understanding and I know he knows there is no other way. My blood rushes with sugar and wine but I am compos mentis. I approach Jet and take the reins from the young girl holding them, but they feel odd and unwieldy in my hands. I reach up my left foot to stirrup and it feels cumbersome and unnecessary. I try three times to mount but cannot coordinate my limbs. Eventually Constantine gives me a leg up. What was yesterday an unquestioned ability, a fusion of horse and human, today feels strange, beyond recognition. I sit slumped on the saddle, reins hanging loose, I can make no sense of why I have them. Constantine laughs and tells me to hold on to the front of the saddle until I find my way. This way of being with horse will take some learning.

Chapter Fourteen

We finally get home after many wrong turns, fallings off and confusion. When we get out of town I want to take off the tack, feel the connection between Jet, myself and the earth uninterrupted but Constantine makes me promise to keep them on, makes me promise to learn how to feel the connection despite the barriers. I agree but really it makes little sense to me. Why make something harder than it needs to be? Constantine laughs when I say this but I don't see the joke.

At the inn, Mary comes to take Constantine's horse to the livery. I take off my hat to greet her and bid her good evening. She looks at me openly up and down and smiles.

'Fine leather work you have there.' I feel a fool, I must look so clumsy, so awkward. 'It will take a while to break in,' she says kindly and I am lost to her. To offer me dignity when I have none - I know then I could give my heart to her.

'It is fine soft leather, so should not take so long to become acquainted,' says Constantine, rescuing me from my lack of words and breaking me from my rapture. He bids me goodnight.

'Goodnight,' I say to Mary. She simply bobs and turns his horse towards the stables and I turn towards home, full of new sensations and feelings.

At home by the fire I show Grandmother the gold coin.

'It is agreed then,' she says, 'you have been called to work for and protect our people.' I can feel her pride and satisfaction in this. 'You must never use this until there is a very clear call,' she says as she takes out her sewing materials. 'This is only for an extreme occasion. You will know when to use it and must resist all other times when it would be easier to use it.' She has never sounded so serious.

'I understand,' I say.

She smiles as if I have no understanding of what I have agreed to. 'Make sure you do,' she says and sews the coin deep into the lining of my doublet. It would be impossible to find if you did not know it was there. As she sews, images of Mary swirl round my head. I would like to tell Grandmother all but somehow the words don't come. I do not know how to share this with her but as we settle down to sleep, Grandmother in her chair, I on a bed of reeds and blankets, she says, 'I hear it's Mary's day off tomorrow.' I look at her and shrug as if to say, what is it to me? 'Sleep well and sweet dreams,' she says and smiles. Within moments she is fast asleep, and I know exactly what I shall do.

I rise early, long before first light and Grandmother. I make sure all my chores are done as the sun creeps into view. I shine Jet's coat so that the early morning sun reflects into a deep dark pool of hair. This morning we do not saddle up, this morning we are as we are. I wash my face and hands, put on fresh linen and dust down my doublet and hose. Grandmother stretches and yawns from the cottage doorway as she watches me mount up and set off towards Mary's family farm.

I hope I am still in time. I wait just beyond the farm towards town. It is her day off but still she will rise early to come and help her mother with the young ones, come to give them her earnings. I find a spot out of sight of the farm and with an easy path into the countryside; it is clear now that it's going to be fine day. I have packed some bread and marchpane, just in case, and we wait. Jet becomes disinterested in our task and becomes engaged in feasting on the roadside foliage whilst Sabby sleeps and I grow more anxious. I think we must look a motley crew, when around the corner she comes; her head is down, she seems fascinated by her boots, so we have a few moments to gather ourselves. It is not until she is almost upon us that she looks up and sees us. She stops, startled.

'Good morrow, Mistress Mary,' I say taking my hat from my head and bowing as best I can on Jet's back.

'Good morrow, Master Raven,' she replies with a smile and glint in her eyes which I know means play.

'We wonder if you would do us the honour of joining us in taking the morning air?'

'Fine, sir,' she says and hesitates, looking towards her family home. Almost on cue we hear the roars of her father and then the shrieks of her mother. 'It will be entirely my honour,' she says.

I offer my hand and, without hesitation, she is sitting astride Jet, close to my back with her arms around my waist. We turn towards the rolling, open hills and as the shouts from her family home grow louder, we speed off into the distance. I did not know that anything could feel so good.

Eventually we reach the forest where Sabby was found and she leads us to a clearing with a small beach to the river and bushes made heavy with their burden of fruit. Sabby takes to wandering. I do not fear her explorations; she will not go too far and will return when I need her. Jet has more than enough to be occupied with gorging on the lush meadow that makes up the clearing. It takes no time for me to collect wood for a fire whilst Mary collects berries and mushrooms.

Every chance I get, I snatch a look at her, unnoticed. She seems so at home and at ease; she hums a gentle tune to herself and I find myself jealous of the breath that leaves her body, of the berries that have her attention, yet at the same time I have no desire to interrupt the scene, so perfect is the vision. I collect fresh water from the river and try to light the fire. The flint does not spark. It is impossible to count the number of fires I have lit, so that is second nature for me, never before has the flint not sparked. I feel a heat rise from the pit of my belly. Why does what I know always fail me?

She smiles. 'You have more heat in you than the fire.' I look up at her with flames in my eyes but she is not frightened or startled or surprised. Instead she laughs but not a laugh that stings, a laugh that releases and I am stilled by her acceptance.

'Here, you have to ask nicely,' she says and takes my knife and flint from my hands. She kneels down in front of the built but unborn fire.

'Please fire, may we light and burn you?' She pauses, then strikes the knife and flint; instantly the flint sparks and the fire catches. 'There see, all you have to do is ask nicely,' she says, grinning a knowing smile at me.

'Is that right?' I ask, holding her gaze squarely in the eyes. We pause, held in delicious tension. Then together we break and busy ourselves with preparing the mushrooms and bread.

We sit on a fallen tree and with wetted sticks we toast the bread and mushrooms. Our chatter falls into a simple easy rhythm focused on our task. Mushrooms and toast will never taste the same again. We come to a natural lull and for a moment we sit held in peace, then a shadow falls across her mind and I know she is thinking of her mother, brothers and sisters and that the shadow that has fallen is her father.

'They will not begrudge you these few hours,' I say. 'There will be much left of the day for them.' She looks at me with an openness I did not think she had. I would take her in my arms right then, hold her till there was no more pain and the memory of the imprint of his fists dissolves to nothing, but it's fleeting and soon replaced by a trickster's grin. She reaches down, takes my knife in her hands and, with the eye of a woman grown with use of blades, she throws it, so it lands embedded in the trunk of an ancient oak.

'Shall be mine if I reach it first,' she says, and we are on our feet and the game begins. I head her off just before she reaches the oak and the trees become our playground as we weave and dodge and stumble amongst them. In the end she reaches the knife first. We pause, catching our breath between laughs and chuckles. Finally, I have breath for words.

'Maid, it is fairly won.' She composes herself and with mock solemnity tries to take the knife from the tree, yet it will not yield. She tries again, still it does not release.

'Perhaps you have not asked nicely enough,' I tease, and she looks at me with a sarcastic glint, then tries again with all her might and still it is steadfast. She steps back defeated; with the utmost gentleness I step up to the tree. I know my knife and I know how it prefers to be treated; as softly as I can, I clasp the hilt and with softness release it from the tree. I turn the blade towards myself and offer the hilt to her. She looks at the knife with disbelief.

'How it yields to your touch,' she says, looking me in the eyes.

'I have taken the time to learn her form, her likes and dislikes, how best to please her,' I reply.

'Such diligence is most often rewarded,' she says, reaching out with one hand to clasp it over mine and the hilt, locking my eyes.

I do nothing. I want to. With all my heart, I want to kiss her, to hold her close, to breathe her in. Yet I do not. If I do she will know, she will discover at least one of my secrets. An uneasy silence falls. Eventually I drop my eyes to study the knife.

'So bold and now so shy,' she says and wraps her other hand around mine.

'It's yours,' I say and pull away, leaving her holding the knife.

There is nothing more I want than to feel her flesh against my lips but I am afeared of what will follow, what could follow. If she were to find out, if she were to tell of what she discovered, it would be the end of everything, not least my life. What was I thinking? I followed my heart and not my head. I turn away, go to gather Jet.

'It is late, we should return before they send the hounds to look for us,' I say, and it is true our absence will soon be noticed. I begin to put out the fire and dismantle it so we leave no scar or trace. I expect her to be doing the same, collecting herself together ready for the ride home.

When I look up to see if we are ready to leave she is standing naked, a vision of beauty. I am frozen. I know I should turn away, but I cannot. I am transfixed. Eventually I come to my senses and am about to turn away.

'I know,' she says. I meet her eyes but say nothing. 'We are alike,' she says, still I offer nothing, but I do not move. 'It is not men I favour,' she says

'But...' I say, does this mean everyone knows?

'Your secret is safe with me. It is only I that know.'

'But…' I say.

'I know because we are alike,' she says, and it is enough.

I do not think then of consequences of rape or beatings or death. I do not think at all. She lets me walk to her, her arms open and welcoming, enfolding me in soft warm skin. I do not think of how I have not done this before, of how I never really thought I could or would but somehow, I know exactly what to do. Our lips find each other, and my body explodes, everything inside me is joyous and awake. I want the kiss to last forever, but I want it finished too. There is the universe of her body to explore and the utmost urgency to discover all parts of it. My desire knows the course to follow and I submit entirely to its guidance. It is flesh that feels, it is flesh I taste and hunger for, but the joining of our flesh transports us to realms that have not been spoken about in any of the books. I have experienced a taste of these in brief snatched moments with myself, but this is beyond any of my imaginings, despite our clumsiness and fumbling as first-time lovers. I am at once lost to the stars and never more in my body. I have no notion of distinct actions, distinct body parts more a shared explosion of energy manifest in the meeting of our flesh.

In the immediate afterglow, our beings spent, I do not know how long we lie in each other's embrace, feeling the soft moss cushion our bodies, feeling the gentle breeze caress our senses back to earth. I find her lips and we kiss long and slow. I would like to tell her all that I am, share every secret I know, her eyes tell me she is the same, but crow screeches a warning and we both of us break, unquestioning. We dress hurriedly. I have no time for binding, so it takes less than a minute for us to be presentable. Jet and Sabby are ready and waiting. By the time we have mounted Jet and taken a last look around to check we have left nothing behind we hear the sound of the bugle, a hunting party from the castle. In seconds we are gone, and they will never know of the magik that moments ago was created there.

Chapter Fifteen

I drop Mary off a little way down the lane, out of sight of the farm. At first she does not move and I do not want her to release her arms from my waist. Yet we hear the cries and shouts of her brothers and sisters and can feel her called by them. Before she dismounts she leans in close and whispers in my ear, her breath hot against my skin.

'Till next time, my love,' she says and dismounts with gentle ease. She does not say goodbye, does not wave, does not turn back but I can do nothing but watch as she nonchalantly meanders towards her family home. When she is out of sight, we take the back-road home to avoid any prying eyes to saddle up; we are already late for lessons.

The rest of the day passes in a blur. I am almost too frightened to even think of what just happened, fantastical and amazing and unexpected, but my whole being is filled with joy and I can think of nothing else. Yet every thought, every sensation is followed by a shadow. What if she tells? What if we were found out? I swing violently from high emotion to despair but always back to high. My lesson is a blur. Grace does not enquire but I know she has noticed. Mother Gray doesn't enquire but I know she has noticed. Afterwards I decide to call on Constantine; he will make sense of all this for me.

I know Mary will not be back at the inn yet so feel easy handing Jet to the stable boy. I bound up to Constantine's room, eager to share my triumph and my confusion. I knock on the door and enter without waiting for a reply, such is my confidence in our comradery. I am greeted by an empty room. The bed is stripped bare, the fire cleaned and cold, no sign that he was ever there at all. On the table there are two letters and a red rose. One letter is sealed and addressed, the other simply folded. I pick it up and read.

My Dear Friend

Please excuse such an untimely and abrupt departure. Yet I know you shall understand and forgive this indiscretion. I ask one final task of you. That you deliver the letter I leave. I know you will know how. As for matters of the heart I am as much a novice as you. Love does not answer to reason but to the heart and that in all things I suggest you follow.

Till we meet again.

Your would-be brother.

Constantine

P.S: Please deliver this rose to the heart it belongs to.

I am disappointed and frustrated. I want to tear up his letter but cannot; as ever I am charmed by his ways. I wanted to drink ale, I wanted to hear his tales of conquest and learn his ways of wooing. I want to smash the table, break the chairs in frustration and disappointment. Instead I pick up both letters and slip them into my doublet. I pick up the rose, for this I discard my anger.

Silently I leave the room undisturbed. I check the way is clear. It is approaching dusk and the inn is beginning to fill. It's not far and I am up the stairs to the attic rooms. From smell alone it's not hard to find Mary's room. Tentatively and as quietly as I can, I open the door. A tiny window lets in a little light, a bed and a small chest of drawers, rough flaxen blankets cover the bed, a bowl and jug on the chest, a hairbrush and a tiny shaft of mirror. The simplicity is calming but already I want to shower her with gifts to soften and cheer the room. I go up to the bed and cannot resist the temptation to breathe in her scent and hold her pillow close. Then a stirring downstairs alerts my senses and quickly I replace the pillow and lay the rose on top. Then we are downstairs and on our way, silently and unseen.

We hurry home, my heart as light as the breeze that washes our faces as we speed along through the dusk. I half want to meet Mary on our way and half hope not to. I fear when we meet again that the magik will be lost, just a passing, fleeting sensation, but all the rest of me yearns to see her. Yet I am saved both ways and we return home without sight of her. When I get home I find the letters in my doublet. The address on the letter is one I do not know, and I show Grandmother.

'Constantine left this for you?' she asks.

'Yes, see the letter he left me,' I offer but she declines and sits down heavily by the fire. I see she is troubled; the letter has significance.

'How time moves on,' she says at last. 'It's a little-known side street in the shadow of the castle walls, make sure you keep to the shadows. If you are seen, you must run as far and as fast as you can. Do you understand?'

I try to hide my concern. 'Of course,' I say. 'I'll be as quick as mouse, as hidden as spider, as silent as panther. Am I not always so?'

'This marks a change,' she says, 'tomorrow will be your last lesson. It is time to work.'

I am filled with pride but also sadness. I have hardly made a dent in the library and am I not to see Grace's face again?

'Your lessons are complete but your time with Grace has just begun. She will have further instruction for you. Come, let us eat; you needs to be rested for tomorrow.' I know there is no more that will be said on the matter. That night my sleep is fretful and broken, my dreams confused. I awake more tired than when I lay down.

The fresh morning air helps clear the fog a little. Crow welcomes me to the day with a squawk and a dance and joy becomes mixed with excitement and fear. I know today everything will change. It is a comfort to do my chores, a grounding and humbling practice on this day. I eat breakfast with a hunger I did not know I had. Before I leave for my last lesson, Grandmother holds me tight. I ask to take a gift to Grace and we both decide a draught of our finest lavender oil is the perfect sentiment.

Sabby becomes impatient with the preparations and soon I am on my way. We take the route by the brook as we have always done, even though with Jet the road is the quicker route. We drink in the scents, the heat, the sun on the cascading water. We reach the ponds and I dismount from Jet. A fallen tree reaches out into the centre of the pond and I walk along and carefully lower myself, so I am lying flat along the tree. I take my knife, pull up my sleeves and reach into the water. 'Will you join us?' I ask the finest of the Frogbit that cover the ponds surface. The flower yields easily to my knife, so I take that as a yes. Before I mount Jet, I place the stem inside my doublet for ease of movement.

Today when we travel through the town each hello is tinged with sadness. We pass the inn and Mary is sweeping the steps. She looks at me and smiles as if I am anyone but in her eyes there is a subtle glint, a fire, and I know she will tell no one of our passion. She wears the red rose in her hair and my heart swells so that I fear it shall break out of my body and dance a jig for all to see. We reach Grace's and I am boosted by love for whatever comes next.

Mother Gray meets us at the door as usual, but she holds a kerchief to her mouth and her eyes are barely dry.

'Never mind me,' she says, 'I am an old fool,' and at that she pushes past Grace and into the hall as she begins a loud wailing. Grace smiles at me.

'Soft on the inside,' she says, 'like good marchpane.' We laugh, sharing the affectionate joke. 'Come,' she says, 'I have something to show you.'

We make our way up to the library. Apart from the usual candles there is nothing on the desk to see. 'Hold these,' she says handing me the candles. She tilts the desk so one end is raised. It is almost on its end when a creaking and shifting of levers is heard and the floor underneath the desk slides underneath the rest of the floor, opening what looks like a tunnel. There is a click and the table is held in place, half-suspended. Grace takes one of the candles from me and goes around to the tunnel. She reaches inside the darkness and brings out a large square book wrapped in oilskins.

'It is a chamber?' I ask. 'Another library?'

'A passageway,' she says, 'leading out onto the street.'

'Of course,' I say but it is not that that interests her. She hands me back the candle and with a gentle wiggle back and forth the table descends as the trap door closes. With a degree of reverence she places the book on the table.

'Place the candles here, not too close,' she instructs. Sabby pants contentedly and we both watch closely as Grace peels away the oilcloth. Laid bare is a thick leather-bound book with thick parchment pages and a smell of the forest.

'Please,' she says and indicates for me to approach. I dare not touch it; the leather binding is thick and beautifully engraved.

'Please,' she says again and stands back to watch me.

Despite myself I am compelled to reach out and touch the cover of the book. It is like touching time itself, so connected I feel as if instantly I am reaching back through the generations to the beginning of time. The leather is thick but palpable, a skin rather than cover. It yields to my touch as if I am caressing a living organism. I am transported to a different dimension, not bound by the ways of the earth but ingrained in all aspects of the earth at the same time. I observe that I am in the library with Grace and Sabby. I am conscious of all physical sensation, but I am also beyond it. Yet I am not scared; rather a sense of palpable peace inside and around me pervades.

I look to Grace; she is smiling. She nods her head and I open the cover. Inside are beautifully illustrated pages, ornate borders hold every page. Inside the words are worlds and universes. The book is a galaxy and inside holds all its secrets. To know this book would be to know knowledge itself.

I browse through the pages, and as I do gaps begin to appear, then whole pages are blank until there is nothing but blank pages. How can this be, is knowledge incomplete? I look at Grace, have I been deceived? She comes and sits down next to me.

'It is our most precious edition in the library. We keep it hidden so it can live and breathe in conditions that favour it but also it is essential that it does not fall into the wrong hands.' I look at the empty pages with a growing sense of despair.

'It is the book of knowledge, but it shall only reveal to you what you already know and what you are ready to know.'

'The blank pages?' I ask.

'The pages are only blank to you.' Before I protest she says, 'Other pages are blank to me. Let me show you,' she turns the book towards herself. She turns back some of the blank pages until a page that was blank for me is full of symbols and pictures and text. I cannot make sense of it, but its beauty overwhelms me, and a single tear rolls down my check.

'If you seek an answer and cannot find it elsewhere, you will find it here.' She stares longingly at the page then closes the cover and, with the gentleness of a lover, wraps the book back up in the oilskins. I take the candles from the table; holding the book, she raises the table again and slides the book back into the hidden shelf in the darkness and then lowers the desk. I return the candles.

'You have a question,' she says.

'Only that if the pages are blank to those not ready then can it fall into the wrong hands?'

'If you seek an answer the book will provide it,' she says. 'Come, there is one more thing.' I know my question has been answered but I am not sure I understand what has been given. She takes the candles from the table and leads the way out of the library. We all turn back and look at the books.

'It is a door that shall always be open to you,' she says.

'Thank you.' I am beaming inside.

I know then that I am no longer pupil but an equal. She puts the candles on the table by the window and blows them out. She indicates for me to close the library door and, even though I have only seen her use the secret lever once, I intuitively know where it is. When I pull the lever and watch the door and tapestry close shut as if nothing was there, I am filled with a sense of responsibility. I have been entrusted with the wisdom of my ancestors and the magnitude of that does not go unfelt.

'Here,' she says, 'I have something for you.'

I join her at the window. She opens her hand and laying in her palm is a three-dimensional six-pointed star made out of a clear stone that sends light in all directions. It's attached to a leather lace tied in a loop. Delicately, she picks up the lace and holds the Merkaba up in the air. Rainbow light fills the room. I gasp, she smiles and opens the loop, I bow my head and she guides the loop over. It feels like the Merkaba has come home. Sabby barks approval.

'Thank you,' I stutter, 'it is too much.' I fear the sentiment of the draught of lavender oil is left wanting compared to such a gift.

'Not for you. Besides I have only reunited the both of you and that is an honour for me.'

'All I have is some lavender oil,' I say and look her in the eyes, hoping she makes the connection to our first lesson together and the last time I offered her lavender oil.

'Then we come full circle, young sir,' she says, and I know the lavender oil shall never be used but always kept. 'Come, let us celebrate, Mother Gray awaits us.'

We go downstairs to the kitchen; in the middle of the table is a huge cake covered in marchpane and sugar icing. It looks like the cake of kings not of a simple Shifter. Beside the cake are three small pewter cups the shape of large thimbles, a jug and a stopper. Mother Gray beams when she sees us. Wiping her hands on her apron, she comes over to me and embraces me so completely I feel the breath leave my body. It is the best embrace I have ever had.

'Now settle yourself, time for cake and fire water,' she says and guides me to a chair.

'Fire water?' I ask.

'A delicacy from Mother Gray's home country, Alba. Known locally by many names but officially whiskey,' explains Grace.

'Brewed by my own fair hands,' adds Mother Gray. She has popped the cork on the jug and is pouring a beautiful golden liquid into the cups. 'Of course, you can't get the real taste down here. It lacks the essence of the land. Still, it's not bad and much better than not at all.' She picks up her cup and we follow.

'Slàinte mhath!,' she says.

'Slàinte mhath,' Grace replies and they take a large gulp from their cups. I follow, and a burning sensation starts at the tip of my tongue and travels all through my body. I blow out of my mouth to cool myself and the others laugh.

'It's an acquired taste,' agrees Mother Gray. 'Have another sip and that should do it.' I look at her with some disbelief, but she is encouraging. I give it another go, and she is right, this time it is more gentle and I feel myself soften as a warm glow glides down my insides.

'Will you cut the cake then, sir, or are we all to be denied?' she asks. I am full of fire water confidence and take the knife.

'And thank you two fine people, I am afeared to cut such beauty,' I say and we all admire the cake for a moment more.

'But it will be more beautiful inside us.' We laugh as I cut the knife smoothly through the cake. It is without doubt the best cake I shall ever taste.

At first it is awkward between us, our closeness unsettled by this change in circumstance, but fire water works its magik and soon our conversation is easy, and we find we are the funniest topic of conversation. We tease and play and reminisce. Yet after two slices of cake and some cool, fresh water to wash down the fire water, it's time for me to do my work. Whilst Mother Gray clears the plates and packs up my cake, Grace gives me instructions.

'Keep Jet a safe distance away. The sounds of hoofs on the cobblestones will resound throughout the castle and it's imperative that you are unseen and unheard. When you see the faint outline of a rose etched into the upper right-hand corner of the door frame then you can be sure you have the right place. Do not knock, make sure there are no eyes upon you and slip the letter under the door. Wait until you have seen the letter taken so do not push it full under. Once you are happy it has been received, make haste and take a long and complete route home making sure you are alone.'

'Of course,' I say. I am a little confused; I am known for my stealth.

'Today you travel in the shadow of the castle,' she says, and I understand the caution.

Until now the castle has had little importance in my life. It is at the centre of our town and much business is built around it, but its owners have been many and mostly absent, so we have learnt to get along without its influence. The keepers of the castle do what they can but it is said that inside the walls the gardens fester and the stone work crumbles. They mostly keep themselves to themselves, so all manner of powers and gifts are bestowed on them by wagging tongues.

It is understood they have a direct route to the king and court and so are in turns feared and hated, then honoured and respected, which amounts to a general sense of mistrust on both sides. Occasionally a cardinal or bishop will take their leave there on one of their grand tours. Then it is said, depending on the wealth and predisposition of the then owner, the castle comes alive with feasts and merriment. Minstrels and jesters travel from far and wide to play, women of all standings arrive from all corners of the country and the whole town is hot with the fever of the occasion. In my life this has only happened once, and I was far too young to pay much attention. All I recall are colourful flags, songs and dances. I do not really understand why such care is needed but I do respectfully follow instruction.

It is almost dark when I leave Grace's. Our parting marks a progression not an end. Mother Gray has wrapped my cake in linens and it is tucked into the leather saddle bag. The letter I slip up my sleeve for easy and subtle disposal if I am discovered. Grace holds me tight and I thank her for the gift of words on pages and for the eternal journey they offer. Mother Gray unashamedly weeps with both sadness and joy; she cannot say goodbye and runs from the room. I shout after her that I shall see her again soon enough, for that I shall. I was but a child when first I crossed their threshold and now I am grown and learned, entrusted with a task of some import. I mount Jet with no small degree of pride and turn into the enriching darkness of the night.

It's not far to the castle and there is no moon. Still we tread carefully, leaving Grace's as usual, making our way until we are sure we have not been followed or seen. Then we double back. Jet chooses a spot near common ground, a short distance from the castle, rich in grasses and foliage. We leave him there and, keeping to the shadows, Sabby and I duck down the back lanes until the presence of the castle is palpable. I do not know these ways, but I follow Sabby's sense and soon we are in a narrow street against the castle walls. Abandoned two-storey thatched houses overshadow the street, shops are boarded up and fallen into disrepair. No light falls between the castle walls and the houses. The cobblestone road is overgrown with an over flowing ditch of human waste stagnating either side. Sabby sinks down onto her haunches. It's hard to believe any one resides here yet there is a strong presence as if everything has eyes and ears.

We pause before we enter, listening, looking, sensing if anything is following, if anything hears us, smells us, senses us. Yet there is only stillness and emptiness. We crouch low; all is in shadow so keeping out of sight is not hard. Still we crawl under windows, take many pauses and in darkness try to find the right address. Sabby stops outside an old shop. The windows are shuttered tight and no light escapes. It is hard to make out the number, so risking being seen, I stand and trace my hand along the door frame and there it is, in the top right-hand corner, so faint it would take a bright sun to see it in daylight. I hear a rustling behind me and freeze. How can we have been caught off guard? The shuffling continues but no words are spoken. Very slowly I look down. Sabby is frozen and focused on something behind me. She is alert but not frightened. Slowly I turn around to face our fate.

Sitting boldly in the centre of the street is a large rat cleaning its whiskers. My whole body softens in relief. Sabby licks her lips and silently hunches down. The rat senses a slight change in atmosphere, stops cleaning and eyes us slowly, taking us in. I lace my hand on Sabby's neck; any sudden movements could alert any of the hidden eyes of our whereabouts. She doesn't want to, but she hears my command and releases her focus. The rat, sensing the triumph, very slowly turns and saunters into the ditch and is gone. I want to get out of there as soon as possible.

Pausing once more to check it was only rat who has spied us, I bend my knees and turn to face the door. I slip the letter out of my sleeve and part way under the door so that only those standing right beside me would see what I have done. We wait, then it occurs to me to wonder how will, whoever it is, know to look for the letter? How will they know when to expect it? Grace said I should wait until the letter is taken but how long should we wait and what if it is not taken? But I have no need of doubt; a few seconds pass, and the letter is taken with no sound either from within or of the letter moving. I feel a huge sense of release and accomplishment. I want to get out of there as soon as possible and it takes all I have for us to creep and crawl again, away and out of the street. Yet following Sabby's lead I manage. I mount Jet without hesitation and as soon as we are free of the town and on the back roads away from prying eyes, we gallop through the moonless night.

Part Two

Chapter Sixteen

Outside we can hear the sound of the livery and the rattle and chatter of the street. Inside the smell of roast meats teases and seduces, alongside the sound of moving barrels and the angry banter of the inn keeper and the patrons. Lying with her in my arms in the still of late afternoon, in this tiny bed, in the tiny attic room, everything in the world feels as it should be. There is no need for anything other than this palpable peace.

Life has continued. I work alongside Grandmother taking the heavy chores, the wood cutting, the digging, the deliveries. I have not been able to leave the books alone. It is not safe to take the books out of the library so when I can I visit and spend the evening reading and sharing wisdoms with Grace and Mother Gray. Increasingly my deliveries require the cover of darkness and reach greater distances, but whenever I can I grasp for the library. Mary, more or less, has run of the inn now and is often left in charge which makes our clandestine meetings easier to arrange. I have not had cause to meet Master Tanner in private, but when occasion causes us to meet in public a quiet glint in his eye reveals our connection and I do not hesitate to reciprocate.

I have begun to accompany Grandmother when she is called to hold ceremony. Riding pillion with me saves her feet and offers protection. Although the utmost secrecy is required, discovery would mean certain death, torture and public humiliation for all. We have not seen or heard from Constantine for the past two years but there is many a time I have felt his presence and his gentle guidance. I feel sure one day our paths will cross again but know it is not in my will or power to decree when.

'I should rise,' says Mary, not rising at all.

'Just a little longer,' I say. Our time is always snatched, always precious. I would stretch time to make our moments last as long as possible if it were in my power, but I cannot shift into the shape of time and to do so would take me from her arms and there is no place else I would rather be than in her arms.

'I must dress,' she says, 'the labourers will be shortly on their way back from the fields.'

'Let them wait,' I say, 'the old man can cope.' Even though I know he can't. She laughs and kisses my chest. 'You are incorrigible,' she says and begins to rise.

'Of course, I am,' I say and pull her back to me and hold her tight.

'Let me go,' she insists.

'What do you offer me, fair maid, for your release?' I tease.

'I offer to box your ears for you,' she responds.

'Promises,' I say, 'a simple kiss would suffice.'

'A price we can agree on,' she says, and we kiss long and deep. I would keep on kissing but eventually she pulls away and suddenly the tiny bed is cold and big and empty.

I watch her gather her hair, search out her linens. I want every day to be full of these rituals, for us to sleep and wake together.

'You could always marry me,' I say.

'Do you still persist?' she teases.

'It would be a wonderful wedding. Of course for decency we would need to do the church bit but then we could have our actual betrothal. A hand fasting in the woods of our meeting.'

'I do not look good in white,' she says.

'But with all my heart, Mary, why not? To everyone I am man and you a woman. They would never know, and we could be open, live as others.'

'You know why,' she says.

'I know but do not understand it. I do not seek to own you. I just want us to be together.'

'And you know I watch my mother, even now, being beaten and raped by the man who is supposed to be her protector. I watch him as he rapes and beats his children. I will be beholden to no man.'

'And you know I will never be that man.'

'And you know what will happen if you are ever found out. I shall not witness your rape too.'

'And that shall never happen.' But we both know I cannot make such a promise. We sit in silence trying to banish this fear that sits too close.

'Besides you know I like the bed to myself. I spent long enough lying on a reed bed entangled with my sisters and brothers.' It's meant as a joke, her tone a gentle tease but it stings. Whilst I have never sought my birth family, I cannot help the jealousy that is stirred when I see others with theirs.

'Do you love me at all?' I ask. It is unkind but part of me is hurt and confused by her persistent refusal. She sighs and sits down next to me on the bed. She takes my hands and kisses them.

'You know how deep my love for you is. I know you cannot mean your question.' I pull my hands away slightly. 'I have good relations now with innkeeper Joe. If I maintain favour, in a few years this inn will be mine; with no siblings or children of his own the inn shall pass to me. He rents and so I shall take over his tenancy. You know this.'

'I know you have it all worked out,' I say.

'In a few years I shall be beholden to nothing and no man. Would you deny me that?' she asks, and I cannot. 'I know you know this. You have chosen men's attire.'

'For comfort,' I say.

'For comfort and freedom,' she says, 'do you deny me that?' How can I when women are little more than cattle to most men and each year our value decreases. In the library, books tell of goddesses and benign matriarchs, but these are not the times we are living in. The freedoms I have passing as a man are vast. I am considered one of them. Mostly this is advantageous.

'I understand,' I say, 'it is not me but marriage you spurn.'

'Yes,' she says, relieved I have finally consented, and we hold each other tight.

'This is my vow to you,' I say. 'I promise never to cage you, never to beat you, never to make you other than who you choose to be.' A tear rolls down her check. 'You shall have your independence. I shall love you, but I shall not hinder your path. Rather be always available for travel reports.' And we laugh, falling and kissing on the bed. Then quickly we silence our laughter just in case anyone should hear.

That night, sitting by the fire with Grandmother, I imagine a time when Mary and I could wear what we want, be what we want, do what we want without the need of disguise and subterfuge. Grandmother says, and the books in the library corroborate, there was a time before when women where equals and we of the third sex were honoured, considered special, soothsayers and shamans. She says there will be a time when this is true once more, when humans will have travelled full circle and remembered who and what they are, but it will not be in our lifetimes. Then she gives me my next delivery. I have been called to the tanner's tomorrow afternoon. We do not say but both know that can mean no simple task. That night my dreams are fragmented and restless. I am afeared for what tomorrow may mean.

The next morning we speak little, the afternoon's calling sitting between us. The sun splits the sky but we do not share the joy that fills all beings around us, rather it jars and we are out of sync with the day. Grandmother encourages me to eat well but I have little appetite, something that we both know is significant, I have rarely not had an appetite. Before we set off, Grandmother says, 'They would not ask it of you if there was another way. Whatever they ask is needed.'

We set off resolved to fulfil our calling but uncertain of what that may be. We travel fast, cutting through the deer park and avoiding town altogether. We join the river and the road a little way out of town, confident that if we meet a fellow traveller now they too will have been summoned. The smell of the tannery greets us long before we see it. Sabby is taught and tense, Jet jittery and easily spooked, whilst I call on courage to fill us all for it's clear we will all require it. I want us never to reach the tannery, despite taking every effort to get there; I hope that somehow it will have been a mistake and in a short while I will be in the arms of Mary, drinking ale, eating marchpane and enjoying the sun.

Yet it is not to be and sooner than we would like the first hanging carcasses and drying skins appear in the trees. Then we hear the sound of the children playing, splashing in the river, then we arrive. Goodwoman Tanner is tending the garden and at our arrival drops what she is doing. She tells one of the smaller children to go to the barn and she comes to greet us.

'Welcome Sirrah Raven, what weather is this?' she says.

'It is a fine day,' I agree but my heart is not in small talk today. She senses my unease and does not press further, rather takes Jet as I dismount.

'I see you three have become friends,' she says, indicating the tack.

'Well, it is the finest tack in the shire, is it not?' I reply, and we smile, a warm comfort.

'They await you,' she whispers as she leads Jet away for water and hay.

'The tanner is in the barn. He should have the repairs ready for you,' she shouts over her shoulder and I shudder a little; are we not safe from prying eyes even here? Still I wave a thank you. I whisper to Sabby to look more at ease and despite herself she manages to look calm and confident.

Inside the barn is cool and dark. It takes some time for my eyes to become accustomed. I look around and no one is there to greet me. How will I know which lever to pull and should I pull it? Is there some kind of secret knock I should use? Sabby is sniffing around where the wall becomes a door when it slides open a crack. Before I can say anything Sabby is through and I follow. It is beyond any of my expectations, but it is Grace that greets us. Sabby is sitting, panting happily at her feet.

'Welcome, my boy,' she says. I want to be held in her arms and can feel she wishes to hold me, but we both know it would not do.

'Madame,' I say and take off my hat.

I look beyond her and sitting at the table is Mother Gray and I cannot help myself but grin in recognition and surprise.

She has been a part of this all along. Master Tanner sits at the head of the table as before, Astral by his side and Philip next to him. Sabby has met with Astral's greyhound and they sit contentedly together, watching from a little distance. This time a jug of ale is next to my seat and I gladly pour a cup; such are my nerves, I do not wait to be asked but no one seems to notice. Mother Gray slides a piece of marchpane shaped like a book to me and I beam at her; she gives me a subtle wink before turning her attention to the tanner.

I follow her gaze. 'Welcome, Raven. I trust you are finding this spell of fine weather agreeable,' he says.

'I am indeed, sir,' I say, somewhat confused by the pleasantries.

'Raven, for many years we have watched you grow,' says Astral, 'and you have grown into a fine adult, you are skilled with the land and you are unsurpassed as messenger.'

'Thank you,' I say and lower my eyes, somewhat embarrassed.

'As accomplished as these skills are, today, we are interested in your other skill,' says Philip.

Instantly I look to Sabby, but she is calmly engaged in licking and grooming. I am not sure if they are to know. I understood Grandmother and myself were the only humans to know of my gift. Many of the local beasts know of my gift as I have played and learnt their ways with them and Grace has been witness, but I know she would not tell.

'Sir, you flatter me. I am a simple man of little talents,' I reply. There are smiles and affectionate titters around the room.

'It's alright, boy,' says Mother Gray. 'We know you are Shifter.'

I look at her, still unsure. It could be a trap. If I am known for shifting I shall be tortured, hung, drawn and quartered with my remains hung from the castle walls as a warning to all who would consider our ways.

'I myself am clairvoyant,' she says.

I would like to leave. Any moment now I expect the sheriff to appear from the barn with a hoard of men to capture me. Yet Sabby is now resting her head on her front paws, her eyelids gradually closing.

'When you cannot sleep,' she says, 'you find comfort in imagining being held by your birth mother.'

I am unable to supress my surprise. I have spoken of this to no one, I barely admit it to myself. I would not tell Grandmother for fear of hurting her feelings and I have kept my silence with Mary because with her it does not matter. Besides if my birth mother does not want me then why should I miss her? It is only at my most vulnerable do I seek her comfort for I have learnt to do without. How can she know this but with her gift? Is this how they know of my gift or has Grandmother betrayed me?

'We have always known of your gift,' says Grace.

'You have been held, you have been protected, and now we need your help,' joins the tanner. Still I am unconvinced. I am confused by emotions that are waging war inside me.

'Maybe we were wrong about you,' joins Philip, 'maybe it was a child's gift and as you have grown, you have grown out of it.' I meet his eyes with fury in mine.

'After all we have done, the lessons, the comfort of your grandmother's home, not to mention the financial investment,' chides Astral.

'It is true he cannot do it,' concludes the tanner. How dare they doubt me?

Without speaking I push back my chair. I look round at the staring eyes, breath deep and begin to shift. Within seconds I am covered in a thick fur, my bones have changed shape, condensed. I am on all fours; my mane is thick. I leap onto the table in one swift agile jump and let out the largest, deepest, loudest lion's roar I can. There is not one of them left seated at the table. Sabby has joined me on the table and together we hiss and snarl at them all.

It is odd when I shift as I am still myself but in a different form. I do not lose my consciousness, but it is joined with the ways of what I have shifted into. I am, and I am not, at the same time. When my skin and bones change shape and form, it is a beautiful sensation of softness and fluidity. I am not fixed or rigid. It is as if I am melting inside. There is always fear, during the change I am most vulnerable, but it's not painful, more a feeling of being completely alive, that energy is flowing freely through my body with no barriers, simply taking on the shape I ask of it, that is needed most at the time. It is when I feel most myself.

Astral's dog is hunkered low, growling. Sabby warns him no but he is built to defend his master and reason may not prevent him. I do not seek to harm but I will do whatever I am called upon to do. Astral tries to calm him, bring him to heel but he cannot make him sit. Mother Gray is the first to approach the table. She reaches out to Sabby, the greyhound thinks Sabby is thus distracted and in lightning speed leaves Astral's side aiming for Sabby's throat, but he cannot move fast enough for my eye. I do not hurt him but before he can sink his teeth into her flesh I have him pinned to the table with one paw and my lion's weight holding him in place. At first, he tries to retaliate but I have him by the back of the neck and there is nothing he can do; within seconds he is lying completely still in submission, hardly daring to breathe.

Sabby jumps down from the table and slowly walks around the group, all frozen in their spot. She completes the circle, jumps back onto the table and sits by my head. I look around at each and every one of the party, making sure they see deep into my lion soul. I let out a roar that is heard for miles around, that becomes the cause of many a local legend for years to come. Then I sit down on my haunches, lift my paw a fraction, just enough for the greyhound to scurry back to Astral. I sit down sphinx-like and Sabby and I both begin a little gentle grooming.

It is Grace who is next to approach. She says nothing but reaches out her hand and I let her pet me. Her touch on my ears feels comforting and known. Mother Gray tries again; she and Sabby make friends and the tension in the room loosens as each of the men in turn approach. I feel the need of this shape waning. I jump down from the table and make way towards my chair and my pile of clothes. I feel my current form slacken and shrink, within seconds I am fluidity again. Sabby, Grace and

Mother Gray form a shield, a screen to protect my modesty as I quickly dress. I do not have time for binding so hide my bandages in my pouch. Within a few minutes I am dressed and seated and gulping down ale. I am tired but feel the elation I always have after shifting.

The Tanner is first to speak.

'Master Raven, I can only speak for myself but to see such a gift, such craft and skill in action. I shall remain blessed for the rest of my days.'

There are rumbles and agreeing exclamations from around the company. The greyhound approaches and I pet him calmly and openly; the entire rooms sighs, there is peace, elation and expectation amongst us all.

It is Grace who brings us to order.

'Raven, we have asked you here today to charge you with a duty,' she says and Mother Gray continues.

'It is a simple book, no bigger than your handspan.'

'But it has fallen into the wrong hands,' picks up Astral, then Philip interrupts,

'They do not understand what it is they have,' he says.

'But should they decipher the code,' the tanner intercedes, 'then all our lives and the lives of many more shall be at risk.'

'Do not spare him,' says Philip. 'There is evidence in the book that will destroy so much, that will be used against us – for all time.'

'The book is being kept in conditions so tight the only way we can think to reach it is with your talents,' says Grace.

'Time is of the essence,' says the tanner.

'Wait,' says Mother Gray, 'he has a choice. Raven, this will be a dangerous task. It will test all you know and all you are not yet conscious of. You do not have to accept this challenge.'

But I do not know how to not accept a challenge. Who would I be if I did not embrace adventure? I feel I could not be more ready; with a raven's eye I have seen the land for miles around, but to go further, to see more, experience more, why would I not do that? Still I do not speak. Sabby is alert and waiting, but at ease.

'Do you not have faith in the boy?' accuses Astral and a stony glare from Mother Gray silences him.

'This young man is more than you shall ever know, but if he is to risk his life then it must be of his choosing to do so,' she counters.

'Soon the castle will be lived in once more and our freedom gained through their neglect will be curtailed. If they crack the code there will be many lives lost,' protests the tanner. I look at Grace.

'If I retrieve this book, shall I be gifted with its secrets?'

She smiles. 'Your thirst and hunger shall never cease to serve you, but there is nothing in this book that is not already inside you, that you shall one day know. This is a book of names also and it is that that risks us all.'

'And Grandmother?' I ask.

'And Grandmother,' she says and then there is no hesitation.

'Where is it I am to go? What form am I to take?' I ask and there is happy relief around the room. Mother Gray secretly beams with pride and Grace looks as if all her years of patience have been rewarded.

'Good,' says the tanner, 'then it is agreed. Make haste, young man, your grandmother awaits.'

'But where am I to go? How do I get there?'

'Secrecy is a skill of yours and will be greatly needed,' says Philip.

'You shall receive instruction as you go,' says Astral.

'That way you are protected from talking if you are captured,' adds Mother Gray.

'Your grandmother has the first set of instructions,' says Grace.

'But how do I-'

'Follow your intuition,' interrupts Grace as if I am supposed to understand what that means. I look around at their faces; surely, they have more for me than intuition, but it is clear in intuition they have faith.

'Don't worry, you have plenty,' says Grace.

Her embrace is warm and confident, and I don't want to leave it. Then there are handshakes from the men. Mother Gray slips me some marchpane and a pat on the back, and we are outside in the fading afternoon light. And somehow, I have agreed to a mission where I don't know where I am going, how I am going to get there or if ever I will come back alive. Yet my overriding feeling is one of peace and contentment. I take their trust in me as conformation of my abilities and it is this where lies my peace. My potential has been recognised and it's now being called upon to be explored and be of use.

Once we are a safe distance from the tanner's we speed home, not least because we are to assist Grandmother in a ceremony that night. I have so many questions for her. What does she know and what shall she tell? When we arrive, hot and exhausted, she is ready and waiting. The tools she will need are already packed up, the cottage closed up; she sits on the bench outside soaking in the sunset.

'Here, take some bread and cheese for you and Sabby whilst I give Jet some hay and water. If we are focused, we shall still be timely.' She does not even acknowledge where I have been. It is somewhat an anti-climax and I am confused that she does not share my joy. Still we are hungry, and it does not take us long to devour the bread and cheese and wash it down with the pure water of our well. By the time we are fed and rested, Grandmother has dried and brushed down Jet; he has almost finished his hay and drank the water trough dry.

'Let us make haste,' says Grandmother.

She has taken off Jet's bridle and saddle - tonight we shall go as we are. I offer to take Grandmother's bag.

'I can manage now as I shall manage whilst you are away,' she says, and it is the first time I understand my great adventure may not be so great for everyone. So full of potential glory my thoughts have been of myself, of how I shall save the day, battle fearsome odds and return the hero. It has not occurred to me the sacrifices we shall all make for such triumph.

Chapter Seventeen

The journey to the ceremony site is long and deep into the forest so as to be out of sight and undiscovered. We travel in silence the whole journey, my head now full of what I shall be leaving behind, maybe forever. Suddenly it is not such a great adventure and being a hero an unwelcome honour when it is due to your way of loving, your way of being now deemed wrong. That those that think themselves above the ways of the earth, that those that think they are the masters of the earth shall do away with everything and everybody that disproves their dominance. I understand fully for the first time that everything I am is evidence that needs to be destroyed and denied. That all the people I love, all the people who love me are evidence that needs to be destroyed and denied. My great adventure is now filled with an urgency and weight I had not at first anticipated. My grandmother's reserve now makes much more sense.

When we arrive at the site there are a good number of folks already gathered. The fire has been set. Before these times the fire would have been set high on a hill as an offering to the moon and the earth, an offering of our inner flame to the earth that holds us but now that would act like a beacon for the men who seek to prove they are now what holds us and not the earth. Yet here there is a large clearing deep in the forest, far out of sight and, with careful planning, we are safe from prying eyes.

The ceremony tonight is one of protection. The family live on land claimed by the castle, for many years they have lived in peace, tending the land with ancient wisdom, communing with their chosen gods and spirits. Now the new masters of the castle threaten all they hold dear and we are calling for the protection of the Great Spirit to leave them unharmed and unnoticed by the new landlord. My role as Fire Keeper usually keeps me occupied so that I do not take part in the activities but tonight I claim some protection for myself, for my loved ones, for the work I am about to undertake. Grandmother exhibits a level of engagement and focus that suggests she is doing the same, our singing, our dancing, our intentions made rich by our need, the same need for the same reasons. The timing could not be more auspicious.

We make our offerings until the moon is full risen and we are spent. In comforted quiet we finally pack away, leaving no trace, mostly in respect for the earth and the land that has held us, but it serves a dual purpose, so that none can point a finger and say we were there. That night Grandmother accepts no gifts for her services.

On the way back we take a slow pace, all of us hoping that our delay will delay the morning. Still she has not given me the instructions and I do not know what or how I am to prepare.

'I shall not go without seeing Mary,' I say at last.

'You shall not be asked to,' is all she replies.

'Will you not say more?' I ask.

'There is time enough,' she says. I want to hold her, to tell her everything will be as it is. That I shall go, that I shall return, and all will be as it has always been but we both know that is not true. I decide to ask no more that night, just to savour the time we have, drink in all that is familiar, so it is there inside me when nothing else is. Home has never felt so good.

I am certain I shall not sleep that night, but the day has been long and full, and I cry out for rest. Grandmother instructs sleep to prepare for the journey ahead and it seems I agree. I awake from a deep, dreamless sleep, feeling cheated out of the night. Grandmother has already risen; the fire is high and I can hear her outside. I hear her cursing and the sound of water slopping. She is carrying in the morning water; it is my job and I leap to my feet and dress quickly. Then I realise I shall not be there tomorrow to complete my chores. I know then that this calling will take some time to answer. The cottage door flies open and Grandmother staggers in with two pails of water, once full, now half of what they were.

'Let me help,' I say and step towards her, but she shrugs off my attention.

'I've got to start somewhere, and it might as well be here and now,' she says. 'My, I am out of practice.' She puts the pails down by the sink.

I want so much to hold her, to feel her comfort, to breathe in her smell.

'If you prepare Jet, I'll prepare your pack. Then maybe an early breakfast before you…' she says and looks at me with eyes of an innocent babe.

'Most certainly,' I manage and rush towards the door before we fill the pails with our tears.

Breakfast is a sturdy feast designed to set us off with full bellies - breads, meats, pottage. I eat ravenously as if this were my last meal. Everything tastes so good, better than any meal before. It's like taking home inside me and therefore with me. Sabby and Jet both eat well; we are all aware of the magnitude of the task that lies ahead. I feel Grandmother's embrace deep into my bones but it's not until I am mounted and ready to leave that she gives me the instructions.

'Take Watling Street towards London. Tonight you are to stop at the Black Bull Inn. There you shall find your next set of instructions,' she says.

'Am I not to know more?'

'The least you know, the least you tell,' she says

'But what am I to say I am doing? People will ask.'

'You are resourceful,' she says, 'you would not have been trusted otherwise.' This is little comfort and I am irked that the last words with my grandmother are ones of frustration and confusion.

'Speed you well, listen to your guides and your voice within. I await your return,' and at that I know I shall see her again.

The sun is now full risen, and I have to see Mary before I go. Sabby is waiting and I turn Jet and we set off on our way.

We do not have time to linger. I would like to stop, to go slowly, drinking in the familiar sights and sounds. Although I am curious and filled with a sense of readiness that now all I have spent my life learning will be put to use, I want to savour what I have lived thus far for I sense when I return none will be the same. It's just after the breakfast rush and Mary will be heavy with chores. I stand with Jet in the back courtyard of the inn knowing at some point she will cross the yard carrying slops for the pigs. It is not long that we wait. She sees me, then sees the pack. She looks at me with understanding and then continues on her way.

'Master Raven, you'll be needing some refreshments for your trip,' she says. 'Come, I'll fill your flask.'

I follow her into the barn.

'How long shall you be?' she asks as soon as we are sure we are out of sight.

'I do not know,' I say.

'Where are you to go?' she asks.

'It's better you know as little as I,' I say, and she understands the danger. She turns to feed the pigs.

'Is not your grandmother's business enough? Do you really need this money?'

As far as I know she does not know I am Shifter; I have not told her, and I shall not put her at that risk.

'It's not always about money,' I say.

'And that is supposed to be enough?' she accuses. 'You leave me, I do not know for how long or if you shall return even and expect that to be enough?'

'And I cannot hold you in my arms in public,' I say.

It is too harsh and in her eyes I see the pain I have caused but I do not look away.

'The cost of independence is high,' I say and we both relent.

Risking everything, I pull her close to me and we breathe each other in. For a few moments we forget about time and there is only us. Shouting from inside the inn brings us back to our senses.

'I must go,' I say. 'I carry you in my heart. Miles will not keep us apart.'

'Speed you home,' she says, 'for there will not be a day when I rest easy until you return.'

'Do not be afeared,' I jest. 'I shall always return.'

'It is true,' she says. 'Maybe that is where my fear should rest.' We laugh and step out of the barn.

'Thank you, this shall be a great comfort to me,' I say and hold up the flask.

'Travel safely and fruitfully,' she says and winks.

I do not know how far away the Black Bull Inn is, so Sabby sets a steady pace so as not to over reach ourselves. It is early afternoon and I hope we make the inn before nightfall.

Watling Street is an old Roman road, straight and sure. It's a busy route and I pass folk we know and folk we don't. It's odd to be so open, usually I would take back roads, out of sight, but the instructions are such. The route is pleasant enough, but I cannot help but feel exposed on such a public thoroughfare. The afternoon draws on and there is still no sign of the inn.

As we have travelled, we have strayed further from houses and towns and for the first time since I was very small we are in territory unknown. It does not look that different to what we already know. Yet as dusk approaches we all grow nervous; with Sabby by our side we are in very little real danger but a sense of unease and uncertainty creeps over me.

We have travelled along alone for some time and night is about to fall when we see an old man bent double. He could be a decoy for a band of robbers. Highways are notorious for surprise attacks from gangs but there is something in his demeanour that suggests otherwise, suggests frailty but wisdom or at least kindness. He has not looked up from the ground since we have seen him so when we approach we are surprised when he says,

'It is not far but make haste, for nightfall is no place to be on this road.'

'Thank you,' I say, scared to say more, scared to ask more. I look to Sabby and Jet, both of whom seem at ease, both of whom seem eager to progress.

'Do you have far to go? May we accompany you to your door?' I ask - we have nothing to offer as a gift. The old man stops for a moment; I think he will accept my offer.

Thank you,' he says, still not looking up. 'I have not far to go but your kindness is acknowledged. Speed you well on your trip.'

He continues to shuffle along the road. Jet and Sabby are persistent in their need to continue.

'Safe home,' I shout as we move away.

When I look back as we are about to turn a corner, I do not see him, yet there was no turning off the road, no place for him to hide, but I do not have time to consider more. He must have known a short cut that took him off the road.

Night is falling fast, and we can see lights in the distance. A carriage passes us at some speed and we can see people outside the inn. The air is getting chill and I am glad we will not have to sleep in the open tonight. I bring Jet and Sabby to a walk so we may compose ourselves before we reach the inn. The warm lights in the deepening darkness look inviting and welcoming; there are sounds of laughter and merriment from within, even some singing.

We go around the back to the courtyard and stables. The courtyard is clean and well kept. I feel at ease leaving Jet here. The stable-hand is no more than a small boy but he has a kind and firm way with Jet and I slip him a small square of marchpane and instruct a full feed and wash down for Jet. I have never done this before and feel my shifting powers of great use as I ape what I have seen others do before me. I leave Sabby with Jet. It's as if my soul is being rent from my body, but it is what we have seen others do.

Chapter Eighteen

I enter the inn via the door from the courtyard. We pass into a dim passageway. The heat and sounds coming from the main bar of the inn are easy to follow. Out of one of the doors comes a buxom young woman carrying too many plates of steaming hot roast meats and bread. We nearly collide but I am swift enough to step out of her way and sharp-eyed enough to catch two of the plates of meats as they fall from the balance of her arms.

'Saints preserve us,' she declares. 'You oaf, can you not see where you are going?' Although the accusation is unjust when it was clearly she that could not see her way, I say,

'Begging your pardon, mistress. May I ease your burden and assist you in taking your wares to their destination?' And I indicate the rest of the plates she carries.

She looks me up and down. She is a plump, homely-build, dressed simply but of quality weave. She is harassed but not aggrieved. She considers my person and what she sees seems to please her.

'Let's call it an alliance,' she says and continues down the passage towards the bar. 'Do not stand on ceremony, sir,' she says when I do not follow. 'It will not get you far here,' and she winks as she opens the door to the bar with her back, a well-practiced move.

A wave of heat and sound crashes across us. Sabby does not hesitate and neither do I. To our left is small bar in the corner of the room, a large fire roars the other end. The room is busy; some stand at the bar but most have seats and sit in groups, some around a table or two. Sawdust and reeds cover the earth floor and the smell of roast meats, fresh baked bread and hops is a heady intoxication. We place the plates on the bar as the barmaid begins to plate up the roast meats on thick slices of bread.

'Thanks, dearie,' she says. 'Master, here's a new arrival for you.'

The innkeeper turns to face us.

He is a square-shaped man as broad as he is tall, his face flushed red with eyes that peep from behind fat full cheeks. He wears a linen apron stained with any manner of unfathomable things.

'What can I do you for?' he asks and all around the bar laugh affectionately.

'A room and board for the night,' I say, trying to sound as if I ask for this a lot and it's not my first time.

'And you are in luck, we have just the room for you,' he replies. 'Settle yourself by the fire there and we'll bring refreshments over.'

There is one spot by the fire left and it is at a discreet angle, so I may take in the room but not be on show myself. Despite this I feel exposed. I have spent many an hour at the inn at home but never in the bar, rather in Mary's chamber. At home it has always been better to keep myself to myself for our business, so I have not frequented the bar. Now I realise I am in a world that is dense with its own customs, a language I am yet to learn, yet the ale softens my nerves and the food grounds me to the earth. We find it easy to sit back in the shadows and observe. After those who can afford to have taken their fill a lazy quietness descends as if the entire inn is taking a moment or two's pause.

Then the warm comfort is broken when a man, obviously traveling on foot, opens the front door to the inn. It seems he is known as a welcoming cheer goes around the bar. He is brightly dressed, with coloured ribbons tied around his wrists and on the lapels of his coat. He looks like a walking Maypole. Within minutes he is given wine and the best place by the fire. He feasts on what food is left while the whole bar waits in anticipation, manging small snatched conversations as their anticipation builds.

When he is full of wine and food he takes out a flageolet flute. My heart sinks. I had been hoping for a grand rendition of eloquent words, of heart-breaking stories. I cannot think what joy can be got from a flageolet, but the room falls silent as he stands. He looks around at all present, greeting them with smiles and nods. He turns to me with a broad grin, places his flute to his lips and instantly it is like being transported to another world or dimension so sweet is the sound. It is as if someone has reached inside me and gently taken hold of my heart, such is the sensation of peace. I am transfixed and for a while the inn, my task, everything, falls away.

I want so much for Mary, for Grandmother to hear this, to share this and I am brought back into the room. I glance around; it is full of men thick with muscles from heavy labouring, grown solid with rain and sun-lashed skin yet each and every one of them is transfixed, every one of them held by the magik from this simplest of instruments. When the song completes I am at once bereft and elated. The room concurs as a loud cheer raises the rafters and almost without stopping the minstrel starts a new tune, this time fast and playful.

Words accompany this tune which the whole bar seem to know and soon Sabby and I are buoyant on a sea of voices. Occasionally, traveling minstrels would pass through home then I remember I have seen one with such talent, such charisma before. It is the minstrel that serenaded me to my first lesson with Grace and I surrender to this joyous confirmation. Hours seem to pass like seconds; he has us rolling about in laughter, tears of joy seen in faces that have seen so much hardship, followed then by tears of sorrow at poems of heartbreak and betrayal. The wine and ale flows.

It is late into the night and we are becoming tiered and spent when one man, standing at the bar, who has been drinking harder than the others, having his tankard filled first, is refused a refill by the barmaid. He does not take kindly to her caution and reaches out to grasp hold of her. Instead she wrestles with him, playfully at first, trying to make light of it and escape without further incident. Yet he persists and does not take heed of her warnings. I can only think of Mary and before I have had time to think twice I am upon him. I push past the revellers.

'Desist, sir,' I command. He is much bigger than me, heavy set, but he does not have full grasp of his faculties. It takes him a while to realise the bar has fallen silent and all eyes are upon us.

'Why you...' he says and releases the maid, so he may take aim at me. Quicker than I would give him credit for, he swings back his right arm. I step aside just enough to miss his heavy, hefty fist. He loses balance and falls head long into the barmaid's fist. He totters and sways and then falls back, sliding down the bar and into a heap on the floor.

'No offence, lad, but I fight my own battles,' she says, wiping her hands on her apron, and the entire bar erupts into laughter.

'No need for concern, master,' says the innkeeper. 'It's a regular occurrence.' A group of regulars pick him up. 'We'll lie him next to the cesspit, where he belongs, to sleep it off. In the morning he will be full of apologies.'

To the barmaid I say, 'Mistress, please do not take offence. I was simply adding number to your ranks,' and I bow humbly. To the innkeeper I say, 'Landlord, you are a master of the most appropriate ceremonies.' I shake his hand and the inn erupts in laughter.

Yet my insides are in turmoil. I am on a secret mission, in a place I do not know with people whose customs I do not know, and I have made a public spectacle of myself. There is not a body in the inn tonight who will not remember my face, who will not be able to tell anyone who asks that I was here. To be visibly invisible should be a choice not an accident. I have no idea of what the consequences of this may be.

Fortunately, as the laughter dies down the minstrel suggests one last song for the road. He chooses a sad sentimental song of the loss of a dear one to war. It is something we can all agree on and have some understanding of. The song tells of undying love and comforts us all with the promise of meeting again once this life is concluded. By the end we are all calm and at peace and ready to find our beds for the night. Some of my fellow travellers head upstairs, most out of the door. In the end it's only the minstrel and I left in the bar.

'Right you are then, sirs,' says the innkeeper. 'If you will follow me, I've but one bed left but the sharing of it will spare your purses and warm your limbs.'

'There's no complaints from me,' says the minstrel. I know this is common practice, but I had never thought of sharing a bed. How will I go undiscovered lying so close to another? I smile and nod agreement, but my distress is not well hidden.

'Have we a man of privilege here? Have you not shared a bed afore?' goads the minstrel.

'I have not shared a bed with one as rare as you,' I re-join. 'I'm afraid my snoring will offend your fine-tuned ears.'

We all laugh. I have lived my life in the veil of secrecy. How, in one night, I have lost all I know is beyond me. This trip will teach me more than I had anticipated.

The innkeeper leads the way with a candle and we are shown to a room at the end of the landing on the second floor, large enough for a bed for two, a small table and a wash basin, no window and a door either side.

'You will not be disturbed,' says the innkeeper, indicating the door.

'Thank you, master, this is most comfortable,' says the minstrel. 'Your generosity knows no bounds.'

'Nay it does, it definitely does,' re-joins the innkeeper and he closes the door as he leaves.

'Have you lost all your senses?' demands the minstrel in an angry half whisper as soon as the door is closed. I do not know how to respond. I do indeed feel at sea as if all my senses are jangled and I have lost my moorings, but what is that to him.

'Sir, it is late, and I have an early start,' I say, but I am not sure if I do have an early start. I am not sure of anything. Still I make to get ready for bed.

'And what would that early start be for?' demands the minstrel.

'Sir, I shall not bore you with my business,' I counter and feel my fists clench in readiness. I look for Sabby and feel her absence acutely.

'At ease young fool,' says the minstrel, 'you do not know you have an early start or not because I have not told you if you have or not yet.' I relax. He is the next instruction. 'Billy Bird, minstrel to kings, queens, lords, ladies, labourers and beggars alike. There's not a soul alive that I shall not play for. At your service.' And he bows ostentatiously.

'Master Raven, messenger for anyone with a message, at yours,' and I too bow.

'And so much more,' he says, half to himself. 'Well, Raven, you are not what I expected, more handsome by far.'

'Thank you, I assume,' I say.

'We can use it. I am travelling to a big house outside London. You shall travel with me and that is all I know. Tomorrow we shall start out after breakfast. I am not known for early starts, one of the few advantages of my trade, so we shall be well rested and make sure you make the most of these soft layers, for tomorrow we sleep under the stars.' And with that he climbs into bed, and as his head touches the pillow so his consciousness leaves him.

I remove my doublet and hose but keep my linens on and climb in next to him. It is the first time I have slept in a bed and not on a bed of rushes, the first time away from home; my head swims with ale and images of the day flash through my head, and the pain of separation from Sabby is almost too much to bear. Sleep, no matter how jumbled, is a welcome release

I am roused by the sound of splashing water, a little light creeps under the doors and I can make out his silhouette as he stands relieving himself. I pretend not to notice and feign sleep. I listen as he adjusts his clothes, smell the perfume he applies liberally, feel his energy expand as he constructs himself for the day ahead.

'You best make haste. We should not leave together, and it makes more sense that you leave first,' he says and leaves the room.

I do not waste a second. I am out of the bed as soon as the door closes. I decide decorum would best serve me and I take the time to wash despite my overwhelming desire to be reunited with Sabby. I too have learnt how to relieve myself standing up and do not wish to disappoint the maid when she comes to clear the room. Afterwards I dress and am out the door, down the stairs, along the passageway and into the barn before a minute has passed.

Sabby greets me with a ferocity I match. It is as if we have been separated for months or years such is our joy at being reunited. I decide then that we shall never be parted again. I stand for a while breathing in Jet, letting tears fall into his coat, unseen by others. It is mid-morning now; I would have done my chores and be sitting down with Grandmother, feasting, happy in the knowledge that I would be seeing Mary later. I am unrested, but for the ale and exhaustion, I cannot understand a bed of layers is of comfort or conducive to sleep.

For a few moments I pause and let Jet and Sabby hold me in their love. They remind me no matter how I might feel I am not alone. My tears dry of their own accord and I sense a focus and determination to complete this task no matter the cost to myself. I am filled with a hunger that knows sustenance is needed and Sabby and I head into the inn for breakfast.

Chapter Nineteen

Billy has no horse or donkey, so we take turns on Jet. After we rendezvous I let him ride first. With his patchwork coat, floppy hat and flowing ribbons he is a one-person carnival. I am dressed in my usual black. Together we make a pretty sight as we set off down the road. Today I think we are hiding behind our ostentation.

At breakfast, when I went to pay for my room the maid bit the coins; I had not seen the custom before, so little have I had to do with money, but Billy says it is common practice for there is many who would seek something for nothing. Sometimes I am overwhelmed with how little I know. How can I be so wise in some ways and so ignorant in others? I know so much about the ways of the earth and the ways of beasts, I am not sure I understand the ways of man.

For most of the morning we do not pass many other folks. The road is easy, and the sun is in the sky and I begin to feel more myself. Billy does not speak much at first, rather slumps a little sleepily, but as the afternoon approaches he begins to liven up, whistling or humming a tune which makes the passage of time a little easier. Gradually there are more people toing and froing on the road. I don't quite understand where they have come from but it's clear we are approaching a town. The energy in the air changes, it jingles and chatters, but something is not as it should be. Underneath the excitement there is a tension in the air that feels it could explode at any moment.

As we approach the town walls, people ae focused, dashing from one place to the next, everything flowing towards the market square.

'We are in luck,' says Billy. 'Must be a hanging or an execution of some kind.' With no lord at our castle we have been left to our own devices; the sheriff has had little cause to visit and most minor transgressions have been dealt with by ourselves. I have never seen an execution before. I am not sure I want to.

'What sort of luck?' I ask Billy.

Sabby is alert, calm but ready at any moment to protect. Jet has become stately, claiming ground, ready to trample and run at a moment's notice.

'What sort of luck?' replies Billy. 'Why the luck of full pockets and full belies, follow me.' And he weaves through streets and people as though this is his home town.

I am not sure if he knows where he is going or if he just knows how to follow a crowd. The deeper in we go the thicker the crowd becomes. People part for Jet and we make short work of navigation. Above the heads of the crowd we can just make out we are in the square.

'You stay here with the beasts. I'll meet you back here after.' Before I have chance to ask after what, he is gone into the crowd offering ribbons and trinkets.

We are on the edge of the crowd and decide to stay as such. From this advantage I can see above the heads and hats. All around the square there are stalls selling ale, roast meats and sweets. Passing through the crowd there are tinkers like Billy selling any manner of unneeded trinkets. In one corner a woman dances to a lute and people throw coins; in another a pink-faced preacher warns us all against the sins of the flesh. Directly opposite us is a large wooden platform complete with gallows. I feel a sickness in the pit of my stomach.

The gallows cast a shadow across the entire square and I wonder how such merriment can take place under such a gaze. The sun in the sky seems out of place. The crowd pack in tighter to the square and we are pushed a little way further back which we do not mind. Sabby is cowering, hiding between Jet's feet.

Jet stays calm amongst all the people, the shoving and pushing, and this somehow means people keep a distance from us. A drum beats and the crowd fall silent as a man, just an ordinary man with a black hood to hide his face, walks onto the stage. He walks around the front of the platform taking in the crowd. He does not respond to the goading of the mob, playing his part of sobriety to the full, yet it's clear from the way his stature increases he has enjoyed their attention nonetheless.

A second drum beat, and the crowd fall silent again. Pushed on to the platform are an older woman and a younger woman, mother and daughter. I had expected a burly man or skinny vagabond not two women small in size and pale in demeanour. They look empty shells; whoever they have been, they are not that now. They look a little confused, bewildered to find themselves on the gallows platform before such a crowd, but also resigned. The marks on their bodies left by torture suggest death may be a release.

The crowd go wild. They shout obscenities, jeer and chide them, laugh and spit at them. 'Witch' is the shout most often and loudest heard. I am chilled to the bone. We had heard that following the Pope's edict, executions had begun of our people, but I did not know it was so close. I cannot understand why folk would believe the words of a man that they have not and will not ever see, above their own experience, above their own wisdom.

The women barely seem to know where they are, their eyes vacant and empty. The ale sellers amongst the crowd are doing a roaring trade, the crowd voracious in their consumption of everything. Sabby moans and whines but her tears are lost in the noise of the crowd. Jet is motionless but taut, ready to spring into motion instantly. I try my best to hide my shock and fear. I cannot bring myself to join the chants, to take pleasure in such travesty. Instead I aim for neutral, an inquisitive traveller passing through, which in some senses I am. Most do not notice us though, their attention blurred by ale and excitement.

I cannot help the feeling that the two women who will lose their lives are incidental, mere symbols for something in each and every one of the crowd that they seek to kill in themselves. I cannot see how this murder will serve anyone in the short or long run. Yet today is not about reason.

The sheriff mounts the platform, a thin man, all angles and all in conflict with each other. He has death in his eyes; I can see through their vacant gaze that he is long since dead inside. The crowd applaud and cheer him; his fine clothes but simple demeanour suggest everyone can reach his heights, suggest power can be everyone's whilst confirming that it can only lie in one man's hands. With a simple raising of his arm the crowd fall silent, expectant of his words, his wisdom.

'Good people,' and a cheer goes around the crowd, 'good people, today we gather as one to rid our community, our town, our homes, of an evil which daily grows more strong, which daily threatens each and every one of us. Evil is everywhere, and it is up to us, each and every one, to rid the earth of it. Despise not these feeble creatures afore you,' he indicates the two women who stand heads bowed, 'do not fear them. Rather look into your own hearts, look into your own souls and there find compassion, there find love. These victims that stand in shame fall on your mercy, call for our help today to release them, their souls possessed, as they are, by the very Devil himself.'

He pauses for dramatic effect and it is as if the shadow of this Devil has passed over the crowd so contrite they are.

'Yet, good people, do not take my words, do not think this is my ruling. I am merely a humble servant of the Lord God Almighty.'

Many in the crowd make the sign of the cross.

'Let the women speak for themselves.'

He walks over to the older woman and with the greatest gentleness and tenderness leads her to the front of the stage.

'Mother Sanders, speak you the truth. Do you not wish to be set free?' he asks. Mother Sanders does not respond. He asks again, 'Mother, do you not seek release from the Devil?' Mother Sanders lets out a frail wail and falls to her knees. The crowd let out a cheer.

He leaves her on her knees and goes and brings forth the younger woman.

'Daughter Sanders, what say you? Do you seek to be free, your soul released for all eternity?'

Slowly she raises her head and looks around the crowd, her eyes a reflection back at them of their own accusation. The crowd begin to titter and jeer under their breath, nudging each other, their hostility palpable. She stands tall and matches it.

'Sister, do you seek to be free?' She turns and looks at him, at the crowd, and then she spits in his face.

The crowd erupt into demands to hang her, kill her, decapitate her. The sheriff does nothing to calm them, instead he motions for the hangman who begins to drag Mother Sanders to her feet and across to the gallows. She does nothing to resist and I want to scream at her, to shout, to kick, to go out fighting but she complies when he places the noose around her neck, her head still bowed, her eyes not making contact with anything or anyone. The crowd are quiet with anticipation.

Then the hangman steps down from the gallows and approaches Daughter Sanders; she greets his eyes. He bows his head, seeking the forgiveness he shall need later that night when he closes his eyes to sleep. She bows too and there is resolve between them. She walks herself to the gallows. The crowd erupt into a frenzy as every insult ever imagined is hurled at her. She bats away the hangman's hands and takes the noose herself and places it around her neck, then tightens it.

This only proves to the crowd that she is indeed possessed by the Devil. Yet at that moment I could not feel more connected to her spirit. Somehow her eyes meet mine. She is some distance away, but I know she is looking at me, that in the crowd she has sought a friend and found one. I keep my face neutral but there is love in my eyes. I know she is facing the gallows with dignity.

The hysteria of the crowd is climactic, and the sheriff gives the signal, and the hangman pulls the steps away from Mother Sanders. She drops silently to her death. He approaches Daughter Sanders who looks him in the eyes and kicks the steps away before he can remove them, dropping with dignity to her death. I see fear turn to joy and peace in her eyes, then she is gone, and the crowd falls silent.

A gust of wind circles round the square and the bodies sway lifelessly. The sheriff and the hangman leave the platform and the swaying bodies. Gradually the crowd begin to chatter and disperse, comparing notes and rating the execution, scoring out of ten for delivery and spectacle. I cannot see Billy, but I am overwhelmed with a desire to get away, as afar as possible away. The image of the girl's eyes as she let her body go are imprinted on my brain. We are soon an obstruction as the satiated crowd disperse and, without thinking too much about it, we turn and follow the flow of the people until we find a small green with enough space for us to wait until Billy finds us.

Chapter Twenty

I dismount Jet and hold Sabby tight; I would like to weep but the pain is too deep, too raw and the location unsafe when everyone else around us is content and satisfied. We all three stand close, holding each other. Eventually the crowd clears, and we are left alone. We do not know how long it will be till Billy finds us. He will be peddling his wares till there is no one left to peddle to. I half fear he will find himself in an inn or ale house full of eager listeners, and we could be waiting until morning.

Yet I care little. I have never seen such a thing. It has always been there, the threat, the shadow of the darkest depths of humanity, but never before have I experienced it first-hand. I am shocked to my core; everything that seemed safe has somehow been violated. There will always be a distance between other people and myself now. There shall never be the easy confidence I had in people. The trust that inside we all share the same truth shall never more be trusted. I feel the loss inside me as if some part of me has forever been killed, leaving me numb and lifeless.

I feel a great fatigue consume me. My head is too heavy to hold up. I want more than anything to be in a soft reed bed by the fire at Grandmother's but so is my sense of tiredness anywhere would do to lie right now. I am about to lie down right there in the middle of the town when I hear Billy singing; it is a jolly song, a tale of a trickster and a king. How can he?

I had thought minstrels keepers of the heart, boosters of spirit and comforters of the flesh but Billy has been nothing but disappointment. When he has a crowd he is joy personified, witty with a piercing tongue for humour that even though daring in its observations it is delivered with such compassion even those insulted feel flattered and understood. I have seen him reduce the bluntest man to tears such is the sweetness of his voice. Yet when he is out of public gaze it is all dropped as if he has taken off a stunning velvet coat, laden with jewels and underneath is just rags. Now he is singing when he should be in tears or at least silent out of respect.

'Come lad,' he says, 'this lucrative stop has waylaid us, and we need to make up time before we make camp for the night.'

Fury fills my being; how can he be so? He sees my distress, who would not, and offers no solace, no comfort. I do not respond but simply mount Jet and look straight ahead, determined not to cry.

'Righty-o,' he says and sets off back through town, this time avoiding the square. We follow and there is not a word spoken or a sound made by Sabby, Jet or me for the rest of the day's travel.

It is almost dark before he decides we should make camp. He has hummed and whistled for much of the way and seems oblivious that we have not spoken. He tells me to settle Jet while he collects wood for the fire.

He has chosen a good spot, away from the road and prying eyes, sheltered by stones but with much grass and foliage for Jet. It is clear he knows this spot well; there have been those before us as the remains of a fire can be seen. Our predecessor's ignorance is piled on top of the disbelief and pain. Each time I close my eyes or let my mind release the tiniest amount I see her face, her eyes. I fear the haunting and do not know how to dispel it. I have used all the incantations I can think of. Internally I have asked her for release, but nothing has worked. How are all my teachings failing me when I need them the most? Everything seems to be happening far away from me, at a distance; for the first time in my life I do not feel connected to the earth. I do not feel her comfort.

Somehow, I untack Jet yet despite the lush undergrowth he eats from need not enthusiasm. We should have unpacked, rolled out our blanket for the night's rest but we sit motionless, lost in a void. Billy has built a roaring fire and is toasting bread and drinking ale before I notice, then it is only because he has passed me a small metal flask.

'Come,' he says, 'this will ease your vision.' I do not even question what it is but drink without consciousness until the harsh sense of fire rips through my insides and I am jolted into awareness through chocking and spluttering.

He laughs but only a little, then, with the greatest of tenderness, he rubs my back, yet I shrug him off. I cannot bear his touch even though I feel his kindness. He turns back to the fire and drinks long and hard on his ale. I hand back the flask and he takes it without acknowledging me. He passes me some toasted bread and some cheese. Despite my expectation I find I have a hunger.

We eat in silence. I share mine with Sabby and there is some comfort in that. It's late now and we shall set off before first light in the morning. Yet I do not feel sleep approaching, just a hollowness.

'It is never easy,' he says. I do not want to listen so make no response, but this does not deter him.

'The first time, it's never easy. You cannot dispel her eyes from your mind's eye, can you?' he asks and looks at me. I look away, ashamed for this truth.

'He had the most beautiful blue eyes. So soft, so gentle to look into them was to know love. Sometimes it is a comfort, the memory of them, sometimes not. But they shall always be with me.

'He had the sweetest smile and the memory of that is always a comfort. We hadn't known each other long but we knew, from the first instance, we knew. We were young and in love. We knew to hide it, to take our pleasures in secret places but they found us out anyway. It was dark in the alleyway and we thought there was no one there, but the local priest had decided to take his pleasure of a whore in the same alley. He shone a lamp in our direction and I hid. I hid my face. He was caught, his beautiful blue eyes dazed in the bright light. "Run," he shouted and I did, sure he would follow, sure he was right on my heels but he did not run.

'It was days before I heard he had been thrown in the goal for sodomy. They take something as beautiful as love and turn it into filth. I cannot fathom it.

'The trail was little more than a farce. He would not confess my name, would not betray me, even torture would not loosen his tongue. Yet I betrayed him, I watched as they humiliated him, as they taunted him, as they tore his body to pieces.

'Worse, in the inn at night I joined in, to save myself. I pointed the finger, taunted and jeered with the worst of them. So precious my life seemed at that moment.

'I too stood at the back of the crowd. I'd never been to an execution before. When they brought him to the hanging tree he was calm, dignified, and I hid my face in the crowd. I could see he was looking for me, I could tell he sought my smile one last time. Yet it was not until the last that I sought his, at the last I raised my eyes and met his and saw only love shinning. It felt the worst cruelty. That I, so unworthy of love, should even now be in receipt of his. I hope above all, that despite my shame, he saw his love reflected back through my eyes.

'After that I couldn't stay, couldn't settle anywhere but I have always had a good voice and a love of pretty things.'

'And every song you sing you sing for him,' I say, and he turns to me and for the first time we look into each other's eyes, each other's souls. Then we quickly turn away.

'Since then there have been many executions, always lucrative but I have no taste for the act itself.'

'Yet how is it possible that man will treat man so?' I ask.

'Try not to ask too many questions or think too hard. You may be unfortunate enough to find the answers. Now rest, it's a long day tomorrow and I do not wish to deliver you looking less than your best.' And with that he lies down where he is and before I can ask any more his snores fill the air. I curl up with Sabby, close to Jet, and find that while my eyes sleep, my mind races.

Chapter Twenty-One

When we wake, Billy has already packed up and is waiting. The sun is rising, my brain is still a jumble and my body aches with emotions, but I know one thing. I shall honour the girl, I shall not try to take the memory of her away. I will not forget, rather make it so I will always remember. I could not save her, but I can honour her. Her life shall not be in vain.

It does not take long to get ready and we are soon on the road. I let Billy ride first whilst I walk. We are mostly quiet but now it is companionable. Billy occasionally sings a song to help the time pass. The road is long with little change in scenery. Gradually, as we walk, my mind begins to settle and clear. The easy rhythm of our walking helps soothe my nerves and I am filled with questions. Who was she? What had she done? 'Yesterday..?' I ask.

'Witchcraft,' he says.

'Were they?' I ask.

'Unlikely,' he says. 'A witch is an invented thing, at least in the way they mean it. A witch to them is someone who has made a pact with the Devil. Yet have you ever met such a chap?' I laugh.

'I know no such teaching,' I say. 'What use a Devil when everything has a use, a purpose?'

'Quite so,' he says. 'Mostly, if the truth be told, it is women and men not liked by the community. Someone to blame.'

'For what?'

'For the crops failing, the rain falling, the fever that kills, anything really, take your pick.'

'For being different,' I say.

'That too. Do we not know how it is to hide who we are?'

'Yet it hasn't always been so,' I say.

'How not?' he asks and it's my turn to tell him of different times, of the third sex, of shamans and goddesses. He says little but when I have finished I see moistness in his eyes.

'It is true then, you learn something new every day.' For all he has seen, all that he has done, knowing that there was a time when we were heroes and not the villains we are now has changed something inside him, for the better and for the good.

In time we come to a stone bridge. A small boy is running from side to side, peering over the edge. Billy would pass without asking but I can hear crying and cannot go on without offering our assistance.

'What ails you boy?' I ask, pulling Jet to a stop just before the bridge. The boy does not respond yet small squeals escape his mouth as he runs from side to side. Again I ask, loud this time, yet still no response. Then I understand he cannot hear me. I walk down to the river's edge. The river itself is some way down from the edge and not easily reached. I cannot see under the bridge very well but it's clear that is where the crying is coming from. I walk back up to the bridge.

'It is not our concern,' Billy says.

'No,' I say, 'yet maybe we can be of assistance; if we do not help each other then are we not our own executioners?' He does not respond, rather dismounts and goes to relieve himself by a nearby tree.

I walk up to the boy. He is simply dressed but clean and cared for. He is standing in the middle of the bridge looking at me with hopeful eyes. I look him in the eyes when I speak.

'Raven, at your service,' I say and bow, sweeping off my hat.

I am hoping to ease his troubles a little with some kind humour, but he simply grabs my arm and leads me to the edge of the bridge. He points down and over, then makes flapping motions with his arms like wings. Then I recognise the cry – it is a falcon's cry. The boy's falcon is trapped under the bridge. I peer over. There is a long drop to the underside of the bridge and little by way of anything to clasp or step onto. The falcon cries again; Sabby barks and Jet munches on grass as Billy lies beside catching, for a short while, rays of sunshine and sleep.

I go over to the other side of the bridge and it is the same there. This would be so easy if I could shift. Any climbing creature would suffice but it's too risky. My mind races, trying to find a solution but nothing seems possible. The falcon cries again, sounding distressed rather than in pain. The boy has sunk down defeated on to the ground. I look over to Billy who is now snoring. I look at Sabby; if I am quick no one will know.

As quietly and quickly as I can I make my way down the side of the bridge. Sabby knows to keep watch and she keeps an eye on me whilst keeping attention on the others. I scramble down the river bank. It's dark under the bridge, yet I can see the falcon trapped in the rafters of the bridge, a bat caught in its talons. I check either side, no fishermen, no boats. I choose lizard for speed and claws that can clasp, it takes seconds. I try to shift so my clothes are left in one neat pile.

I scale the wall easily, despite the wet, dripping stone. I hope the bat is feast enough for Falcon, I don't plan on becoming seconds. I weave in and out of the other resting bats and reach Falcon. He has flown into a tight spot in the rafters and cannot get through or turn to fly back out. It is taut, frightened and panicked. It lets out another cry. To get out he will have to go out the way he came, but this time backwards. I will need to startle him to make him fall and thus release him from his trap.

I drop down onto the rafters and, rising onto my hind legs, wave up and down. Falcon is startled and tries to fly but is knocked off balance when there is no room for his wings to spread. As I had hoped, he topples backwards thus releasing himself from his trap. He drops his catch and the bat hurtles towards the river, but he recovers and catches it again just before it hits the water. Falcon lets out a triumphant cry.

I move quickly back to my clothes. I have learnt to dress with the utmost speed and in seconds I begin to scramble back up the river bank fully clothed, thinking this would be so much faster and easier if not in human form. By the time I reach the top I am covered in mud, my hose torn, leaves in my hair. Sabby barks and Billy takes one look at me and laughs head back until he has to hold his sides. I look over to the bridge and see the boy and Falcon reunited. Falcon is feeding on the bat held now in the boy's hand. They are oblivious to the rest of the world. I dust myself down as best I can. I shall not make a good impression tonight.

'Shall we?' I say in an attempt to encourage Billy to compose himself.

'Yes, let us not tally any longer,' he says between laughs and we set off.

As we pass over the bridge, the young boy looks at me with gratitude in his eyes. He sends the falcon up into the sky and runs to me, flinging his arms around my legs, his clasp is tight and full of love. Gently I peel him away as the falcon circles overhead, this time making an elated cry. I smile and look into the boy's eyes, a beautiful green, and know that no words are necessary. I turn, and we continue on our way.

'How did you do it?' asks Billy when he has composed himself.

'Stones, I threw stones.'

'Cruel to be kind,' he says but I get the feeling he doesn't quite believe me.

It is late afternoon and apart from the bridge incident we have not stopped all day. We are all tired and hungry, when we see in the distance the big house. I look to Billy for conformation and receive it. This is our destination.

The house is set back a long way from the road; a coppice wood circles it and trees line the driveway which is heavily laid with compact gravel. We are not used to such a smooth surface; as we walk Billy begins to prepare pulling out his coloured ribbons and bells. The nearer we get to the house the more underdressed I feel with my mud stains and torn hose. I have half a mind to ask for an hour or so to do some laundry but know this is not an option.

It is early dusk when we finally reach the house, a large stone building three stories high. I have never seen such a beautiful building before. Flower beds burst with all manner of plants and flowers that I do not know, which assault the eye with colour. In front of the house is a large circular raised bed of flowers in the centre of the path. I did not know such splendour existed. I sense someone watching us and look up in time to see a woman's face draw quickly back from one of the second-storey windows. I go towards the front door, but Billy simply laughs at me again and proceeds around to the back of the house. The courtyard is large, the stones washed clean, the stables look full until Billy points towards a barn the opposite side to the stables.

As stately and splendid the front of the house, the back is a hive of activity. Stable hands, maids, gardeners, all manner of trades come and go, all with something to do, all with somewhere to be. Billy simply walks into the centre of the yard, arranges every bell so it's of maximum volume, and begins to dance. The sound of the bells are amplified by the stone floors and brick walls so that it sounds like fifty Morris dancers have taken up their dance. It is not long until he is surrounded by all manner of maids and grooms.

They greet him with a familiarity and expectation, clapping and stamping their feet to his rhythm. The noise echoes off every surface and suddenly a carnival is taking place; back windows of the house fly open as people lean out, joining the celebrations. Eventually the chef, red-faced, round and jolly, comes out of the kitchen wiping his hands on his blood-stained apron. He lets the festivities continue for a little while, enjoying the spectacle, then with a clear clap of his hands three times order is restored. Windows close and the crowd disperse but without fear, relaxed and ready to return to work.

The chef waits until everyone has cleared. Billy turns to him with a smile that speaks of years of friendship and they embrace. The chef clicks his fingers and a groom appears to take Jet and Sabby to the stables and I follow Billy and the chef into the kitchen, only half-listening to their easy enthusiastic word play.

The kitchen smells hit me like a gale-force wind - every delicious smell I have smelt before and many more that I have not. The heat is extraordinary. I have no experience of hell but surely it was visioned by someone who has worked in a kitchen. At least three fires roar and ovens blaze behind iron doors. There is a constant coming and going so that it's hard to tell who is who and what is what, a constant clattering of pans and knives and chatter. The chef corrects and sometimes praises as we make our way through.

Sabby has been sent with Jet and it will be the stable I sleep in tonight. We leave the kitchen behind and enter the servants' parlour - a large room to accommodate the live-in servants furnished with a large table. The chef takes a jug of wine and three tankards and we sit at one corner of the table. A maid brings us fresh bread and some roast meats. I am offered a linen napkin for my left shoulder. I have only heard of the custom, never seen it in practice, but Billy takes his and I copy as best I can. I do not pay much heed to their conversation so intent am I on my belly. The bread is so soft and light and the meat so tender, flavoured with herbs and spices Grandmother and I have only dreamed of. Every bite is a new sensation, a new experience and I wonder how I shall ever eat simple pottage again. When I can no longer eat another mouthful, we are shown to our room.

Billy knows I shall sleep in the stables with Sabby, but we thank the groom anyway. We open the door to find two steaming hot baths, a groom and a maid at our attendance. To bathe in hot water would be a first. The air is filled with the most delicious fragrance of rose and petals float in the water, but I cannot bathe. I cannot be seen. If I am seen for what I am and not what I project I am all shall be lost. Billy senses my concern, but I am not sure how much or what he knows.

'Afeard of a bath, Master Raven, feared for your health maybe?' he suggests.

'Indeed, it is not a practice I am familiar with,' I agree. The maid and groom approach.

'What are your pleasures, masters?' asks the slightly-built groom in a soft voice that suggests much more than toiletries and hot water are available.

'Mistress says whatever you require we shall provide.' It is exactly clear what Billy would like and he seems unperturbed, almost expectant of such treatment.

I can tell it pains him, but he says, 'Thank you, if you could leave us, that will be all.' They look at us both confused and hesitant; this is not what was expected.

'Wait,' I say, 'do not trouble so, it is I that is at fault. I shall take the clean linen and leave you in peace.'

'We can place a screen between if modesty is your concern?' he replies but I have already picked up the linen and am heading out the door.

'Best I make myself a bed and prepare for tonight.' When I say that I realise I do not know what the plan for that night is.

'Come find me here when you hear the supper call,' Billy says and practically pushes me out of the room. Laughter and squeals follow me down the passageway.

It is a great comfort to find Sabby and Jet settled and at ease in the stable. The hay is clean and good, and for the first time since leaving home I feel a comfort as I lay my blanket down. Sabby and I sit whilst Jet munches hay. We are at peace and the comfort I feel reminds me of home. It is then I feel such a yearning, such a wave of homesickness washes through me, breaking and retreating to break again on my internal shores.

I long to hear Grandmother chide me or to hear her words of wisdom. My body feels it shall break if I do not feel Mary's touch or breathe in her smell and hold her in my arms, the warmth of her body reaching in and softening the bones inside me. There has been so much to absorb, to understand, and I have not allowed myself to wander into sentimentality, to even think of home for fear of the pain but now it takes hold and I begin to understand what loss feels like.

Even though I am sure I will return home, even though I am sure I will hold Mary in my arms once more and feel the lash of Grandmother's tongue again, in that moment it is too long till I will be home again, and the loss is palpable. I feel myself sinking into a despair that I know no way back from when I hear the kitchen gong. Supper is to be served and I am not washed and changed. Quickly I push my pain aside. Checking that there are no prying eyes I undress and change into the clean linen. I take a horse grooming brush from the pile and the dried dirt is soon clear of my clothes. I try as best I can to hide the tear in my hose and hurry as fast as I can back to Billy's room.

Chapter Twenty-Two

I knock on the door. 'Come,' shouts Billy from within. I open the door and find him sitting by the fire, a goblet of wine in his hands, dressed in fine and colourful velvet, adorned in ribbons. The baths have been taken away and the covers on the bed roughly made. I take the seat opposite him by the fire. The room is heavy with the scent of perfume and sex.

'Tonight, Master Raven, we shall be the after-dinner entertainment,' he says and hands me a goblet of wine. I am about to protest but he cuts me off. 'You shall be my assistant. Do not concern yourself just do everything I tell you and you shall make a grand impression, well, satisfactory anyway.' He laughs to himself and to the fire.

'I cannot sing and know no jokes,' I say.

'And you shall not be asked for either. Rather hand me instruments when I ask for them, take my ribbons and scarfs when I am done with them. It will come easy, a new role for you to play. Surely you can take on new forms when the need arises?' He says this with more weight than I would like. Is he saying what he knows or is he fishing for confirmation of what he suspects?

'I would not want to disappoint in front of such important guests,' I say.

'You shall not,' he says, getting to his feet. 'The guests tonight are those of noble status.'

'God-fearing folk,' I say.

'Are we not all?' he says and we both laugh. To fear a god makes no sense to me when reciprocation is the basis for all the good relationships I have with all the gods I know.

'Lady Bamford, widow, runs this estate, her brother owns it, but he finds more sport in London's Cheapside than here in the country, she is a long-time patron of mine. We shall not disappoint her tonight.' He has gathered together his props and instruments and stands at the door.

'Are those the only clothes you have?' he asks. I look at him, perplexed. Why would I have more than one set of clothes? For what purpose and from what purse?

'Never mind, we will use it to our favour, pity and wine might make the coffers flow from our esteemed audience.' He indicates for me to get the door for him.

'Tonight, be vigilant. We must appear a team, the slightest slip could be disaster for us all.'

'What joy,' I say and open the door. 'Let the show begin.'

The heat from the great hall can be felt a long way down the passage. The air is thick with chatter, laughter and the constant toing and froing of maids and grooms. We follow two carrying jugs of wine and ale into the hall. The room is ablaze, candles and lights hang from every part of the ceiling, fires blaze; it is the hottest summer's day inside.

Rows of tables are laid, lowest to highest, people dressed in unimaginable finery, furs and jewels – it is the most sumptuous carnival. We join the waiting staff standing around the room and I take time to observe the splendours. Sitting at the top table is Lady Bamford and I can see it was her face in the window. She is grace personified, beautiful but in an unassuming way as if it is the most natural thing in the world to be that beautiful and that at ease with it. She is attentive to her guests, regularly giving instructions to her staff to ensure everyone has too much of what they want. She laughs at jokes that are clearly not funny and makes witty but gentle retorts.

The room is full of sights and sounds; lascivious clergymen, fat lecherous older men, gregarious older women, not used to such abundance, bored younger people who are only waiting for the dancing to begin, all manner of dress and conduct yet I only seem to see Lady Bamford. She is captivating, and I am captivated. Yet I do not seek to woo her; this is a connection I have not felt before. I cannot describe or explain it, to feel something so deep for no reason.

Then the room falls silent at her gesture, the doors fling open and a huge cake covered in marchpane in the shape of an angel is presented to the room. The intricate detail on the marchpane is overwhelmingly delicate and precise. Gasps and sighs ripple around the room. It is far too good to eat and yet I salivate none the less. The cake is placed in the centre of the room. Lady Bamford and her special guest, what looks like the bishop of the area, stand and walk over to view closer. Lady Bamford is offered a knife, but she demurely declines and passes the honour to the bishop. There is recognition and approval around the room. He takes the knife with a mock modesty that hides a sense of entitlement, and with a grand, practised gesture pierces the cake right where the angel's heart would be. There is happy applause from all present. Whatever the myriad of personal feelings people have towards this man in the room it is clear his position is challenged by no one. The cake is taken away to be divided amongst the guests and the boisterous conversation returns.

Billy leans in close to me. 'Prepare you, once the cake has been consumed we are on. Let me lead, do as I say and do not take any of it personally.'

I want to ask what he means by that but do not have the chance as we are jostled and distracted by the delivery of the sumptuous pieces of cake. It is unlikely, but I hope the kitchen has made enough cake for all of us for clearly there will be no scraps left by the invited company. It does not take long for the cake to be eaten and the glasses to be refiled. Then a natural satiated lull falls on the company and that is our cue. Without waiting to be invited, Billy cartwheels, a vision of rainbow colour across the room, the bells a cacophony of joyous sound invigorating the senses. He is warmly welcomed by the crowd.

'Lords, ladies, noblemen, clergymen, gentry men, yeomen, labourers, four legs, two legs, creepy crawlies.' Billy makes a grand gesture of winking and his humour is received by all.

'Tonight shall thrill you, tonight I shall woo you, tonight I shall titillate the senses, tonight expect to be entertained; Minstrel Bird at your service.' He takes an over large bow as the audience applaud expectantly.

'And my assistant, Jester Jay.' He indicates for me to join him. I have never performed in public before; I do not know what to expect and have understood myself to be on the side-lines, not in the public gaze. I shake my head, terror has shot through me like a cannon ball, I am frozen to the spot. Billy lets the silence of the crowd build, he gestures again for me to join him, again I refuse, again he demands, again I refuse.

'Kind, dear, gentle folk, it is Jay's first time and he is a little shy. Will you help me?' asks Billy, and in this way, he turns it into a game and then I understand I am to be his fool - a part I shift into far too easily. He asks the audience to ask me nicely to join him. A cacophony of sound and then gradually he gets them speaking in unison whilst I play back, aping a shyness I no longer have. He has the whole room in his hand by the time he has got me on stage.

We then take up a back and forth, slapstick mostly with me coming off worse. He builds it, so the crowd are almost hysterical and then senses exactly when to dismiss me and take the crowd to the darkest depths of despair with the simplest of love songs. He receives a standing ovation and there is not a dry eye in the hall. Throughout our act, Lady Bamford has paid close attention to me; she has enjoyed our antics, yet something has pained her and I cannot tell what. Yet we leave the hall heroes, rich in purse and ego.

'Why did you not warn me? We could have prepared?' I ask Billy once outside.

'It is better when it's unexpected, really, when no one is acting.'

'Yet a high-risk approach,' I say.

'I knew I could count on you,' he says, shrugging his shoulders and making haste towards the parlour to see what is left of the leftovers.

Despite the astonishing array of dishes that has been served that night it is only the cake I am interested in. I am about to follow Billy when there is a tap on my shoulder and Billy's groom leans into my ear.

'My lady requests you join her in the gardens,' he says and indicates along the passageway. The next set of instructions. I nod slightly to let him know I have understood and with as little fuss as possible I head down the passageway.

Quietly I open the door and before me is a sophisticated display of raised beds, the moon is high, and it is a clear warm night. I cannot see anyone so take a step onto the fine gravel path. I do not know how long I am supposed to wait or where, so I begin to wander slowly, breathing in the softness of the night. I reach the end of the raised beds and there is a path arched in vines.

Lady Bamford steps out from the shadows; I am a little startled but modestly drop down on to one knee. 'My Lady, at your service,' I say.

'Please,' she says, 'there is no need.' She offers me her hand. I think to kiss it but when mine joins hers she uses it to guide me to my feet.

'Come, it is such a beautiful night, let us take some air.' The sounds of music and dancing are carried on a gentle breeze and I think she must love dancing.

'As is your wish,' I say, and we turn and walk down the archway. Two maids follow but just out of earshot.

'Master Raven, such a beautiful name, tell me a little about yourself. You are betrothed I understand?' Fortunately it is dark because I blush once for modesty and once for concern – how does she know?

'Perhaps,' I say, 'betrothed is too strong a word but my heart is spoken for.'

'She is a lucky maiden then,' she says.

'Thank you and who might it be that holds your heart?' I re-join and she laughs with a gentle satisfied sense.

'Oh, the story of my heart is a long and tragic one, not a story for such a beautiful occasion.'

'Show me the braggard that has so abused you. I shall make short work of him,' I say. Again she laughs, somehow satisfied with my response.

'Oh, he has been long ago delivered to history, but you, tell me of your love.'

'Mine, well where to start when someone holds your heart?'

'With her name perhaps?' she offers, and it is my turn to laugh.

'Of course, Mary.'

'Beautiful?' she asks.

'Does that not go without saying?' I re-join and we both laugh. 'Her eyes are deep blue pools to be lost and never found in. Yet she is bolder and braver than most would give her credit for,' I say.

'An excellent choice then. And your grandmother, she fares well?' Again her knowledge is disconcerting; she must be deeply involved in the resistance to be so informed.

'She is well, busy and cranky as ever.'

'You are lucky to have such love in your life,' she says, and it is both a question and a statement. I sense her pain again and think she must have wanted for love in her life.

'I am indeed, my lady. I have not wanted for anything. All that I am I owe to her.'

'And your parents, your mother? Has she not played some part?'

''Perhaps,' I say, 'but I cannot credit that which I do not know.'

'Indeed that is so,' she says and her tone changes to one of business.

'Tomorrow you shall journey to the Port of London; look for the ship the Black Gladfly. In your pack you will find all you need. Captain Langan will be expecting you.'

'Thank you,' I say. She gestures to her maids and they turn back towards the hall.

'It has been an honour and a pleasure,' she says.

'For me more than you,' I say, and she smiles a sad smile and turns away. I watch her for a little and am about to turn back myself when she stops and turns towards me.

'Your clothes?' she asks. 'You only have one set?' What is this obsession with clothes these people have?

'Yes,' I say and resist the temptation to ask why I need more.

'As I thought,' she says. 'Sleep well, you have a long journey tomorrow.'

'Thank you, my lady.' I bow. We both turn to go our separate ways. That night wrapped around Sabby on the soft straw next to Jet, I sleep the best I have since leaving home.

I am awoken at first light by Jet and Sabby who seem to sense an urgency to our travel. Sitting on top of my pack, neatly folded, are a brand-new pair of black hose, a brand new black leather doublet and a set of the finest linen I have ever seen. I quickly change from my own clothes. The feel of the linen against my skin is a pleasure I had not expected. How will I ever wear rough cut cloth again? The hose fits me perfectly but when I put on the doublet it is as if I have grown six feet high. Until then I had understood clothes to fulfil a simple need of protection. Now I understand why the laws state in such detail who may wear what and how. To wear this doublet fills me with the power of the seas - the cloth has a power and I am imbibed in it. It is a sense of completeness and I am bewildered as to how a simple piece of clothing can make me feel so.

Yet there is not time to dwell. Hidden inside the doublet is a map to the Port of London and a small pouch of coins. From the map I should be at the boat by nightfall. I memorise every detail of the map, so it is a picture imprinted on my mind. The sun is now high. I go into the kitchen and, whilst no one is looking, I burn the map in one of the roaring fires. It must take a small forest to maintain this kitchen. There is still no sign of Billy so, treading gently, I find his room. I knock and receive a mumbled groan in response. I open the door and find him still deep under the covers. I crouch down near his head.

'Billy,' I whisper, 'it's time for our farewells.' He groans and rolls over, pulling the pillows over his head. I stand, why disturb his slumber and his luxury.

'Thank you,' I say. 'A friend you have been and a friend you shall remain.' I walk towards the door and open the latch.

'Travel safe, my friend,' he says, and I pause. Then I hear an almighty snore. I smile and close the door behind me.

When I get back to the yard, a stable hand has groomed and saddled Jet, a maid hands me an oilskin bag of ale and the largest piece of marchpane cake I could have hoped for. I check Sabby, she is ready and waiting. I mount Jet and in the early light of the day, we set off for London, a place I had never expected or wanted to visit.

Chapter Twenty-Three

The road is easy and the route as before. The day passes quickly although I feel the loss of Billy. It feels too quiet without his tunes to pass the time. Soon the road begins to fill; as if from nowhere the traffic increases and we know we are approaching London. There are carts full of livestock and vegetables, women carrying huge packs on their backs laden with wares to sell, beggars line the roadside, carriages loaded with goods and people trundle by in both directions. The atmosphere is not unfriendly but there is indifference in people's eyes. They see so many that they see no one.

The smell of the city is the first thing to reach us and received long before the carts and people. It is unmistakable - a mixture of urine, faeces, of beasts and man, smoke, cooking food, sweat and perfume all mixed together. It is frightening and overwhelming; never has the smell of man been so strong. Soon the fields fall away, and we enter dark roads deep in mud and excrement. There are so many people. If I had not seen it, I would not think it possible. I had feared we would stand out, but everyone seems too busy with themselves so that other people seem of little import. It is clear this would be a place to hide and never be found in.

Despite the dark narrow winding streets, the endless stalls of trinkets with no uses or food that looks weeks old, we find our way; the map in my mind and our sense of direction serve us well. We keep our eyes to ourselves and are soon assaulted by a fresh smell of rancid fish and thick water filled with every type of waste you can imagine. The din of shouting, laughing, deals being done, and fortunes lost and made is extraordinary. We stop in an alley way just to pause for a moment. It is exhilarating, the streets are bursting with life yet empty of it at the same time. We hide in the shadows to avoid being seen and take it in.

I breathe in deeply and the smell hits the back of my throat and I have no choice but to turn to the side and empty the contents of my stomach. Jet is skittish and Sabby overly proud. Until now I have always thought myself a lover of people but now I am not so sure. I have half a mind to turn back, to travel as fast as we can back to Grandmother's. Back to when I understood everything or thought I did.

A young man dressed in a long red velvet coat that has seen much better days stops and leans against the wall next to us.

'Have you the time, master?' he asks. It seems in London every taste is catered for.

'Not today,' I say.

We set out on our way again. Dusk is falling, and I want to find the ship before nightfall. Slowly we make our way through the crowds. Along the riverside there are boats and ships of all shapes. People of all skin colours mix together and although I had heard tell and seen pictures in books in the library it is still a wonderment when I see black skin for the first time. The way the light is reflected is one of the most beautiful things I have ever seen, and I am ashamed for I cannot help but stare. I mean no harm, but I have some sense of how that must hurt.

We pass a spice ship unloading and for once we are assaulted by a beauteous smell promising delicious foods. We are almost at the end of the port, the crowd is thinner here and more watchful, when we see the Black Gladfly. It is not the largest or grandest ship, but it is well kept. I dismount and begin to tie Jet to the nearest post when a small boy dressed in rags appears from nowhere.

'Penny to watch your horse, master?' he says. I am about to reach into my pack when Captain Langan appears on deck.

'Away with you, you scoundrel,' he says, and the boy is gone as soon as he was there.

'He meant no harm,' I say.

'He meant to steal your horse,' says the captain and places his first two fingers in his mouth and lets out a piercing whistle. Almost instantly two ship hands appear from below deck.

'Take the horse down below,' he orders, and they come and take Jet's reins. 'Well, don't stand on ceremony, lad, let's be having you.' Sabby and I follow Jet.

I step on to the gangplank with some trepidation. I have never been on a ship before; I expect it to sway and dip constantly, but I am disappointed to find it feels hardly any different, solid yet not solid.

'Welcome, welcome.' He clasps my hand and pats my back. 'You have made good time. All is set so we shall not linger.'

He whistles again, this time two short whistles and one long one, and from below deck, from behind barrels, from other ends of the ship, appear a squadron of sailors of all nations, and the ship that a moment ago looked peaceful and deserted is now a hive of activity. It feels like a miniature London about to set sail.

'Let us get out of the way,' he says and leads us below deck.

He leads us down a narrow passage and suddenly we are thrown against walls as the ship lurches.

'Do not fear, you'll soon find your sea legs,' he says, not faltering in his step once. I recover my step and pat Sabby to reassure her. He opens the door at the end of the passage.

'Please take a seat,' he says, and we enter a wood-lined room, furnished with one small desk, narrow windows looking out to sea and chairs that are fixed to the floor. He reaches into a cabinet built into the wood panels and brings out a jug of wine and two tankards.

'We travel by night and should reach our destination by afternoon tomorrow. That should give you time to plan. It will probably be best for you to attempt the salvage under cover of the moon.' He has poured the wine and raises his glass. 'To our ships, to our men and to your success.' We clink tankards.

I have so many questions but have learnt by now there is no point in asking them; information it seems is dangerous. The ships boy brings us a fine meal of biscuits and pottage which I feel comfortable with. Night has fallen, and the ship has taken up a steady motion. We do not dip and sway exactly but there is a sense of fluidity. I find this gentle rocking most soothing.

'It's your first time on board a ship?' the captain asks.

'First time at sea.'

'You have never seen the ocean?' he asks with such disbelief I can tell he considers this a great injustice. 'Come,' he says and there is no arguing with his order.

We step out of the candlelit passage up on to the deck and into a star-lit night. All around it is completely dark but the moon is bright and almost full, the stars light up the sky with such intensity I cannot help but gasp and look up in wonderment. He is happy with this reaction.

'Come see the main attraction,' he says, and he leads us to the wheel. From there we see a huge black undulating mass. The wind is strong and in our favour. We are at first hesitant to trust our lives to such a moving beast and then we see it, the reflection of the stars in the water, dancing on the surface, the moon smiling at the moon. We are held by the sky and the sea whilst the wind clears our minds and cleanses our bodies. For a few moments there is just this all-encompassing beauty. I wish with all my being that it was shared with Mary and I experience at once sublime beauty and visceral pain.

'Not bad for your first time?' says Captain Langan as he offers me the wheel and guides me on its use. The crew are welcoming and friendly, happy in their mission and I wonder how much they know of what they are part of.

I had thought all sailors to be rugged men of no principle yet that it is not what I experience. They are a fine collection of individuals indeed but joined together by a common goal, a common way of life. The captain must rule by carrot rather than stick for it is clear every one of his crew feels a connection to their ship, each other and this rugged life. It simply adds to the sense of beauty and peace.

'I expect you'll want to see that horse of yours, make sure he is settled,' says Captain Langan and it is as if he has read my mind.

We travel down through so many passages and ladders that I feel we have travelled to the depths of the sea. When at dock there is direct access to the hold but at sea it is a different route. The hold is a vast space, with a low ceiling, a cargo of crates and boxes fills most of it, then some supplies and then in one corner what could almost be mistaken for a small yard. Chickens and pigs roam freely and a cow munches on hay.

'The light and air down here is not the best for them,' says the captain, 'but when we can they get a roam on deck. It is good for our hearts and good for our stomachs.' Jet is tethered next to the cow and is companionably sharing his hay. He looks at ease, if not at home.

Captain Langan leaves us and we three spend a gentle time together. I would lie down and sleep with them, but the ship's boy comes to collect me. He takes me and Sabby to the mess where wide benches line the walls, three high. It is a small room and we lie check by jowl. My pack has been given a spot on the bottom benches. It's not the softest bed I have ever slept on but the heat from the other bodies, the gentle sway and Sabby lying beneath my bench sends me into a sleep of gentle dreams.

I awake with a start; nothing has disturbed me and down below there is no daylight. My disturbance is the undeniable sense that today is the day we have been journeying towards. There is a fire of nerves in my belly and all my senses are alert and expectant. Sabby feels it too and to know I am not alone is the greatest comfort.

We step out of the mess as quietly as possible so as to not bother the others. Down here it's impossible to tell what time it is but as we approach the deck we can tell it is daylight. I lift the hatch to a dull overcast sky; from the quality of the light we can tell it is early morn, but the clouds may distort our reading a little.

All is quiet; the watch go about their business with a gentle peace. We look up at the bland white sky; the wind no longer cleanses but rather chills. We go over to the edge of the ship, excited for our first sight of the sea in daylight. We are greeted by a vast nothingness. The horizon is flat and far into the distance; a mass of undulating greens and blues is all that lies between us and it. Small white horses ripple the surface but otherwise it is still. How can something which was beauty personified last night be so bland today? Our disappointment is palpable, the only consolation being that should the clouds remain we will have greater cover tonight than on a clear moonlit night.

We are awoken from our dismal contemplation by the ship's boy ringing a bell. Breakfast, a simple meal of ships biscuits and ale has been prepared and the entire crew are called. Captain Langan is the first on deck, greeting his crew, checking all are well and have what they need for the day. There is constant joking between the men. The ship's cat sits aside, washing and watching. I think the captain bold and the crew courageous to host a cat when to do so risks death. I think they must have a healthy disregard for laws and notions that do not serve us. Cats have always been our allies; they know no evil because evil is an invention of man alone.

After breakfast we go to sit with Jet in the eternal night of the hold. It is good to gather ourselves. I feel the energy around and, in the air, full of disquiet, pulling in different directions and it is important that we have a strong connection to the peace within, so we may be successful in our task.

It is not long before the captain joins us.

'It's a good spot for planning,' he says and sits down next to us.

'The wind has been in our favour and we fast approach our destination. We shall anchor as far out at sea as possible so as not to raise suspicion. I shall travel with you to shore. The cardinal's residence is vast and well inhabited but it's the vaults of the chapel we are most concerned with. There he has a private chamber and there you shall find the book. The book is hidden within a tomb inside the chamber, the chapel is in full view of the house. The loosely guarded entrance to the vaults for the uninitiated leads to certain death such is the design.'

'There are traps?' I ask.

'There are traps. We do not know the full details, but the mechanism is so sensitive that without the exact combination of movements death is certain, spikes appear from walls and floors,' he says.

'You do not know the combination?'

'Only the cardinal knows the combination. The plans have long since been destroyed and the combination is passed directly and only from cardinal to cardinal.'

'And no one has witnessed the combination?'

'We have friends but not that close to the cardinal. Anyway, it is part of the passing that no one else witnesses it, ever.'

'And what do you think I can do?' I ask.

'The chamber is not completely sealed.'

'And if I gain access? I cannot carry a book through cracks.'

'Once inside getting out is easy, a simple lever.' I nod.

This will be a challenge, yet I cannot help but feel this brings a sense to my gift. That the gift that I have, that brings me so much joy, that is feared by so many, can now finally be of value to more than just myself.

'When you get out make your way to the shore. There Sabby and Jet will be waiting for you,' he says.

'And then?' I ask.

'Then as fast as you can directly to the tanners. Go across country, avoid all and everything, resting only when you must.'

'I shall have provisions?' I ask.

'You shall have all you need.'

'I am ready,' I say.

'And I believe you,' he says, and we smile, a subtle smile of resolve.

Chapter Twenty-Four

We wait until dusk before setting off. It is heart-wrenching to leave Sabby and Jet. It is the greatest trust I put in the captain to ensure their safety and our reunion. He rows the boat himself, but I know the instruction to the crew is to sail round the coast to a deserted cove and there disembark Jet and Sabby; it is there I am to meet them.

We do not speak, each lost in our own fears and expectations. It is not only my life I risk, not only my life I have responsibility for. I feel my blood pump round my body. I hear a million conflicting voices in my head and yet at times a complete clarity and focus. I have chosen mosquito to shift; that way I am able to fly, crawl and see in the dark. I can think of no other beast to fit the purpose. The gentle lapping of the oars help calm my nerves and it is easy for a moment to think we are out for a pleasure trip, then we see the shore.

He has brought us to a dark forgotten part of the estate. We make our way down a narrowing of the sea into an overgrown river where he works hard to avoid the overhanging trees and dense river reeds and plants.

'They think this is unpassable,' he whispers, proud of his own seamanship. I think I'm sure they do and concur with his ego - for a lesser oarsman this would indeed be unpassable.

Before I know it, we have reached our destination. Somehow, I had hoped it would never arrive, the rest of me is relieved wanting this to be over as soon as possible. I step out of the boat on to marshy ground. Darkness is nearly upon us and the clouds have lingered. I can just make out the outline of the chapel in the distance. I can see no one. We have timed it well as the estate will now be concerned with supper or ale or both.

'We have faith in you,' he whispers. 'We shall wait until midday and then assume the worst. I shall not wish you luck as you do not need it - the gods travel with you.' We laugh a gentle knowing laugh. I turn to look at the chapel and when I turn back he is gone as silently as we arrived.

Keeping to the shadows, I make my way towards the chapel. I have decided to wait to shift until I am inside; that way my clothes will be close at hand, a naked woman being easier to spot than a man dressed all in black. I try not to think of dangers, the what ifs, but I am alert to every sound, every movement, every smell. I sense a presence. I am but feet away from the chapel. I duck into the shadows.

Standing outside the chapel door is a guard. Is this new? What should I do with him. I wait, deliberating attack or flattery. If I shift now how will I get out? Then the chapel door opens, and the cardinal comes out, his aides carrying lanterns. I sink further into the earth under a bush and hope they walk the other way. The cardinal sweeps past the guard and heads directly towards me; it's a stone path and his shoes clatter. I hide my face as the feet of his aides pass directly by my nose. I glance up as the cardinal passes; he looks troubled - deep in meditative thought and I am relieved he is so occupied. The guard makes sure the coast is clear then follows the party into the great house.

I pause a little longer, waiting for the stillness that will be my cue. When I feel it there is no hesitancy; as elegantly as I can I crawl from my hiding place, take one last look around and duck through the shadows to the door of the chapel. The door is fastened shut but not locked. I open it just enough, so I can slip through. Inside it is cold and still, almost pitch black, so I close the door behind me and wait a moment for my eyes to adjust a little.

Gradually I can see the pews and altar. Following the wall I make my way towards the altar. The chamber is behind it, the entrance next to the vault where I should be able to crawl through. I find a corner where my clothes will not be easily discovered. I pause for a moment in the darkness, half-hoping for an intrusion, but all is still. I take a deep breath and let the shifting begin. It is slow to start, and I fear I have lost the gift, then I feel hairs sprout on my arms and the familiar sense of liquidity and, despite everything, that sense of coming home. In seconds I am airborne. I buzz around where the entrance is meant to be; at first, I sense nothing, seeing is different - less vision and more feeling. But then it is there, and I can feel an opening. I land on the stones above it, getting a sense of the size and direction.

Then I crawl; the smallest irregularity in the surface becomes a mountain to surpass but I am light and agile. It is a joy to move and suddenly I realise I have no fear only impulsion. I enter the tiny crack between stones, keeping as light and as nimble as I can in the space that I have. It feels an eternity - the stone is a foot thick and it takes what seems like a lifetime to reach the other side. I crawl out and find I am in a tiny room, the chamber. I fly all the way round to make sure this is not part of the traps, yet I can see a table and the outline of what seems to be books.

I find a spot on the ground with enough space and shift back as quick as I can, forcing myself not to linger in the change. It's harder to see but I can just make out a candle and holder with flint and knife. I light the candle. I am in a small stone room, completely bare except for a table and a chair. On the table there are five or six books but then it is unmistakable - a small leather-bound notebook. By it are pages where the cardinal has tried to crack the code, attempt after attempt has been made. I fold up the papers and slip them inside the notebook.

I find the only thing that looks like a lever, take a deep breath and pull. Almost silently the door slides open towards me. I check up and down and around. I see iron spikes in the walls around the doorway. I do not take time to think but step through as quickly as I can.

The air in the chapel is cold against my bare skin. I still hold the candle and wonder how I should close the door. I step on the vault stone looking for a lever and the door begins to slide back into place. For a moment I consider throwing the candle into the room and letting the flames devour it, but my training is to leave no trace and I cannot dishonour that. I find my clothes and dress as quickly as I can, tucking the notebook into my doublet. I place the candle holder amongst the others on the altar and blow out the candle.

Again I pause to adjust to the light then make my way towards the door. I open it a fraction and listen, all is still. I squeeze out of the door and close it gently behind me. Then I am as swift as I can be. Darting though the shadows I make my way back to the shore line. There is no path and the going underfoot is hard. It takes all my attention to tread in the dark, not knowing what is underfoot. I fall many times. It is some relief that the clouds begin to lift.

I do not stop, traveling as fast as I can through the night. I reach the cove just as dawn is breaking. To see Sabby and Jet waiting is a relief and a joy beyond expression. They are on their own, no sign of Captain Langan or any of his crew. I hold Sabby tight as if it has been years since we have been parted and stand with Jet, soaking in his peace and confidence.

The ship is just visible on the edge of the cove. Catching the early morning sunlight I signal to the boat with one of the coins Lady Bamford gave me. They signal back, and I do not waste any time at all. I mount Jet and we are about to set off when I realise we have no map. Captain Langan has said travel by the back roads but I do not even know where the main roads are. For a moment I panic, lost in despair. I search the pack that the captain has left me but find a few simple supplies to get us home, a blanket and some ale, no map. Sabby and Jet are eager to get going but, how can we? I feel lost and abandoned and stupid. Why did I not think to ask? Yet Sabby does not let it be so; she nudges my leg and when I do not respond she barks, and I am started out of my indulgence. If she is heard and we are discovered. Then I see her find a path and Jet begins to walk it. Then I realise we have all we need. Sabby will find our path.

'Let's go home,' I say, and we do not hesitate.

Sabby sets a steady pace, not too fast and not too slow. We fall into a trance-like state and keeping to the pace and rhythm we are able to travel long distances without rest or exhaustion. We travel through the day and night; taking regular rests of an hour or so every four or five hours maintains our focus, strength and energy. We see few people, mostly treading faint paths or forgotten trials and byways. When we do, we either hide, or when that is not possible, I avoid all eye contact. Others travelling these routes have also chosen anonymity, so we do not seek to pass the time in idle chit chat.

I do not really see the landscape we pass through and if asked I'm not sure I could follow this route again such is my focus on our destination. It feels an eternity since I heard Grandmother's laugh or held Mary in my arms. I feel the notebook next to my heart burn to reach its rightful home. For substance we just have a few ship's biscuits and a little cheese, but it is enough. What took five days and nights takes us merely two days and one night. We approach familiar territory around dusk on the second day and the sense of relief is sublime and triumphant - we have almost completed our challenge.

We know the routes now and know how to reach the tanner's unseen. We keep our pace for fear if we stop or if we slow we will not make the final stretch, although we do allow ourselves to feel our fatigue and I sense exhaustion mingled with fast running energy. I think I could lie still for some time but be wide awake.

We reach the tanner's as deep night has fallen. We slow our pace so as to not cause suspicion should we come across another as we approach. There is smoke coming from the chimney and candlelight sneaks out from the cracks in the shutters. Before we have reached the cottage, Master Tanner comes out to greet us. He is alone and has deliberately kept his family at bay. He signals towards the barn and we oblige.

Inside I dismount, he lights a candle and gives Jet a feast of oats, Sabby some fresh venison and to me he hands a star-shaped piece of marchpane.

'Master Raven,' he says, 'you are a sight for sore eyes,' and we embrace.

'I have it,' I say, cutting to the chase and reaching inside my doublet.

'Haste you not,' he says and glances round. Even here we have to be on guard. He pulls the lever and we step into the secret chamber.

We leave Jet eating oats and seal the door behind us. Inside he lights some torches.

'Now,' he says, and I take the notebook out of my doublet and place it on the table. I feel a lightness in my body as if I have been carrying a tremendous weight next to my heart. I sit down, overcome with relief. I could close my eyes and fall into a deep sleep on the spot but that I need to see my home.

'This is it,' he says as he holds the book with reverence, soaking it in before he opens it and strokes the pages. He finds the notes hid inside.

'What's this?' he says, eagerly unfolding the pages. He lays them on the table and, taking the candle, scans them.

'They were with the notebook,' I say. 'I thought they would be of use to us.' He is delighted, and he beams at me.

'This is their notes, this tells us much. From these we can see who they have employed to decipher our code. Who holds and how far this knowledge goes. Well done, lad.' He shakes my hand and slaps my back. 'This will serve us well.' He takes the candle again; scanning down the pages, he chuckles. 'The good news is they have not got far, in fact they could not be more confused,' and at that we both laugh. 'Congratulations, Master Raven, you could not have been more successful.' He pats me on the back again but this time with the respect of an equal and I know I shall return in my mind many times to that moment. 'Food, you must be starved. Come, we have plenty to share,' he says, walking over to the lever.

'Thank you,' I say, 'but it is no offence, my grandmother would not forgive me.'

'Of course, how unthinking of me. You must go and go directly,' he says, folding up the papers and placing them and the notebook in a hidden slot in the wall.

'Thank you,' I say, and we turn on our heels and make our way to Jet who has sensed our approach and is ready to go.

For caution we take our time leaving the tanner's but as soon as we turn off the main road we speed as fast as we can to Grandmother and home. Seeing the cottage, the smoke from the chimney, knowing the safety and comfort inside, we stop a little way off to savour the moment, but the joy is tingled with loss. We know that in some ways now everything has changed. Still we do not linger long on this wisdom but soon speed as fast as we can down the hill. By the time we reach the yard, Grandmother is outside waiting for us. I jump off Jet as Sabby bounces around, checking all is how she left it. I pick Grandmother up and twirl her round as we laugh, and she squeals.

'Put me down, you buffoon,' she says and reluctantly I oblige. She holds me at arm's length, surveying my new attire. 'Very proper,' she says, 'a seafarer's look. Come let us feast.' And we go inside.

Everything seems new and familiar at the same time. The fire welcomes us, and we do not hesitate to take our place by it. Grandmother brings us wine and bread and pottage made rich with rabbit; she even has cake and marchpane. We feel triumphant warriors given a hero's welcome. We exchange news and I tell her what I think cannot harm her to know of our adventure.

She asks a lot about our visit to Lady Bamford's. I did not know she had such interest in the gentry. For all her dealings with gentry in her business I have never seen her show reverence, only compassion. Still I answer her questions as best I can. I notice she has not made up my bed, nor offered to unsaddle Jet. After the meal I know we shall not rest and so does she. We sit for a while after eating and talking, letting the peace of companionship settle between us. Then without speaking we know it is time for us to leave. The look in Grandmother's eyes when we embrace is of such pride and joy and satisfaction. I am becoming the person she knows I am. I hope she sees reflected back the love and recognition and respect I have for her.

The moon is high, and the stars play patterns in the sky. We take our familiar route to the inn, not dallying but not rushing, taking the time to breathe in the familiar smells and sounds. They are not the same as afore, enriched by our knowledge of the world as a bigger place. I know then we shall travel far in our life, but we shall always be connected to this, our home.

It is late now, and the inn will be deep into the night's festivities. Quietly we sneak Jet into the stables; his usual spot has been kept and he takes up residence happily. Sabby settles down next to him and I sense her fatigue and her releasing into the safety and comfort of home. I leave them to rest and creep up the back stairs of the inn.

The ruckus from the bar tells me I'll not meet anyone on the stars and soon I am in Mary's room. The smell of her washes over me like a wave, it reaches inside me loosening every last bit of tension. I quickly slip off my clothes and slip under the covers of her bed. It is my intention to wait for her to retire, to be an unexpected delight, a living bed warmer, ready and waiting with open arms and an inviting smile.

I awake to her sweat caress, her lips on my lips. She has undressed and has joined me under the covers. I open my eyes and to see her face, her eyes glinting in the moonlight, is such joy I cannot help but beam.

'Seems I have an intruder in my bed,' she whispers.

'Madam, is this how you greet intruders?' I ask.

'Sir, if you were an unwelcome intruder you would know.' We kiss as if we are inventing kissing so deep is the kiss between us, a kiss that entwines our insides.

We abandon talk, abandon thought, and speak of our longing for each other with our bodies. Her caresses start with my skin but speak to all my senses so that I cannot tell flesh from sensation, her smell is returning to something known deep inside of me, her body, the feel of her skin beneath my fingers inflaming every part of me. To be inside her, for her to be inside me, at once an explosion of energy. We are entwined but distinct, a union not a possession, and for moments, that seem an eternity, we are joined as pure energy and consciousness. Afterwards we lie in each other's arms in a state of deep peace till the first rays of light creep through the shutters.

'It is but a week,' she says.

'Felt longer,' I say and think of the week that has passed and all that happened and feel it a lifetime. 'Much has changed, and nothing has changed,' I say.

'True,' she says, and we kiss.

'They've moved in,' she says.

'Sorry?' I ask.

'The new occupants of the castle,' and with that she gets up, pulls out the bedpan and crouches down to urinate.

Part Three

Chapter Twenty-Five

Although my spirit seeks only the body and bed of Mary, her life does not stop for mine. I rise reluctantly from her embrace and leave the inn before any of the others have risen so I go undetected but with the knowledge that Mary approves of my new attire. Light begins to creep across the land and I take the opportunity to tread gently through the streets that once seemed so imposing but now are quaint and pleasing.

For all of my life the castle has been an empty shell. The odd caretaker has come and gone as the castle has been passed from the ownership of one disinterested lord to another. Each more involved in the intrigues of the court than a castle several days ride from London. It has fallen into decay, its walls crumbling and scaled by adventurous children in games of love and war.

We circle round the to the gates. The walls, now, surrounded by scaffolding, a small city of tents has grown up and around the castle walls out of which sleep-laden labourers stagger out of to greet the day. Now I understand why the inn was so raucous last night. It will be the best business the inn has ever known. We pass by the street of the secret delivery; everything so far is undisturbed. I stop at the castle gates and greet the watchman who is nursing the dying embers of the night's fire.

'It's a big job?' I ask.

'That it is,' he says.

'A pretty penny too,' I say.

'That it is,' he says.

'It will take time,' I say.

'That it will,' he says.

'The new tenant must be invested,' I say and for the first time he looks at me. He takes a long slow look up and down, taking us all in. He does not respond, instead gets to his feet, takes a few steps towards the castle walls, turns and makes water. The castle has a tenant then who has no intension of ingratiating with the local folk. We turn away and head for home. We shall be in time for our morning chores. It is with some joy and some disappointment that we proceed.

It feels good to be down to the earth again. Chopping wood, fetching water, it gives me time to let all I have learned over the last week sink in, keeping what serves me and letting the rest go. It feels good to slip back into the regular routine and share breakfast with Grandmother. We sit in comfortable silence and I do not understand how she has not mentioned the castle since my return.

I break the quiet. 'The castle?' I ask. She shows no response and simply continues to chew, staring into the fire. She has never been like this before. Never not spoken.

'New tenants I see.' Still nothing. 'They have wealth,' I say.

'I cannot talk of this,' she says and gets up, packing away the breakfast things, cutting short our time together.

I do not push further, so surprised am I by her response. Never before has she not spoken. I look to Sabby; her eyes offer softness and I know I must treat Grandmother with compassion on this subject. It does not bode well. Intuition tells me I need to know more and know where I must go next.

We take the old route to Grace's, indulging in the memory of times past. Times that now seem much simpler. Worries over the ordering of letters now seems a preferable agony. We make our way through town and it is a joy to be greeted by familiar faces but the newcomers to the town are many, the streets full of comings and goings, mostly labourers and their families. There has never been such noise in the town. It is invigorating and exciting yet not the town I left. The market place is a hive of commerce, everyone has something to sell, it feels, and I half expect to see Billy deep amongst the crowds, selling, singing, telling stories but the minstrel that takes that spot is not known to me.

It takes much longer than usual to make our way through the crowds, but it is a welcome sight when we arrive at Grace's door. Slightly off the main streets we find some quiet away from the crowds. Jet settles into his usual spot and we knock expectantly on the back door as always.

Mother Gray answers and her face explodes into a wide grin. 'Come, come away in,' she says and ushers us into the kitchen. It seems we are expected; a jug of ale and three tankards are on the table and a plate of delicately flower-shaped marchpane.

'It's her,' Mother Gray shouts as she ushers me to a seat. She lays down a plate of meat for Sabby. Grace does not hesitate; as soon as she sees me she embraces me, enveloping me in love, pride and relief. Eventually, she releases me.

'My, how fine you look,' she says. I turn to Mother Gray and against her better judgement she too comes in for an embrace.

'Let us sit,' says Grace and we take our places. 'Congratulations, Raven,' she says, and we raise our glasses 'to the ways of the Earth.' We clink glasses and drink.

'It was quite an experience -' I say but Grace stills my tongue.

'Do not tell us that which can betray you should we feel the torturer's touch.' I nod, a little ashamed I had not considered this. The heady rush of my return leaves me as I slip back into my body and the earth. The depth of the danger we are all in begins to sink in, sobering my thoughts and humours.

'The notebook?' I ask.

'It is safe,' she says. I ask with my eyes. 'Not here,' she says, and I know she does not know where it is now either.

'Will you not try my flowers?' asks Mother Gray.

'Try to stop me,' I say and make a show of choosing the first flower. I do not reach for the showiest in the centre of the display, rather I reach for the shy flower, simpler but inviting in its honesty.

'A wise selection,' says Mother Gray who then takes the centrepiece for herself and we laugh, the tension broken. The marchpane is the best she has made yet, far superior to the master cake at Lady Bamford's. I cannot say this so instead I say, 'The finest I have ever tasted by far,' and she blushes but does not seek to hide her pride.

'A lot has changed in a week,' I say and Grace and Mother Gray exchange glances.

'The castle?' I say, and Grace puts down the marchpane.

'The castle,' she says. 'The king has ordered improvements.'

'Indeed,' I say, 'and the new keeper of the castle?'

'A very noble, Christian man,' says Grace and we all know that this means he is not a friend.

'And his authority?' I ask.

'Absolute,' says Grace. Suddenly the carnival that engulfs the town takes a sinister turn. The neglect of the castle is in part what has protected us, enabled us to maintain our ways, our traditions; through discretion we have gone unnoticed, easily overlooked when there have been more pressing matters at court. Our geographical place has been ideal for linking all four directions of the country. It is not just happenstance that there is a call for my services. As messenger I link communications from across the isle for our "historical society".

'And the reach of his authority?' I ask.

'To be determined,' says Grace. Silence falls upon us as we each consider the implications. Mother Gray is the first to speak

'There has been an addition to the library,' she says and Grace's face lights up.

'Yes, it's an ancient work of such delicate beauty.'

'Let us go,' says Mother Gray and we make our way upstairs.

It is the first time I have known Mother Gray to take an interest in the library. As we step inside I know I have come home. It is a tight fit but Sabby makes room by slipping under the table. The book is wrapped in silk and Grace carefully peels back the outer layers to reveal ancient parchment with a script I have not seen before. I am speechless in the presence of such teachings.

'Sanskrit,' says Mother Gray, her sense of satisfaction resonating around the room. I want to reach out to touch them, but they look so delicate I dare not.

'Priceless,' says Grace, 'the journey they have travelled to be with us.'

'Aye, they have had a will to join us,' agrees Mother Gray. I have never questioned how the books have made their way to the library before but now I have a sense of the risks that have been taken, my appreciation of the library increases tenfold.

'What do they say?' I ask.

'They speak of a spiritual path, the first to be written down on to page,' says Mother Gray.

'I have spent a little time in India,' continues Grace. 'It will take some time to decipher but will be a joy.' The two women look adoringly at the sheets, their new-born. I feel humbled to be in the presence of such knowledge, such wisdom and such experience.

Until this moment I had understood these two women to be of this context, contained and moulded by it, by my understanding of it. Now they are people who have histories that reach far beyond our little town and quiet shire. I want nothing more than to spend hours hearing their stories, tasting their wisdom, getting to know them. They exchange a look of affection, I think I recognise, then Mother Gray begins to wrap the sheets back up in their silk.

'More ale, Master Raven?' she asks but the evening is fast approaching and already I have new deliveries for Grandmother.

'Thank you but I must work,' I say, and the two women do not question it. I want so much to spend more time, as I leave I say, 'Maybe one day we shall take supper together?' and they both look delighted.

'It will be our honour,' replies Grace. I have no idea how or when but the principle comforts and pleases all.

We are about to take the quiet back roads to avoid the crowds when we hear a commotion in the square. We have had our fill of excitement, but the screams of a woman draw our attention. Most of the stalls and stall holders have left, a few are still packing up and a small crowd has gathered in the centre of the square, they are laughing and jeering. Whatever it is, it is fine entertainment.

Sitting atop a fine grey dappled horse is a stern-looking man with a long thin face that looks as if it rarely feels a smile. His clothes are sombre but impeccable and of the finest cloth, his cloak of the finest weave draping his horse's back like water flowing over rock. Next to him, sitting astride a white Arab mare, is Ben Lovell. Whilst no expression passes over his companion's face, Ben is revelling in the show - a greedy satisfaction fills his checks and eyes. He refrains from joining in the chorus of abuse but only just. He too is wearing the finest clothes but his are loud in colour and heavy with decoration. The two look like two sides of the same coin. It does not feel good.

The butcher is standing in the door way of his shop looking on with reserve. Quietly we work our way to stand next to him.

'Quite a commotion,' I venture.

'That it is,' he says. 'He's only been here a week, and this isn't the first,' and he indicates the thin man. Then we understand he is the new keeper of the castle. We take the time to consider him once more and it is as if a storm cloud has passed across the sky, blocking out the light. My heart sinks, my spirit fears, Sabby's silence is focused with intention.

'Still, good for business,' I say.

'What price prosperity?' he counters, and our eyes meet. He turns into the shop and returns post haste with a large bone for Sabby and as they share a little light relief, Jet and I push a little further into the crowd to see what all the fuss is about.

In the centre of the square is Mother Lovell; her clothes are torn and covered in dirt and dust, her modesty revealed. Her hair, usually hidden well beneath her bonnet, is loose flowing, wild, thick with mud and leaves. Around her face they have fitted an ordinary horse's bridle, only slightly adapted to fit her head rather than a horse, an iron bit forces her mouth apart and clangs against her teeth, her check bleeds where the bit has torn the flesh and lips.

Behind her, waving the reins wildly up and down, with whip in hand, is her husband. He does not have mastery of the whip, his wild flailing causing both merriment and fear amongst the crowd as they at once dodge its trajectory and urge on its use. Mother Lovell does not seem present in spirit, her body as torn and ripped as her clothes. Her husband is whipped into a frenzy by the crowd. We cannot comprehend what is happening. Gradually we are able to make out a common thread amongst the shouts and jeers. It seems Mother Lovell has been accused, tried and judged by the crowd for adultery. Yet I do not see her accomplice in such an act anywhere near. For who would even consider seducing Mother Lovell?

I think it will not be long till her husband has killed her when the sheriff arrives. He has two deputies beside him and I think now this will be put to a stop. Yet he simply observes the scene. He looks to the castle-keeper and is met with an unflinching stare which he holds for as long as he can before bowing his head and turning away, his deputies following, reluctant to be missing the show. It is clear whose word is now law in the shire.

I look at the castle-keeper and can see no flicker of emotion on his face or body. I have never seen such a thing before. I turn back to Mother Lovell, now on her knees, crawling round in a circle. I am filled with rage at such injustice and horror at such barbarism; we had heard tell of such treatments, yet they seemed fantastical. How could people treat their neighbours so? Many laws have been passed, too many to keep count, but we in our quiet backwater have been left largely untouched, our way of life undisturbed with a few adjustments to allow for the fashions of the times. Now ways unknown to us have been unleashed and I cannot understand how this is so, how are those I considered neighbours so easily turned to foes?

I want to do something, I want to stop it, but I am transfixed. Mother Lovell staggers to her feet, one last attempt at a semblance of dignity, and she looks me straight in the eyes. I look back but with apology; I do not know how to help her.

What can I do? I am feared to move away for fear the crowd will turn on me. I am afeard to stand next to her for the crowd turning on me. I see her spirit leave her soul as the whip lashes round her face bringing her to her knees. Her husband finally exhausted and satiated falls to his knees too.

The castle-keeper signals to Ben and he dismounts and, as if he is the returning prodigal son, the crowd part like the red sea at his approach. He picks up the reins and kicks her as he passes, dragging her to the well and tying her there to be left for as long as we are entertained. Her skin and bones broken, battered and torn, she heaves herself, despite her pain, into a sitting position and glares with unmitigated disgust at each and every one of us. Ben spits in her face and she does nothing to remove or respond to it, simply lets it slide down, mingling with her blood. I am not even sure if she felt it.

Ben walks away as the crowd watch in a self-justified silence. Without a word he mounts his horse. Still without any sign of emotion the castle-keeper turns his horse and nonchalantly walks away, followed closely by Ben. Gradually the crowd begin to disperse, some coming to their senses and their shame, most staying true to their judgement - whatever they have done she has deserved it. I have never felt such shame in my life and never felt more ashamed of people. We turn away, hollowed inside.

Chapter Twenty-Six

'In a week,' I say, 'how has this happened in a week?' I sit on the edge of Mary's bed

'It is not a week though,' she says. 'Why have you lived your life in secret? If not for what you have just witnessed?'

'But I did not think it so close. Mother Lovell? Adultery?'

'Nobody liked Mother Lovell,' she says.

'Exactly, who would have her?'

'Nobody and nobody has but now the law decrees a woman and not a man is punished for adultery all the nagging wives of the shire will be whores and adulteresses.'

'There must be something to be done. We must be able to do something.'

'It will pass, this castle-keeper shall come and go like the rest, the king does not care for us, as long as we keep our heads down we shall ride this out as we have done before. It is but a fashion.'

'A fashion? And what of the damage done in the meantime?' I ask.

'It will pass, and things will return to how they have always been.' She is trying to calm me.

'Even if that were true it would not be enough,' I say. 'This is deeper and more dangerous than a hard winter that must be endured. To release the shadow side of humanity for such little cause is a road of no return.'

'Well, people like nothing more than exercising their darkness,' she says and turns towards the window.

I have gone too far, pushed too hard. I know she still feels the sting of her father's fist even though it is years since she has let him hit her, even though if he even tried now she would knock him from his feet as easily as a ball topples a skittle. I stand and approach her. Gently I enfold her in my arms.

'There is something we can do,' I say. 'Come.'

We tread lightly down the stairs and into the kitchen. Sabby keeps watch as we trim a few thin slices of meat, so they will not be missed, take some of the left-over bread and a small flask of wine. It is dead still in the streets now everyone and everything is at rest. We slip through the streets to the square.

Mother Lovell is slumped on the ground. She is not able to sit in comfort as the reins are tied just too tight for her to find a spot. Still she has curled up as best she can. The bit is still tearing her flesh, but she cannot feel it anymore. Sabby approaches. First, she sniffs all around Mother Lovell but there is no response. So she sits peacefully by her side and we approach. Somehow, Mother Lovell is sleeping, not unconscious otherwise Sabby would have tried to raise her. We place the food and wine close to her but hidden from public view and are gone as quick as we can.

If we left a blanket or a cloak it would tell all of our identity. For the next night I shall collect fire water from Mother Gray to warm Mother Lovell's bones and in this way, we shall keep her from death. We return to the inn; that night our love making is tender and gentle to soothe our souls and ease the threat of death.

In the morning my anger returns, burning in my belly. I exorcise it chopping wood, but the anger blurs my precision and I make clumsy work, risking my own arms and legs in the process. Frustrated, I throw the axe to the ground and slump down next to it. Grandmother stops picking herbs and comes to join me. She sits on the tree stump used for chopping kindling. She picks up the axe and toys with the blade. I watch her for a while and then decide I would be better served doing anything else. I go to stand when she breaks her silence.

'Are you going to give up so easily?' I stop and turn, my anger reignited. I would answer her, but she continues,

'It's a long road to travel. If you fall at the first hurdle what are you to do?'

I sigh. 'Get up and try again.'

'As long as that is not forgotten,' she says, placing the axe down, getting ready to return to her labours.

'How can I forget when everything is a struggle, when everywhere there is danger?' I snap. She sits back down.

'Mother Lovell,' she says.

'We must stop them,' I respond. 'How do we stop them?'

'We are doing all we can,' she says.

'It is not enough,' I say.

'You risk your life and it is not enough?' she snaps. 'Your mother -'

'My mother? I have no mother,' I interrupt, surprised at my own venom. I have never thought I have felt her loss till now.

'Your mother entrusted you to me, so I would teach you the ancient ways from which you are born, from which we are all born.'

'You know her?' I ask.

'I know of her,' Grandmother says.

'Tell me all you know.'

'I know only that she cannot live as our kind, but she did not want the same for you, the shame, the confusion and denial she lived.'

'Lived?' I say. 'Has she passed?'

'I do not know,' she answers. 'I never met her, never knew her. I was entrusted with your care and I thank all the Gods for you. You are a gift to me and to the world.'

'A gift that was given away,' I say.

'A gift that was protected,' she counters.

'I do not care,' I say. 'I have no need of her as she has no need of me.'

'She would not have given you up if her choices had been different. If she was free to live as we could all be free to live. We all must do as best we can. This is a long road and there are no short cuts.'

'And if I choose not to walk it?' I say.

'It is not a choice; we each are what we are and must play our part to the best of our ability.'

'And if it is not enough?'

'You are enough, know you are enough. Have you not felt my love of you?' she asks. I have felt her love, I have fed on her love, grown strong and bold on her love but in that moment, nothing feels enough.

'I have never had cause to doubt your love,' I say, and she holds me tight into her body.

'Know you are enough, know that you have everything you need in you.' I do not understand how this is so but say nothing and release into her hold, its offer of comfort too great to resist. We part, and she looks deep into my eyes. Satisfied with what she sees, she says, 'When you are finished with your work the council expect you at the tanner's.' After that I make short work of chopping the wood.

We do not take the usual route to the tanner's, rather detour through the town to pass by Mother Lovell. The town has gotten used to her - already she has become part of the background. Occasionally someone thinks to spit at her or take out the frustrations of the day on her with some abuse or other. Then she spits back or snarls or curses under her breath. Any movement near her, fast or slow, she recoils, expecting pain. Otherwise she sits staring at the world as it goes about its business as a beast stares from its cage, for beasts is what we all are. I do not try to make contact with her, simply observe. She is a warning to us all, women definitely but men too, what makes us human is being corrupted so some may rule us, and they will stop at nothing to establish their domain. Tonight we will leave her some marchpane to feed her spirit.

We are welcomed at the tanner's as old friends. Jet knows where his hay is waiting for him and I am happy to leave Sabby at play with the tanner's offspring. I pull the lever and walk confidently into the room - the full council is waiting, and I am greeted with handshakes and congratulations. We take our seats and Master Tanner calls us to order.

'Members of the council we are all aware of the recent events that have brought us together; the new keeper of the castle and the king's renewed interest in our shire offer a unique opportunity.'

There are a myriad of responses around the table, but the underlying unease and concern is palpable.

'What say you, Raven, are you not curious? Do you not want to see what lies behind the castle walls?' asks Captain Langan.

'My interest in architecture and historical building methods is always refreshed with a visit to one of England's great establishments,' I parry and the tension in the room is released somewhat.

'It is an open mission, find what you can,' says Astral. 'We have word that the cardinal is outraged as a result of your last sojourn into a building of historic interest.' We all laugh.

'The secret nature of the room and his activities in it mean he cannot openly seek retribution, but we do expect some form of response,' says Philip and sobriety returns to the room.

'Do not tell us what form you take,' says Grace and I understand I am to report back but have responsibility for planning my own approach. I feel trusted and recognised.

'Consider it done,' I say and there is happy agreement around the room.

'I hear the old fat head nearly burst when he found the notebook gone, so purple with rage was he,' says Mother Gray, and we all laugh.

Chapter Twenty-Seven

The rest of the day I help Grandmother, gently falling back into the regular routine. It is a comfort and an occupation to fill the time. I have decided to waste no time and plan my sightseeing trip for that night. I dread the approach of darkness yet cannot wait for its arrival. Grandmother senses what is going on, but we do not speak, rather keep a tacit silence for safety and protection. We eat a quiet, companionable supper and as night falls I take to the hills with Jet and Sabby.

There is a camp built up around the castle of labourers who are heavy with ale and hard work. We send Jet to mingle unseen with the beasts that have accompanied them and make our way through the camp. The men chat and laugh, happy to be in work. They tell stories, joke with mock rivalries and ale-fuelled chatter. There cannot be a wife in the area that is not brewing their own ale now to meet the demand. The women cook, tend the children, tend the spinning and weaving, their work never completed.

We pass through the encampment largely unnoticed, hiding in clear view. We deliver a poultice of herbs from Grandmother to a young pregnant woman. A young marriage still fresh with new love and our legitimacy is confirmed; from then on it is easy to walk through the castle gates.

Inside, scaffolding covers the walls like ivy. Masonry tools of every description line the ground, some dropped, some tossed, some carefully stored. Flame torches provide a little illumination to find a way amongst the organised chaos, casting a stunning yet alarming array of shadows in every direction. Soon a pattern of toing and froing becomes apparent in the shadows and we follow. We soon hear music and laughter and observe the empty and full jugs of wine, coming and going from what must be the great hall.

We find a workbench covered in a large oilskin hidden in a corner near the entrance to the hall. We slip under the oilskin. Sabby is to keep watch and alert to any danger when I am inside. I begin to shift and feel the ecstasy of the softening. I have chosen mouse - the Pope's edict against cats makes it safe from predators; they are quick and not unexpected. It feels good to be in this light and playful body.

Keeping close to the walls and shadows, I follow the servants into the hall. Inside is a blaze of candles and fires. Every dignitary and official in the shire, down to the lowliest clerk, sits at their place. The ale and wine flows, faces are flushed and rosy. A band of musicians play dance tunes as male and female acrobats dressed in tight-fitting woollen and silken tunics create all manner of shapes for anyone, not too drunk, to notice. The bishop and Ben sit at the top table next to the castle-keeper, each with a woman, not known to these parts, draped around them.

There is much coming and going so I keep to the edges, the outskirts, to avoid being trodden on or causing alarm. I make my way up to the top table. It's dark and quiet behind the seats and I am able to follow the shadows till I am behind the table. I hide inside a dropped tankard. The bishop and Ben are much engaged with the women on their laps, but the keeper absent-mindedly fondles his whilst keeping a keen eye on all that he surveys.

'The cardinal,' he says, and the bishop's attention is caught.

'He is certain, amongst this motley crew of yokels,' and Ben's attention is pricked, 'are heathens intent on practicing the old ways. Intent on ways that do not recognise the word of authority. The word of God spoken through the Pope to the king to the church.'

'We have been left to our own devices for too long,' says the bishop. 'There is only so much we have been able to achieve but now you are here and with the king's support the word of the Pope shall rule.' Ben chokes on his wine.

'You have doubts, Master Ben?' questions the keeper. Ben tries hard to compose himself.

'My lord,'

'Stephen, please,' says the keeper.

'Stephen, these are simple folk. Do they really have the powers the cardinal claims?' Stephen takes a long slow drink of his wine, maintaining eye contact with Ben the whole time.

'Do you doubt our intelligence?' he asks. Ben quickly retraces his steps.

'No, no my lord, Stephen, I meant merely that it's hard to imagine this motely lot are capable of such things. I mean, look at them, it is hard to imagine they could ever be a threat to men of philosophy such as yourself, I mean look at them.' And all three peer around the room.

I see a room of people honest in their humbleness seduced by rich food and wine made of grapes from lands they will never see but Stephen begins to titter, and the others join in until all three are laughing loud. Stephen stops suddenly, and the others follow suit.

'Tomorrow we clear the back lane. Our intelligence tells of an ancient apothecary hidden amongst the midden. We shall bring this "motely lot" under the protection and guidance of the king and they shall leave behind all that does not serve him. We shall be ready for when the cardinal graces us with his presence.'

'We have struggled in darkness, thank the Lord that he has sent you as our saviour,' says the bishop and Stephen looks at him with unashamed contempt but he bows his head anyway and says,

'Thank you, bishop, your support is the least I'd expect.' But he says it so sweetly the bishop is confused and receives it as a compliment.

'Ben, make sure you are ready for sun up tomorrow.'

'My lord, Stephen,' he says accepting the command.

Stephen stands, dropping his whore to the ground. The whole room stands.

'Let the dancing begin,' he declares, and a cheer erupts as people grab their partners and the band pick up their pace; in the commotion Stephen leaves the room.

I waste no time and take the opportunity to hurry back through the shadows. I am a short distance from my clothes when I come face to face with a rat. It is a large rat, its large red eyes locked on me. I freeze; normally I would make a swift movement and a sharp noise, and the rat would flee but now I could be dinner. The passageway is empty as all are consumed by the dance. We shall not be disturbed but still it is not the place to shift. We stare at each other, not making a sound or movement, waiting for the other to move first. The tension builds. I can feel the energy about to explode. The rat senses his moment, I am convinced of my imminent death and the rat's jaws are wide as he springs towards me. As he does, Sabby's jaws close tight around his body and within seconds he has passed. Sabby drops the body lifeless on to the floor. I race towards my clothes and slip under the oilskin. I shift and dress as quickly as possible. I know I must tell Grace.

Sabby welcomes my return and I know it is safe to emerge from under the oilskin. We dance through the shadows yet as we pass the chapel we hear a strange sound. The door is left ajar, moonlight streams through the stained-glass windows and we tread lightly so we can peer round the door.

There, kneeling in front of the altar, is Stephen, his doublet and linen removed. His back is scarred many times and fresh blood trickles down the through the scars as with his right hand he lashes his back over his left shoulder with a cat-o'-nine-tails. We stare in disbelief – to hate the body so. I had read in the books that for some this hatred was their path, but it breaks our hearts to see it. To reject one's self so is to reject all the world has to offer. It is no wonder Mother Lovell is tied to a post by a rein when he treats himself so. We turn away in shame for him, but with a sinking sensation; this is worse than we thought.

Most of the labourers have taken to sleep so we make fast work of returning to Jet. It is late, so we tread softly through the town so as not to wake and cause suspicions. Jet takes his place when we get to Grace's. In the dead of night it would cause suspicion to bang loudly on the door. We peer up into the house and spot a faint light in the upstairs chamber. We stand in the street and make the sound that Grace and Mother Gray will recognise but others will sleep through. I sing the song of Raven.

I see the light begin to move and we make our way to the back door. Mother Gray snuffs out the candle as she approaches the door which she opens and silently gestures for us to go inside. We maintain our silence until we are in the hall way, away from windows.

She relights the candle. 'Master Raven, what ails you?' she asks. 'It must be important at this hour.'

'I knew no place else to go,' I say.

'Of course, of course it is best you did.'

'Come lets us go to the library,' says Grace who has appeared at the head of the stairs, a cloak thrown over her linens.

We make our way to the library with quiet speed. Once inside she lights the candles and we close the door on the world.

'I'm sorry, I did not mean to disturb you,' I say, 'but we must act now.'

'Spit it out, what is to occur?' asks Mother Gray.

'Tomorrow morning, they are clearing the back lane next to the castle.' They exchange glances. 'The castle-keeper, Stephen, he knows of the apothecary.' Their faces turn a stony shade of grey. Mother Gray sits down slowly and Grace turns to face the books, lost in thought.

'I'm sorry, I did not know what was best to do. Should I have gone directly to him?'

'No, no you did right,' says Mother Gray. 'It is just they know more than we had hoped.'

Grace turns back from the books, 'We must move fast. Raven take the back roads, travel with speed but gently so as not to wake the shire. Tell the tanner all that has happened and then make your way home. Mother Gray and I will approach the apothecary. Tell the tanner we shall salvage what we can.' We stare at her. 'Come, we have no time to spare.' And we each are stirred into action.

We know how to travel with speed and silence and it takes little time to reach the tanner's. I sing Raven's song again and again we are heard so accurate is the sound. I tell him all that has occurred. He thanks me and tells me to do as Grace has instructed, to go home and await further instruction. We do not want to, there must be something more we can do than sit and wait but the tanner insists we need to be ready should we be called upon and we cannot disagree with that. We make haste towards home.

Grandmother is awake on our return and we tell her the night's events. Together we spend a sleepless night watching the flame tease and soothe our humours. We do not know who or what resides in the old shop, but we can sense its importance. By first light I cannot be patient any longer. We think to find a hiding spot near to the lane from which to witness and be at hand if required. Grandmother does not say but I know she will follow on foot once we are out of sight.

Chapter Twenty-Eight

When we reach the town it seems we are not the only ones to have heard the news and a large crowd has gathered, one at each end of the lane. There is much superstition around the lane and many of the yokels will not tread along its boards for fear of what lies in wait behind the closed and abandoned doors. It was supposed to be a highly desirable street next to the castle, a home of those aspiring for the allegiances and protection of the castle owner. Yet the design meant no light ever reached the street and the energy was such that no person could sit long in its shadows. The street was deserted as soon as it was built.

I think whatever has been hidden there has been hidden in clear view, an apothecary who works with shadow. We find a spot in the crowd, at the back some way out of the clear view of others but that affords a view of the street. I search the crowd and spot Mother Gray, face and head covered, then Astral, then the captain. Each of us sees the other but does not acknowledge for fear of discovery. I do not see Grace but think she may be at the other end with the other crowd.

There is a huge commotion, much shouting and then a strong repetitive chanting. The crowds part as either end of the street two large battering rams are lined up at the first houses. The crowd cheer and joke in nervous anticipation. Stephen and Ben take to the ramparts of the castle with clear view of the street. Stephen raises his right arm just a fraction and the crowd falls silent.

'Good morrow,' he says, 'it is well we are met on such a fine morn.' The crowd cheer and stomp approval. 'Today we will rid our town, our shire, our country of an evil that has plagued our people for centuries. Evil surrounds us, the Devil ever watchful, ever eager to steal our souls and condemn us to eternal damnation. Today we rid our town of one of his lairs.' A huge cheer erupts from the crowd. 'No longer shall this shadow fall upon us, no longer will our crops suffer, our babies sicken. No longer shall outsiders take what is ours for in these the Devil resides.'

Again a cheer. Yet I am confused - we have never been rich in coin, but our lives are abundant. Never have our bellies been empty, yet the people around me fear starvation? Travelers have come and gone creating trade and those that have stayed have found a home, yet now they are said to bring evil? I understand not the contrast between what appears to be in people's minds and the world that surrounds them.

'Today we shall exorcise the street for it is in this street we have been complacent. We have let a home for evil fester. In the clearing of this street we evict the Devil from his home and welcome freedom and prosperity to this town.'

Another cheer. Again he speaks as if we are deprived but where is our deprivation? Our lives are hard but that is no different to the next person. How can we be deprived when the earth offers us so much?

'Today we send the Devil and all his followers a simple and clear message. He is not welcome here.'

Another huge cheer, the crowd in an almost frenzy. I do not know this Devil or what he is supposed to do. There has been no Devil, no evil in my teachings. I cannot think who it serves to fill people with such a fear.

Ben gives the signal and the men raise the battering rams. In unison they run at the houses with a triumphant cry. Wood splinters, daub crumbles, dust explodes in clouds all around us. So thickly interwoven are the buildings that as soon as one begins to fall so the strain on the others begins. The sound of wood and structure splintering, tearing, breaking apart is deafening. People scatter as bits of rock fly in all directions.

Still the battering rams withdraw and attack again. Rats and bats and all manner of beasts that have made this forgotten backwater their home scatter in all directions, forcing the crowd to turn, to run, some laughing, some afeard, all exhilarated in one way or another. Within minutes there is little more than a pile of rubble and a cloud of smoke left behind. The sun's rays cut through the dust, shedding a clarity on such destruction. The loss of a forgotten street does not seem such a tragedy. Yet I cannot help but feel we have lost a home for difference within our town. Not all creatures that serve us thrive in the sunlight.

The crowd disperses, congratulating themselves on their success. Mother Gray passes us and for a brief second makes eye contact and I know that shall be our next port of call.

We follow the crowd and then take a detour and approach Grace's house from the rear. Grandmother opens the door. I am shocked to see her there and looking so at home, but reason tells me it is no surprise she is no stranger there. Yet I cannot help a sense of slight humiliation and violation. I had understood this as my place. I had never stopped to consider Grandmother's relationship would predate mine. Mother Gray and Grace are sitting around the table and a jug of ale is in the centre, but it looks like there is little appetite for its offering. The mood is sombre – it is clear the demolition has caused some distress.

'Raven, thank you,' begins Grace, 'thank you so much for your warning.'

'It is the least I could do,' I say.

'Tonight you have a very special delivery,' continues Grandmother.

'Anything, anything I can do I gladly will,' I say.

'It is a delicate package,' says Grandmother.

'Hardly a package -' says Mother Gray.

'Tonight we need you to transport a friend of us all,' cuts in Grace and the others fall silent. 'He is old and frail and will need the gentlest of care,' she says.

'The apothecary?' I ask. They exchange glances.

'The least you know the better,' says Grace.

'Of course, as always,' I say.

'Good, then meet us here tonight at the first fall of light.'

'Of course,' I say and look towards Grandmother to see if she intends to leave with us.

'Take all the more advanced herbs, tools and remedies, hide or destroy them and I will join you shortly,' she says, and I nod. 'Leave the basics, the common remedies.'

'I shall,' I say. I hesitate but it is clear we are expected to leave.

We decide to travel back home our usual way to seek comfort in routine but even the brook, so familiar, seems changed and distant. I can see it looks unchanged yet somehow it is completely different. Everything is changing and changing so fast. The town, our neighbours, seem overnight to be different people. We do not know them and everything which seemed certain now is not.

Still we stop by the brook at our usual spot. Jet and Sabby drink and for a moment it is possible to forget, to snatch a pause of peace amongst the turmoil. The sun shines, the water dances and it is hard to believe that just a short while ago person had turned on person for no substantial reason. Then our thoughts are shattered by the approach of three horsemen, Stephen, Ben and another. They are travelling at some speed but come to a halt when they see us. I stand but am unabale to mount Jet before they reach us.

'Good afternoon, gentlemen,' I say.

'Raven,' acknowledges Ben.

'Ah, so this is the mysterious Raven I have heard tell of; pleased to have finally met you.'

'My lord,' I say, 'it is an honour.' I bow my head. Ben and the other titter.

'Oh, the honour is all mine,' he says, 'to meet the grandchild of such an esteemed cunning woman.'

'Thank you, you are too kind. We are but simple folk and my grandmother simply offers the wisdom of local roadside plants.'

'Interesting, then the local roadside plants must be particularly magical for she is known for her powerful magic or so I've heard it told.'

I laugh. 'Sir, you afford us power beyond our measure. We know not of magic. Perhaps local legend requires heroes and villains of its own choosing.' He laughs and Ben and the other follow suit.

'Of course, one cannot take gossip for evidence. It is well for there is no place for magic in this shire.'

'Indeed not,' I say.

'We must away,' he says. 'There is much work to be done.'

'Thank you, my lord, it has been a privilege and a pleasure,' I say.

'Good day to you,' he says.

They turn their horses and continue on their way and as we watch them leave Ben looks back and we lock eyes for the briefest moment. We wait till they are out of sight and then waste no time in speeding home. I am becoming no stranger to feelings of shame. I have denied all that I am and cannot reconcile such betrayal of myself. I want to bathe in the most ferocious of waterfalls, wash away all that I am and all that I have denied but there is no time to dwell, we must do as Grandmother has asked.

Sabby keeps watch as I take all the ingredients but the most common to the hidey hole I used as a child. I dig the hole deeper into the ground. We have a small iron chest that has mostly been ornamental, a gift from a customer who could not afford to pay another way, and I place the ingredients and equipment inside and bury them. I scour our small cottage for anything that could be incriminating, anything that could say magik.

Fortunately trinkets and ornaments have never been Grandmother's way. When I am contended there can be no accusations made, I sit with Sabby by the fire. We sit in a shell - the heart of our home has been ripped out and I am numb. There has been an element of play with our secrecy. I have enjoyed knowing whilst others have not, but this is another thing. This secrecy for this survival feels very different. It is late afternoon as we sit by the fire but can feel no heat.

Grandmother returns; we do not speak as she enters. She takes a while to check all around.

'It's a fine job you have done,' she says finally and sits down by the fire with us. We sit like that in silence for a while, each lost in our own singular pain. Eventually Grandmother gets up and out of her bag she takes a heavy fruit cake topped with marchpane. She cuts a large chunk for Sabby and I but neither of us have much of an appetite. For the first time I do not salivate at the mere suggestion of marchpane. Grandmother does not comment or try to persuade, simply takes back the cake. She wraps it in a linen.

'Take it, you might need it later. It will be nightfall by the time you reach Grace's, it is time.' I stand and look at her. I take the cake and place it inside the pocket of my cloak and without speaking we head out into the dusk.

The moon has risen by the time we reach Grace's and Mother Gray opens the door on our arrival. She does not greet us but ushers us inside in silence. Sitting at the table is a person dressed in black, small and old by demeanour. I cannot see their face, hidden as it is inside a hooded cloak. Grace is clasping their hands and I see fine wizened skin that looks a million years in age, experience and wisdom. Both Grace and Mother Gray proceed with the utmost gentleness and reverence. This must be the apothecary.

Grace smiles affectionally at me and indicates for me to sit. Mother Gray places a tankard of ale and a small tumbler of whiskey in front of me.

'Drink,' she says, 'it will be a long night and you shall need the sustenance.' I do not hesitate to down both. 'Travel directly to the clearing on the moor. Let Sabby guide the route and set the pace. You will be met there, you will know you have been met well and by our friends by their smell. From there they will take our special delivery.' Mother Gray indicates the apothecary. 'Speak to no one, not even at the change over.'

'I understand,' I say.

I am relieved it is this task I am to undertake. There is familiarity amongst the change and confusion. Mother Gray and Grace help the apothecary to their feet. I see the fragility and worry that the journey, even if we could go slowly, would break every bone in their body. I stand; it seems to take an age to for them to reach the door so small are the steps they take. I open the door and Mother Gray takes it from me, ushering me on to prepare Jet. I mount and wait.

Mother Gray approaches Jet and whispers in his ear. He nudges her with his nose and then with careful but steady movements he lowers to all fours and Grace and Mother Gray lift the apothecary on to his back behind me. I expect to feel no weight at all, but I can feel, despite the frailty and weightlessness, a density in their body. They wrap their arms around my waist and I feel a strong grip. We do not fear they will fall. Jet stands and in silence we turn and follow Sabby. It is the last I see of Grace and Mother Gray.

Chapter Twenty-Nine

I do not know the route to the moor and the moon shifts in and out of cloud. I am happy that Sabby is our guide. We make good, steady speed. I speak no word to the apothecary and they no word to me. Yet I feel a communication between us; a part of us is deep in conversation and a bond is forming between us that I cannot explain but do not resist. It is powerful and beautiful and makes the shame of the day worth the pain. I am filled with a sense of certainty that I know he has given me to sustain me.

The moon has just begun to wane when we reach the moor. We do not have to wait long before two figures emerge from the bracken. I smell the air and it is a smell I remember but cannot place, it is a smell of comfort, of home. These are the people we are to entrust the apothecary to. I check with Sabby who is calm and greets them warmly. Without being asked, Jet gently drops to his knees and the men lift the apothecary off his back. I am given a final squeeze before they release, and I receive the thanks and the love that travels with it. I barely see the men and only a flash of their faces as they carry the apothecary off into the night. Jet rises, and we speed off, Sabby taking us a different route to avoid trace and suspicion.

It is just before dawn as we approach the town. Soon Mary will be up and about her duties. It is risky, but I cannot resist the sweet embrace of her. As quietly as we can, we enter the yard and Sabby and I make our way silently up the stairs. As we approach the door we hear the sound of muffled tears. Gently we ease open the door. Mary lies on her side in a foetal position, streams of tears flowing down her face. She does not sense us, so lost in her pain she is. Silently we approach and as softly as we can, I climb in next to her and Sabby takes position resting near her feet. She does not seem surprised to see us, nor does she resist, rather she lets us hold her. We lie like that till her tears run dry.

We lie in peace for a while and I expect sleep to come but she turns to me and seeks out my lips. Our love making is deep and soft and gentle but fuelled by a passion that amplifies each sensation, so I am lost to the world as I give myself completely to the moment, completely to her. It is a healing we both need. Afterwards we lie in comforted, companionable silence. I know she will not tell me the cause of her tears. She knows I will not ask. We both know that the shadows of her early years still torment, that life as an innkeeper can be too similar at times. We both know that soon we shall have to leave the warmth of her bed and our embrace and go about our business.

'There is a fever it the town,' she says, 'that has spread fast.'

I say, 'How can it be so that one man can release such fire. I cannot fathom it.'

'It was all underneath waiting to be released,' she says as she eases herself free of my clasp and begins to dress.

'Yet I do not understand who it serves,' I say.

'Because it does not serve us but there are those it serves, or they think it serves them.'

'In a war nobody wins,' I say and reach for my clothes.

'Be watchful as you leave. There is not a place in town now that does not have eyes.'

'You know I will,' I say. She pauses at the door with her hand on the handle.

'Some of the more militant are holding a meeting here tonight,' and she turns and looks at me, her expression a mixture of fear and openness and I know if she could she would tell me she loved me, to take care so I am not lost to her. I smile at her and wink.

'The secret to a long life is knowing when it's time to go,' I say. She relaxes her fear and, smiling, shakes her head.

'Make the bed afore you leave,' she says and opens the door and goes.

We are not the most domestic, but we make the bed as best we can. I take the slice of cake from my cloak and place it on her pillow. The sun is high in the sky but if we are careful we shall make it back home afore anyone else is the wiser. After morning chores we shall take the afternoon for sleep.

Chapter Thirty

We do not need to call the council to know we should attend the meeting at the inn. We are not regulars at the inn and do not wish to draw attention to our presence. We decide with Grandmother to wait in the shadows and when the numbers begin to arrive for the meeting we will slip in amongst the crowd. After supper we head into town and wait.

The moon is high by the time people begin to arrive, at first dribs and drabs, one or two folks, folk I would expect, bullish men who seek dominance over all things. Yet then others arrive, men and women who I have always thought mild in their ways, God-fearing folk, but ones I thought to have a milder stance. In they come and soon it is clear I shall not stand out in the crowd. The meeting may be led by militants but the whole town has come to hear their words. We leave Jet in the yard, not out of place, as we had feared, but at home amongst the rest. We take the back entrance. Mary, carrying a tray heavily laden with ale tankards, passes us by; her eyes flash a warning and we brace ourselves.

We follow her into the bar. A wave of heat washes over us, the fire blazes and every inch of space is taken. The air is brimming with an edgy conviviality. People joke and laugh, catching up. Usually we are a disparate lot but today we are all fake friends. We manage to work our way through the crowd to a corner where we have a view of the room, but it does not have a view of us.

Tucked away in the opposite corner is the man who was with Ben and Stephen at the brook. He keeps an even lower profile than us and is overlooked by everybody who is more concerned with what they think is the power or the problem when it is exactly what they are not seeing that is the genuine threat. I spot the tanner in amongst the crowd and our lack of acknowledgement of each other is our acknowledgement.

Eventually we are brought to order by Master Lovell who is flanked by the bishop and the sheriff.

'Friends, friends,' he says and gradually conversations are ceased. 'How it cheers my troubled soul to see so many of you here tonight.' A ripple of justification and self-importance spreads across the room. 'For too long the decent, law-abiding, Christ-abiding people that have made this community have lived in the shadow of evil.'

Around the room there is agreement. Yet I do no recall any such shadow, I recall contentment, hardship for some but no more than the next. This discontent has been introduced not grown organically in the hearts of the people who until yesterday were friends and allies.

'For too long our crops have failed, for too long the winters have been harsh, for too long we have been forsaken. Yet we are good, honest, hardworking people; we deserve more, and we can have more. The mighty Lord has sent us our redeemers and we must seize this day, seize this chance to rid our land, our community, our people of those that bring evil and worship the Devil.' The crowd explode in a frenzy; there are one or two unsure, the butcher is one, but no one will speak out against this tidal wave of fear.

There is not a person in the room that has not sought and benefitted from the services of my grandmother at one time or another, yet now that wisdom is evil. I have never been more confused, more frightened or more angry in my life.

'Yesterday we saw the destruction of a corner of our town that had been the home of evil and what have we found? All manner of corrupt wrongdoings.'

He holds up a skull. It is most probably some sort of monkey skull used to connect to our ancient ancestors. The crowd are shocked, all claiming piety when there is not one of them that has not lived their lives check by jowl with beasts that live and die by their hands.

'What evil incantations, what demons are conjured by this monstrosity? Demons that shall destroy all that we have built, all that we have created. Do you seek a life of suffering and an eternity of damnation for your children? Or do you seek the protection of the Lord and an eternity of heavenly bliss?' A cheer of confirmation bounces round the room; the energy is high and the crowd thirst for blood. 'We must be vigilant. We must seek out those amongst us who have been corrupted by the Devil. We must save them and if they cannot be saved they must be spared. Be vigilant and report what you find. We must rid our town of the evil that has been and the evil that threatens.'

'What about those two spinsters. They're not from these parts?' a voice from the crowd contributes but I am too slow to see who.

'That's right and it was after they came our troubles began,' shouts another, but Grace and Mother Gray have lived in this town longer than I and our harvests have never been bad.

'Good, good, thank you brothers,' says Master Lovell. 'What else, who else?'

'I heard they are murderesses, that they killed their husbands for money. Widows but by their own hands,' says a voice and from then the allegations escalate, becoming more extreme and more ridiculous.

Within minutes, Grace and Mother Gray become prey and we the hunters. I see Master Tanner quickly slip out of the back door. I think him a coward but then the crowd decide to take the law into their own hands and we are being bundled out the door, swept along by the crowd. Then I realise the tanner has not run away but rather has run to warn Grace and Mother Gray. As we are pushed through the door, I glance back and see a look of satisfied congratulation pass between Master Lovell and Stephen's aide; this was an intended outcome.

Someone starts the chant of "Witch" and then there are no end to the insults. "Whore", "Hag", some words I have not heard before. The streets are narrow and the crowd, forced together, begin to act as one body. We manage to fall to the back and follow.

It does not take long to reach their house. Master Lovell steps to the front, his desire for vengeance ignited.

'Widow Buccan, open your door to the salvation of the Lord,' he shouts, and the mob support him. 'Be you not afraid, surrender yourselves and let us set you free.' The mob clamour. I see the flicker of a candle in the upstairs chamber and remember the secret passage. Then from nowhere the tanner appears in the crowd.

'Let them burn in hell,' he shouts and throws a lighted torch on to the roof of their house. It takes seconds for the fire to catch. Again a cheer goes up amongst the crowd. The house stands slightly alone, and it is a still night so little chance of sparks flying and the fire spreading, so the crowd relish the flames.

'Let them burn,' cries Master Lovell. 'If they are innocents they shall seek refuge in our arms.' And so we watch and as the flames engulf the house I feel part of my soul go up in flames with it, as I feel each one of the books in the library turn to ash and dust.

We cannot move as we watch my childhood dissolve into nothing. I hope against hope that they have been more prepared than I that they have had an escape plan all along, otherwise it is more than memories and wisdom that has been lost. We stand in the shadows watching as centuries of wisdom go up in flames.

It does not take long for the mob to break up; some return to the inn full of high spirits, others return home justified but saddened none the less. The butcher waits till the peak of the blaze has passed; as he passes us he pauses. I feel he wants to say something, maybe to warn us or commiserate but in the end, he says nothing but looks us briefly in the eyes and then walks on. It takes till early light for the blaze to completely die out and all that remains is a smoking pile of ash and rubble. We turn away before we are spotted, and head for the comfort of home, devastated by loss.

That afternoon, after a few broken hours of rest, we go to the tanner's. We know there will be a meeting and for the first time Grandmother joins us. We ride pillion and I am surprised how well she understands the ways of horse. We take the back roads, and the bright sun and the earth bursting with life seems an affront. How can everything continue when such tragedy has occurred?

It is still and quiet at the tanner's, almost too still. A sense of mourning pervades the entire place. Once in the barn

Grandmother jumps lightly off Jet's back and I cannot help a sense of pride. I do not know her age, but I know she is well for it.

We step through to the secret chamber and Astral is the first to his feet.

'Aluna,' he says, full of joy and welcome and love.

'Astral,' Grandmother responds, and they embrace, an embrace of histories untold. In turn she is greeted by all with embraces and love. I have always known her as Grandmother and am ashamed to discover I had never thought she had another name. Aluna fits her perfectly and as it is spoken I see not my grandmother who chides and nags and comforts but a spirit that has seen many full lives. I see the fullness of her experience, her wisdom, and realise my fortune to be raised and held by such intelligence and depth of compassion and love. I know then she shall always be a guide, that she will always in some ways be present for me.

We have barely sat down, and I cannot stop myself.

'You threw the torch?' I accuse the tanner. There are looks around the room. I lose patience with never knowing, always trusting when so little of anything makes any sense. When I am told so little.

'Where is your answer, Master Tanner?' I ask again.

He breathes deeply. 'Steady yourself, Raven, it broke my heart to do so.'

'Then why so?'

'Raven,' chides Grandmother and her betrayal stings. How can she not support me? How can she side with others when she was not even present? I cannot help but glare at her, my heart filled with anger. A moment ago I was full of pride and gratitude, now I feel betrayal and disgust.

'They are safe, Raven,' Astral soothes. 'They were safe before Master Tanner threw the torch.'

'But the books?' I protest.

'The only book that matters is safe with Grace and Mother Gray.'

'But the library?' I say.

'Hence the fire,' says Master Tanner and I look around the room and for the first time I am able to see their pain, their loss.

'Captain Langan?' I ask.

'With Grace and Mother Gray, northward bound,' says Master Tanner.

'We must be more vigilant, their thirst for blood will not be satiated till they have taken life. When the remains reveal no bones we can expect hysteria. Do not keep hold of anything that can incriminate. Have all your senses alert at all times and be ready to flee at all times. If in doubt rendezvous here,' instructs Astral.

'If captured take your life if you can,' adds Grandmother and all in the room understand.

We disperse one by one with distance apart so as not to cause suspicion. Each to our own sorrow, each to our own grief. We ride in silence back home. Her clasp around my waist offers comfort but I have no taste for it, no trust in it. What good our "society" if it cannot protect our treasures? Grandmother slides gently off Jet when we reach our yard. I feel she lingers as if she does not wish for the moments to pass. She looks up at me.

'Know that I love you and always shall,' she says. I look at her but do not verbally respond but turn Jet away and speed as fast as I can to the only place of comfort left.

I leave Jet in the yard, not even thinking if the stable boy will tend him. I know Mary will be taking her afternoon pause. Despite my desire, my passion, I manage to just about retain my discretion, although I care little for the words of instruction from Astral. I ease open her door; she is standing by the window and I know she has been waiting for me. We do not speak but our bodies meet beside the bed, our passion hot and furious, our love making an explosion of emotions we cannot contain.

Chapter Thirty-One

Afterwards we lie in silence, holding each other. There is release but no peace. Eventually Mary breaks the pact.

'They were close to you, the widows.'

'Taught me to read,' I say.

'You read?' she says. 'I don't believe it possible.' We share a gentle laugh.

'It's a useless talent,' I say and turn and begin to dress.

'It will be useful when you are an innkeeper,' she says. 'Can you do figures too?' And for the first time I see a future, a future I never thought she would offer me. I search her face for confirmation and find it there. We kiss, a kiss that should never have ended but we are interrupted by a commotion outside in the street. It sounds like the whole town is on the move. Quickly we dress and hurry to the front door of the inn.

A squadron of cavalry men from the castle, led by Stephen and followed by the howling mob of last night, march past with intent. The cavalry men's eyes are empty, and their lips closed, the mob focused but chatty as if it's a holiday. The butcher drops out of the crowd to join us.

'You do not know?' he says, looking into the crowd and not at us.

'The castle-keeper, they found no bones in the ashes. Master Lovell cried witchcraft.' I do not need to hear more.

We turn, and I am through the inn and into the yard as fast as I can go without caring who knows I am there. I find Jet in the stable; the boy has removed his saddle, and I do not wait to re-tack but leap on to his back as we speed as fast as we can. It will take longer to go the back route, but we hope their bulk will slow them down. I do not see the trees passing, do not smell the flowers or hear the brook. All there is, is getting home, getting to Grandmother before they do. Her last words to me repeat in my mind, over and over. She must have seen this, must have expected this. What use clairvoyance if you see but cannot change?

I know Jet and Sabby are going as fast as they can. I know they too know why and still I push them harder, ask more of them than I ever have before. At last the cottage comes into view. We see the horsemen, the mob, are they coming or leaving? We watch from a distance as they surround the cottage. Coming. I am paralysed. Am I to intervene, to try and stop them? Am I to wait to witness? In my hesitation I am too late.

Minutes later we see Grandmother walk out of the cottage. She is composed and proud, walking tall, indifferent to the shouts of abuse thrown at her by people whose lives she has saved with her “witchcraft”. We watch powerless as they tie her to one of their horses to be paraded and shamed through the town. We wait till the last is out of sight and charge down the hill to our home.

I jump off Jet and go inside. We have lived simply all our lives but everything we have is broken to pieces, strewn across the floor, remedies and herbs thrown into the ground, nothing is in one piece, nothing is reparable, everything is destroyed. I leap back onto Jet’s back and do not stop to think if I have ridden him too hard, just demand to be taken to the tanner’s as fast as possible. I do not feel his sweat soaking my hose. All I feel is that it takes too long to get anywhere.

We thunder into the tanner’s, the usual care we give to secrecy and discretion abandoned. Fire rages inside every pore of my body. I can barely see for the rage in my eyes. Yet I feel the most conscious I have ever felt. Nothing is heard but the blood that feeds the fire inside. Jet just about stops in time and I leave him panting. I charge into the meeting chamber, expecting action, expecting weapons, a plan, a stratagem, yet they sit speechless, Astral, Master Tanner, Philip, Theron, Fergus, Robin. ‘What’s this?’ I demand. ‘Is this not a call to arms?’

‘They move faster than we expected,’ says Astral.

‘We must not act in haste,’ says Master Tanner.

‘You are but afeard,’ I retort. ‘Where is your metal?’ No one will meet my eye.

‘There is much at stake, Raven, what we do must consider all,’ says Robin.

‘It is simple,’ I say. ‘I can shift. I can free her.’

'You must not,' demands Master Tanner. 'The risk is too great. If you are discovered, it will be the death of us all.'

'I shall not be discovered,' I reply. 'You know my gift is better than that.'

'Whatever you do you must promise us not to shift. You do not know what is at stake.' I stare at all of them, taking in their worried, frightened faces stricken with broken pride. I have no patience for their stakes, no patience for their secrecy which once seemed courageous and now seems just plain cowardly. We are being made extinct and they fight so little.

We have such gifts as can run circles around those that would stop us, dullards frightened of magik, not seeing it as an aid but as a threat, as competition. They create evil and then call us so whilst we stand by, hiding books, meeting in secret and denying what we are, when I can see nothing about what we are that needs hiding. We are fighting the wrong war.

'Of course, you are right,' I say. 'Forgive me, such is my shock. I shall return home, try to salvage what I can.'

'No, we must get you safe,' says Master Tanner. 'Philip will escort you to a safe house. You will need to travel quick.'

'There are people I must see before I go,' I say. 'Do not fear, I will heed you. I shall not shift but I do not know when or if I shall return. There are those I cannot leave without a word.'

'Then to the inn only,' says Astral, 'then return.' I hide my surprise that my love is known but act to take it in my stride.

'Sir,' I say, 'as you instruct.' And not giving them time to reconsider I turn and head out of the chamber.

The youngest of the tanner's children has fed and watered Jet and is wiping him down when I exit the barn.

'Thank you,' is all I manage to say, such is my haste, such are my emotions that I cannot spare a moment more. This time, with our usual caution, we leave the tanner's. We take the back route as they would expect then when we are safely out of sight we turn, all of us, knowing where we are actually going.

It takes little time to reach the banks of the river that runs alongside the castle. They will have taken Grandmother to the dungeon and with what knowledge I have from my previous visit and my senses, I know where to start. We find a clump of bushes and trees nearby and it takes seconds to shift into river rat. I do not even take time to enjoy the shifting such is my focus and intention. I slip into the water, leaving Sabby to keep watch and hide. I find the first small gap in the castle walls and swim through.

I find myself in a small dark passage in the cellars of the castle. The smell of the dungeon is pronounced, but a clear guide, and it takes mere minutes before I am able to squeeze through a small hole in the base of the wall and I am with her. She sits composed, leaning against the wall of the cell. Her eyes are closed. A small window high above her head is the only light in the room.

It is a fair-sized cell, the floor thick with human faeces and waste. She has been given no blankets or bedding despite the damp coldness and lack of furniture. She is alone.

'You should not have come,' she says, opening her eyes and looking into mine and I know she sees me, know she is looking at me through my form. 'They will be here soon, it is too much risk.' I let out a frustrated high-pitched squeal. 'Hush, you must go. Do not let them take both of us,' she says.

I want to tell her how much I love her, how full of gratitude I am for the life she has given me, the life we have shared. I look into her eyes and hope she can see the love I have for her. She smiles at me and for a moment we are transported to a place of peace, far removed from our material circumstances.

Then we hear the guards, heavy footed and clumsy, keys rattling.

'Hurry,' she says, 'they will think little of killing a rat.' I want to shift to bear, grasp Grandmother in my arms and storm out of the building, terrorising all in sight. Yet I know in my heart they would simply kill us both and claim the Devil had a hand, then who knows how many of the villagers would face the noose when fear of the Devil is supported with so much evidence, when my body returned from bear to human flesh on death. Then I know that Grandmother chooses this, chooses the loss of her life to save the lives of those that will see her hang.

As the guards fling the door open I take refuge in the hole. I stare wide-eyed as she stands, ready to be escorted. Yet they hit her to the ground, kick her and drag her till she looks as demented as they say she is. I watch, and the feeling of powerlessness rips apart my soul. I want to leap from my hiding pace and chew at their faces. Yet I do not, cannot. They shove her out the door; before it slams shut she turns to me and winks and I know no matter what they do they shall never break her spirit.

The stone door slams shut behind them and I can bear it no longer. I turn and speed back through the tunnels and passages, through the water and up on to land and without taking care of who or what is around I shift back, not caring about my nakedness or who might see it. I'd like to cry, to weep, but my tears are buried deep inside and I cannot reach them. I lie panting on the ground. Sabby comes and lies beside me; she nudges with her nose into my face, licks when I turn to face her. Her soft fur is against my skin and I pull her tight to me.

We sit together, Jet standing above us, sheltering us until the chill in the air reaches my consciousness. On steadier feet I dress. They will expect me back, will have already checked the inn. Yet I do not seek their protection, not tonight. I shall witness the fate of my grandmother. They shall not take that away from me to protect themselves. I know exactly where to hide.

It is dark by the time we reach the picnic spot in the woods, the spot where Mary and I first lay. There is water; I shall not light a fire for fear of discovery, but my cloak shall shelter, and the moon is bright. I hold Sabby close to me and prepare to return Jet to town. He will know the way and will be unseen amongst the shadows. She will know when she sees him. I trust she will not misunderstand and think I am passed, and Jet escaped. I trust that when she sees him she will answer my call. Jet does not hesitate, he takes my instruction, but I think he understands without my words. He is off into the night without a flicker of delay. We find a spot out of the moon's rays thickly laid with comforting moss and settle down to wait, each giving each other warmth.

I would not think it possible that we slept but it seems so as we are awoken from a dreamless sleep. The moon has passed over, so it is into early morning when we feel Jet's breath upon us. My eyes snap open and my startled face melts into a smile of relief and joy at the sight of Mary.

'I came as soon as I could,' she says and slides off Jet's back.

'It is good to see you,' I say and pull her tight. Her embrace is to return home.

'You must be starving,' she says and we part. She has brought bread, ale and meats. We feast in the first sun's rays.

'The town is in a frenzy. Most have taken a side, those against evil vociferous and dominant. Anyone who differs is keeping a low profile.'

'And Grandmother? What news?'

'There is to be a trial at first light.'

'A trial? Then they have condemned her.'

'They have hung the rope,' she says.

My rage renders me motionless, the sense of helplessness crashes over me, a tidal wave of despair. That morning we do not make love, rather hold each other. Each in our own torment, each for each other, in turn we are held by the peace of the morning and the earth. Held by that which has spawned all life. Held by that which they seek to dominate and control but cannot nor will ever be able to. They make an enemy of all that is alive in the name of a God of their own creation. Then they expect us all to pay the debt they have birthed. I have never been prouder to be that which I am and never more ashamed for mankind. I think that one day things will not be so, that mankind will one day look back on these days and consider us foolish. I think I will not see that day but vow to myself to spend my life fighting for it.

When the sun is risen we begin to stir without words; we know this time has come to an end. As we stand and our bodies part I feel as if part of me has been torn away, a part that shall be forever with Mary. She packs away our picnic, Sabby stretches and I prepare Jet.

'Raven, you must be careful, you know what they will do.'

'It will never happen. They will never know, I promise.'

We kiss a long slow deep kiss of love that has no words. Both of us clinging to a promise that is really more of a hope. Then we mount Jet, Mary riding pillion, her arms around my waist, a warmth and comfort I shall never forget.

We travel in quiet, the beauty of the morning caressing the land a cruel joke when the day will bring such horror and sorrow. Before we reach the town we stop and Mary slides off Jet's back and onto the earth. She has not said but I know she will walk to town via the woods and fill her basket with mushrooms and fruits; that way she will not have been in the arms of her lover but will have taken an early morning stroll to gather supplies for the day. Later she will cook beautiful dishes with these ingredients and feed the people who will have broken her lover's heart and ripped apart the town and she will have no choice but to do so with a smile.

Chapter Thirty-Two

The sun is full high by the time we reach the town. It is already humming with the expectant excitement of an execution. From miles around every manner of pedlar and merchant has set up shop. Wine and ale flows as if from a multitude of tiny waterfalls. There is laughter and merriment, music and dancing. I do not understand how something so ugly can create something so joyous.

We are on the outskirts of the town passing a narrow dark alley when we are not sure, but we think we hear a whistle. We stop and there it is, and we know that whistle, that cadence. It is odd to feel such joy amongst such pain. We turn down the alley and into the arms of Billy Bird.

'Master Raven,' he says, 'my old friend. I feared and hoped to see you.' I dismount, and we embrace.

'We greet you with joy but wish it was not so,' I say.

'It is so,' he says. 'Come, you shall be soon for the gallows yourself if they recognise you.' Out of his pack he pulls a bright red cloak, a mix of the finest wool and silk with a deep hood.

'Openly hiding,' I say and gladly take the cloak and hand him my black one.

'And well it suits you,' he says. The cloak feels good and for a moment I forget why I am wearing it, then the remembrance returns, and I feel ashamed of my fickle mind.

'You must think of yourself now, Raven. Above all else you must watch out for yourself. It is survival now,' he says but I cannot hear these words, cannot feel their good intent.

I am about to lose the person who has fed and clothed me, shared her wisdom, kept me from what harm she could and comforted me when she could not. Nothing makes sense and as she is about to be lost to me and the world, so I am lost to myself. Yet I do not say this to him, do not dare express this despair for fear it will engulf, for fear it will take hold and never let go.

Instead I say, 'Yes.'

'Promise me?' he insists.

'Of course,' I say.

'Your grandmother would want it so,' he says and at that I have to run away and hide the tears that have come to my eyes. I mount Jet.

'And you too,' I say, 'make sure this day is lucrative.'

'You know me, I have no shame.' And we smile.

'Anon,' I say.

'Anon,' he says, and we step out into the crowd.

The cloak is loud and stands out and in doing so does its job; we are invisible. The crowds are so dense we cannot get very close into the square. We can see a stage, Stephen stands at the front, my grandmother to the side, her head high and I can tell from her stance that she has already left, her spirit free, it is only an empty body that remains. Ben stands beside her, acting like the rightful guard and accuser, to the side sits the sheriff and his deputies. The crowd are hungry, and Stephen is happy to feed them.

'For too long this evil has lived amongst you. For too long this evil has corrupted your children. For too long this evil has brought ruin to your homes.' The crowd cheer and shout, 'Burn her', 'Witch', 'Hag' and any insult they have to hand.

'Speak woman, of your innocence, or condemn yourself,' Stephen commands and Ben pushes her forward. I could tear off his hands for his ill treatment of her. The insults increase and with a slight raise of his hand Stephen quietens the crowd.

'Let her speak. Let her save herself. Let us hear of her innocence.'

A deathly silence falls. In this pause I scan the crowd and they are all there. The tanner, Astral, Philip, men of consequence, men of stature, yet not one of them speaks up, not one of them will stand up and be counted. How can they call themselves men?

'Speak woman,' says Stephen. 'Your silence condemns you.' Still she does not, still she maintains her dignity. I know her, know her stubbornness, know it in me, I know she will not speak.

Stephen turns to the sheriff, who in the silence stands. It is easy to see he is reluctant, easy to see he is trying to hide his disdain for these proceedings. He looks over to Grandmother and the sound of his heels on the wooden platform is like the loudest crack of thunder. He stands and stops by her side. He leans in close to her, his lips barely move but I can tell he is asking her to speak, pleading with her to renounce all that she is so her life may be saved. But I know Grandmother and know a life which she has gained by betraying all she holds to be true is not a life that would interest her.

The crowd grow restless. 'What say you, sheriff?' prompts Stephen and the sheriff has no choice.

'Widow, you offer no defence, and no one here will speak for you,' he says, looking directly at her. 'You leave me no choice but to find you guilty of witchcraft,' and the crowd erupts. He shakes his head, his anger and disgust now aimed at her.

'To the gallows,' cries Stephen and the crowd surges.

It is all we can do to step back, step out of the crowd. I want to turn, I want to run, I have no stomach for this. I steer Jet away, it would be impossible to follow the crowd anyway but when we get to the outskirts of town Jet will not go, will not take my instruction, rather he chooses his own path and there is nothing I do that can stop him.

He guides us to the opposite side of the river across from the castle. He stops near a clump of bushes and trees. He lowers his front leg, instructing me to dismount, reluctantly I do. I do not want to see, do not now want to witness, still Sabby insists and leads me to a small clearing by the river. We have a clear view of the bridge. Three nooses swing in the breeze as the crowd swarm onto the bridge. I hope their weight shall bring down its structure, but it holds fast and I curse the ingenuity of the town's engineers.

We see three woman - Grandmother and two others, Mother Lovell, now sent mad by her time in the stocks and then a poor beggar woman whose name no one knows but she has never caused any harm. We hear chanting as the rope is placed around their necks. Then silence falls as the cart is driven away and they drop, first the beggar woman, then Mother Lovel, then Grandmother.

I watch and feel nothing, can feel nothing, the pain is so deep it has no voice, no song. I cannot scream, I cannot cry but the world will forever be frozen in that moment. I watch helpless, yet we have so much power. How can we have the power of the earth and be unable to stop such travesty? Why can we not stop them?

There is not a part of me that is not numb. We watch the crowd disperse, watch the bodies swing in the breeze. Even though I have seen it with my own eyes I cannot accept that it is my grandmother left to billow in the wind, a warning to all who dare to think differently. In time Sabby leads me to Jet and I mount but do not know how as I cannot feel anything. We move away but I do not care where we are going. There is nowhere to go.

I watch the leaves on the trees pass by, the bank, the deserted back roads, in the distance we hear the celebrations and merriment in the town. Yet I feel none of it, sense none of it. It is as if I am passing through the pages of a book I cannot read. It all looks pretty but means nothing to me so disconnected I am. It does not take long to realise we head towards the tanner's.

I recognise a deep resistance inside. I want to be anywhere else than amongst the cowards that have sacrificed my grandmother for their own skins. After all she has given to them, to the people of the town, to people far and wide. Yet not one of them stood up, not least me. Yet the resistance lies buried deep with no access to action. So I do nothing but sit and watch as the tanner's cottage comes into view. Everything appears deserted with no one in sight. Yet we make our way to the barn as usual and Jet takes his usual place. Sabby bites and pulls on my cloak and in an automated way I dismount, and my body remembers the way to the meeting chamber.

They are huddled round the table deep in whispers and secrets. I stand in the doorway and their conversation stops.

Relief washes over all their faces. Astral is the first to approach, followed by the others.

'Boy, we are well met,' he says and embraces me, but I cannot return his embrace. I do not understand it. I do not appear to have control of my own body. They sense my emptiness and Astral guides me to a chair at the table. They give food to Sabby and I feel betrayed by her appetite. They pass me some wine and if they could show me how to drink it I would oblige but otherwise it is just fluid in a container on a table.

'Where have you been?' asks Philip.

'He's been at the execution, clearly,' says Master Tanner and he is met with reproachful stares by all.

'What? It will not serve him to pussy foot around,' he says.

'It is true action is what is needed now,' says Astral. Philip sits down next to me.

'Raven, we must get you to a safe place. Are you ready now?' I look at him, as if any place will ever be safe again, but I cannot respond - there seems so little point in doing so. He takes my silence as agreement.

'Good, then once Sabby and Jet are finished eating we shall set off. They will be looking for you. Time is of the essence.'

Again he takes my silence for acquiescence. They exchange concerned glances but soon I am ushered to my feet and led to Jet. I feel a flicker of recognition on seeing him, a tiny flicker of comfort and it's the first feeling I have.

I mount because my body remembers to do so. As I take my seat in the saddle sensation returns to my legs. I am filled with curiosity as I wiggle my toes in my boots. I take hold of the reins and the memory awakens something in my mind. I look down at Sabby and something like the memory of connection awakens in me. Philip mounts his horse and they approach.

'Come, follow close, Captain Langan awaits.' And without another word from him to the others we set off. His steed is fast, and we are soon ducking under trees, swerving round corners, galloping along straits. We are circling the town heading from my memory towards London or the south. With each step we take a little more of me is awoken, a little more of me is remembered.

Then we see it, hanging in the tree, its wings caught holding its lifeless body in place, the breeze gently swaying a dead raven. Its feathers are torn and bloody, the loser of the fight. Yet it is not a raven I see but my grandmother's face, her neck broken, her eyes staring. There is not even thought, not even intention, we simply turn on the spot. Philip is some way ahead and has not seen the raven corpse. Alive and awoken now, I speed Jet and Sabby on - we have a purpose and it is clear. They cannot take my grandmother and my only response be to run.

We take a different more direct route than we have come, hoping to lose Philip, who has now realised we are not following. He will not call out, but we can sense he has turned and is in pursuit. We cut along by the river as we did when we visited Grandmother in the dungeon. Yet I shall not shift this time, vengeance shall be savoured in human form. There is no plan, I have none, but my head and heart are clear.

We come to stop in our previous hiding place. I jump off Jet and follow Sabby to the castle. We know that all will be otherwise engaged in celebrations. The courtyard is deserted, and we can hear sounds of revelry from the great hall. I know exactly what to do. I take a torch from the wall and, using my dagger as a flint, light it. I take another and light it. I take aim and throw the first torch on to the roof of the castle over the great hall. It takes a moment or two before it catches. I throw the second into the wood pile. I light another and toss it on another part of the roof. I light another and throw it at the foot of the great hall. In seconds the roof is ablaze, and I stand triumphant. If they seek hell, then I shall give it to them.

Soon there are screams and shouts, the alarm has been raised but I care not. I am feasting on the flames that greedily devour the restoration that has been done to the castle. I am grabbed from behind. I think I am caught and am glad of it for I shall not be a compliant prisoner. But I am being dragged away out of sight. I turn and see Philip. I struggle and we wrangle.

'We must go,' he says. 'We must go. It is enough. You have done enough.'

'I have only just begun,' I say and try to get past him back to the flames.

Again we struggle. He is bigger and stronger than me, but I am driven by a will to destroy and will not be stopped. He has dragged us away towards the edges of the courtyard, but our commotion does not go unnoticed and soon we can hear shouts and guards thundering towards us. By the time we realise, it is too late. They will be upon us before we can escape.

'Go, you must go,' insists Philip. 'Go and I will hold them off.' I am at a loss. A moment ago I would not have thought anything of taking his life; now he offers it to save mine.

'I cannot leave you,' I say.

'You must,' he says and pushes us on.

'I'll not go without you,' I resist.

'Then come,' he says, and we turn.

I think we are travelling away together, Sabby leading us away to safety, but when I turn at the castle walls there is no Philip. All we can see in the distance is two guards dragging a body towards Stephen and Ben who are conducting the control of the fire. I am frozen; what should I do? Try to rescue him? Go and get help? But how am I to tell the others that I have cost a man's life. The guards and Stephen converse, they drop Philip to the ground, discard him as if he is nothing more than forgotten waste.

They turn in our direction and I duck out of sight. I hide. Their attention is taken by the fire and I run. Outside the castle walls we go as fast as we can to the inn. I cannot think, I only know there is nowhere else to go.

There is no one in the courtyard. The whole town has gone to view, to help put out the fire. Jet knows his place in the stables and Sabby and I rush to Mary's room. I should not put her at risk like this, but I cannot leave without seeing her. I plan to leave. We have no choice but to run as fast and as far as we can. We shall tell no one and seek no help from anyone. Least of all the "society".

I shall never see her again. Grandmother was snatched way, Philip I abandoned, I cannot leave Mary without seeing her, holding her one last time. I am sure the fire will soon be extinguished and the inn heaving with smoke raw throats with a thirst to match. I think she will be home soon, and the town will be engaged, and I shall be able to slip away unnoticed. I am shaking and restless but seek comfort as we crawl under the sheets. I am muddled in my head, so it seems the safest place should we be discovered. A young man awaiting the arms of his lover seems innocent and justifiable. I do not remember how or when, I only know that we have slept when we are awoken.

Chapter Thirty-Three

I feel Mary's breath in my ear. I breathe in her smell and in half sleep turn to her with welcome in my being as I open my eyes my consciousness awakens. I see the fear in her eyes, her being. I look around, we have not been discovered.

'Quick,' she says, 'you cannot delay.' I scramble out of bed. Sabby is already at the door waiting.

'I had to see you,' I say and we kiss passionately but hurriedly.

'They come for you, search for you,' she says. 'You must go.'

'Come with me,' I say. 'We can be free.'

'We both know I would slow you down.'

'I'll return for you.'

'And I shall wait,' she says, and we kiss again.

'Raven, please, please hurry, you know if you are discovered-'

'Here,' I say reaching for the Merkaba around my neck. 'A keepsake.'

'I can't, I know how much it means, it was gift from Grace, it is too much.'

'Nothing is too much for you,' I say and place it around her neck and we stay, locked in embrace for as long as we dare.

'Jet is waiting. I shall distract them. Go!' She pushes me out of the door.

I hurry down the stairs, not thinking this shall be the last I see of these walls, these walls that have held us in our love. These walls that one day we plan to be our own. All I can think of is escape.

Night has fallen, the sky clear and the moon just rising out of the horizon. The stable hand holds Jet and I see we have been given a pack and some blankets. I take the reins from the stable boy and we look into each other's eyes. His quiet discretion has enabled my love, our relationship. We owe him so much but all I can muster is a simple 'Thank you.' To give a gift would be to endanger him and I cannot sully his gift with mere coins.

'The pleasure has been mine, sir,' he says, and I could weep at the simple pleasantry that says so much more than is implied. Instead I briefly clap his shoulder and leap onto Jet's back and we turn and head out into the night.

I do not know where we are heading, where we should go; to London would be too obvious, they are bound to block that route. I let Jet and Sabby take the lead and we head out towards Grandmother's, towards home. Then I realise we are heading north. We shall go in search of Grace and Mother Gray.

All is quiet, and I think we are safe as we reach the outskirts of town and the brook we know so well. Then we hear them. They are a little way behind. It is clear they have been lying in wait as one after the other they emerge from the shadows and corners of the town. We turn and look - they are a little way behind. We know this route well and they do not; as soon as we get past Grandmother's we will be undercover of the forest and they shall never find us.

We turn and speed on. We hear their dogs, their shouts, their horses' hoofs tear up the ground. We speed up. One of their dogs, a long-haired greyhound, comes up behind; it makes a play for Sabby but with one precise bite the dog is lying dead amongst the reeds. It barely slows our speed. We turn the corner; we are only a short distance from home. Standing before us are two guards on horseback. We do not pause, do not hesitate, do not stop as we are supposed to. Sabby leaps for one of the guard's legs and takes out a chunk as she passes. Jet takes a bite out of the other guard's leg and we continue on our way as they reel in pain and surprise.

We can hear the others hot on our heels, but we are approaching our home and soon we will be in the safety of the trees. I see the shell of our former home and feel the memory of all the times I have returned home before; somehow it does not make sense for us to be passing and not stopping. We are about to reach the forest when we hear a loud bang, a sound we have never heard before. I feel a wetness in my shoulder. I see a hole where there should be flesh, blood pouring when there should be dry wool. This is what it must mean to be shot. There is a moment of pause, the force of the shot and the pain send me reeling and I am thrown from Jet.

I land face down in the briars at the edge of the forest. For a few moments I cannot move. The pain is nothing I have experienced before. I am beside myself, almost unable to do anything I am so engulfed. I am losing blood and I can feel the life force draining from my body. I know that if I stop, if I lie down and succumb to the pain, I shall never rise again. Somehow, I manage to stagger to my knees. I crawl to the bank and grab handfuls of blood moss and pack my wound.

On the horizon I can see the silhouette of a herd of horses and I know what I must do. They are not far behind and I have little time. With their fire weapons they can take us all and that I cannot allow. It is one thing for me to suffer at their hands, but I cannot let them take the lives of my guides and companions, gifts from the earth that I must protect as they protect me. Such is the resolve that I push the pain to the far reaches of my being and free Jet of the bridle and saddle. There is no time for goodbyes, yet I kiss his forelock, hug his neck then send him away. His herd are calling, and he must return. He is reluctant, he bows.

'Thank you, you are released,' I say and turn my back on him and begin to walk away. I hear him hesitate then to relent, turn and speed towards his birth family.

I am getting weak, but the energy of the moment keeps me moving. I take more blood moss and change my dressing; the blood has stopped flowing but my shoulder is seizing up. They are seconds away and above all else they must not take Sabby.

'Sassaba, thank you for serving me, you are released,' I say, yet she does not go.

'Go I tell you. You must leave,' I shout with all I have left but she will not leave my side. Our connection is so deep, our love unconditional, she must be protected. I pick up a rock and throw it - she simply dodges it and returns.

'Go away,' I scream, falling to my knees, but it is too late - the thundering of hooves surrounds us.

I am grasped from behind and Sabby leaps to defend, a second shot, the bullet whistles past my ear and she falls. She is shot, and I cannot tell how badly, she cries out and falls to the ground. She does not move. I want to go to her. Is she living? Is she dead? There is blood, but I cannot tell how bad or where the wound is. I try to reach her, but they pull me back. Ben triumphantly jumps off his horse, gun in hand and still smoking. He walks over to her and kicks her lifeless body. Then from deep inside his body comes a rumble that explodes into victorious laughter. All the men join in.

'Bring him,' he says then pauses. 'Sorry, bring her,' and again they all laugh, pushing and dragging me in to the centre of the circle they have created with their horses in the courtyard of my home.

The moon is high now and I can see all their faces. Some are new but mostly labourers from the town, old faces that a few days ago I would have sworn would never be thus before me. Stephen sits in confident and satisfied silence observing. Next to him I see a dull, frail figure slumped on his horse, barely conscious, Philip.

The blood stains down his body, his twisted shape, all markings of torture, and I know he has spoken. How much he has spoken I do not know. I have been dropped on my knees and am unable to stand.

'What's this, you cry just like a girl,' Ben says, and two henchmen drag me to my feet.

I can feel nothing; Sabby has been shot and every part of my being is numb. I have no senses in body or mind; I can barely stay conscious. I had not noticed that silent tears have been falling from my eyes.

'Just like a girl because you are a girl,' says Ben and rips apart my doublet. Taking his dagger he slices apart my bandages and I am exposed to all. My bare flesh, my bare breasts exposed to the moon, to the earth, to these men. A chorus of laughter and jeers surround me. I think that later I will feel shame. That later I shall rage against this inevitability but now there is nothing.

'Gentlemen,' says Stephen and they fall silent. 'This woman is confused and needs correction. Her malady requires immediate treatment.'

He reaches over and clasps Philip by his hair and holds up his face, so he has no choice but to watch, an audience for their power. Stephen nods his head and Ben rips off my hose. I am naked to the earth. He pushes me down and kicks my legs apart, one by one they take their turn.

It does not take long, such is their excitement. Some take me from behind, some want to come in my face, some cover my eyes, my head. All twelve take their turn, Ben the first, Stephen the last. By the time they have finished I am covered in fluids and mud and bits of earth, my flesh torn asunder and my shoulder immovable. Yet I feel none of it. I am not present, I am nowhere, and I am not there. I can distinguish little of what takes place, just snatches, fragments cut and jar into my consciousness but mostly I am somewhere in non-existence. At some point I just cease to be there at all. Stephen, the last, takes his time, savours his pleasure and in my half consciousness I fear he mistakes this for love making. As he puts himself away, Ben asks 'What now?'

'Bring her,' says Stephen. 'Her execution will be good sport for the cardinal's visit.'

Chapter Thirty-Four

I awake, a single clear beam of sunlight streaming through the cell's bars. I do not move, cannot move. I am naked and lying in the spot where my grandmother lay before me. They have left a pitcher of ale and a stale biscuit by my side. A rough piece of sacking has been thrown over my body and I feel fresh straw beneath me. I do not understand such special treatment. Then somewhere in my mind the word cardinal floats to the forefront and I think I remember being a gift for him. Still I feel nothing, I barely remember the night, but I remember Sabby's last cry and that pain is the only thing I feel, and it sends me back into unconsciousness.

I do not know how long it is, but I drift in and out of consciousness, sometimes the moon is shining, sometimes the light is fading, sometimes growing. I move little, there seems no point and I do not have the strength anyway, mind, body and spirit are defeated and destroyed. I cannot lift myself to drink and cannot contemplate eating. Still I feel nothing but always flashes of memory send me deep into the still darkness to escape.

There is no order to the memories and joyous memories of my life flow in and out of memories of breath against my face and hands across my body. I am lost and have no desire to be found. Always the loss of Sabby, of Grandmother, of Mary pulling me deep into nothingness. I have no sense of time; this could be days I lie like this, hours or minutes. It does not matter to me. My life has ceased to have value to me. I do not fight for it, do not fight for myself, rather, I wait, expecting to either pass over or awake fresh and revived as if nothing has happened. I no longer expect to have any agency in either outcome and have no preference. I am suspended in torment and it is the only thing that makes sense. I have no desire to heal.

I awake to the feel of water on my skin, the smell of lavender, the sound of Mary's voice. Still I do not move but she has moved me. She has been hard at work; my legs and arms are cleared of muck, but they are many colours from the bruising. She has arranged the straw and sacking and placed me on the best bed she can make for me with the materials she has to hand. I know I should feel joy, feel love. I should seek to take her in my arms, but everything is happening miles away. I can see myself in the room, witness what is happening, but I feel no connection, at the most a slight annoyance that I have been disturbed from my despair. I close my eyes again; she has not seen my consciousness and carries on her work.

She begins to unpack the blood moss from my shoulder. I see she has more, and I can tell by the smell of my wound I have been in this state for three days. I can feel her pause as she looks at my face.

'Where are you?' she sighs. 'It has cost me a lot to get to see you. The whole town is awash with your discovery. No one would come to you. No one dare step up, no one has the stomach for it. Lucky in a way as in the end they had to order me to come. A barmaid already considered of ill repute. Forgive me for I protested but only for protection. Hiding in full view as you always do.' She pauses, and I can feel her wipe away a tear.

'What have they done to you?' She pours cold, clean water on my wound and I cannot help but react. Still I play unconsciousness.

'You are in there. I knew you were, I knew I would feel it if you passed. In the end they needed someone to clean you up, make you presentable for the cardinal. He is expected tomorrow and the day after your... they plan to…why do you do nothing? How can you lie there? Surely your grandmother taught you something, some way to escape.' and she shakes me. 'Wake up!' The pain shoots through my body; against my will I recoil and my eyes snap open. She is relieved.

'Raven, Raven, I knew you were in there,' she says, looking into my eyes, searching. I try to look away, but she follows. I am filled with anger and resentment that she has pulled me back to this reality. Despite myself I clasp my shoulder.

'Of course,' she says and quickly returns to tending the wound, cleaning and packing.

'I looked for her,' she says. 'Sabby, I thought to fetch her body, thought you could be together, but she had already been taken. The birds must have feasted because there was a fair number of black feathers at the scene. I'm sorry.'

A tear falls from her eye and into the wounds it seeps inside and feels as if a kiss has been planted deep inside me. It is the first sensation, other than pain, that I have had since Sabby's parting and it feels like a violation, an intrusion and an insult. How can she shed a tear for Sabby when her death has ripped my soul from me? I would lash out, I would strike her if I could remember how to coordinate my body. Instead I close my eyes.

She finishes packing my wound, brushes my hair.

'I have always loved your hair and I have always wanted to dress it,' she says. 'There, as handsome as ever.' She kisses my head.

Still I do not respond but I feel her warmth begin to reach me. She wraps me in a blanket and sits down next to me. She has brought a rich pottage, still warm in its clay pot, and wine. She brings the tankard up to my lips and I open my eyes, but I do not understand the value of sustenance. But she holds the wine to my lips and it wets my tongue. Yet I cannot swallow, and it runs down my cheeks.

'No wine, I should have brought ale,' she says, wiping up the wine. She offers me pottage and I take a mouthful, but I cannot chew and it sits there, a foreign body on my tongue. I try to swallow but nearly choke; again, she wipes up the mess.

'It is here for when you can,' she says.

She places a kirtle and linens by the food. 'I can't make you wear these,' she says. 'It's all they would let me bring,' and she smiles. 'You will look like a Mummer, will you not?' I wish I could smile too. She dabs lavender oil on my temples, a little in my hair. 'I leave this too. When you decide to return it will be a comfort.'

We sit then for a while. I close my eyes, but I can feel her gaze on me and I cannot bear it, cannot receive her love. Cannot accept her kindness when I am so shamed. My promises have failed us both. I hear her tears.

'Raven, where are you? What has become of the courageous hot head Raven that I love… You must fight. Your grandmother, she would expect it. If you cannot do it for me then fight, fight for her, for Sabby.'

I look at her square in the eyes with fury. Can she not see it is because of me that they have lost their lives? It is their association with me that has lost them everything. For the first time in three days I manage to move as I turn my back on her.

'What's this? You turn your back on me? Raven, this is the last time I shall see you. The last time afore the gallows. You must do something. You must, you have power, you must use it, please.' But her pleading is lost in the sound of the keys turning and the guard approaching. I hear her dry her tears, try to compose herself to avoid revealing herself. I drift into unconsciousness with her pleas echoing though the empty chamber I have become.

The next time I surface moonlight streams through the bars. I feel the warmth of the blanket and the cushion of straw. Despite myself thirst gnaws at me and I reach for the wine, gulping it down till it is all gone. I feel I have betrayed my pain but the wine softness everything. I am able to move and curl up now into a tight, comforting ball under the blankets and sink into the refuge of emptiness.

The next time I feel the jolt of leather on my skin. I recoil as much as I can and open my eyes. Ben's boot has kicked my side. I follow with my eyes the length of his body and meet the stupid smirk on his face.

'Is it conscious?' asks a plum, well-spoken, older voice.

'It is now,' replies Ben. I move the smallest amount, so I may take in the room, Stephen, the cardinal and Lady Bamford. I show no signs of recognition, simply close my eyes and hope the emptiness will claim me again. Let them come, let them stare at the freak, I care not.

'It is good work, Stephen, this shall be an example to all who do not follow the edict of Rome.'

'My lord,' says Stephen and follows as the cardinal sweeps away, leaving Lady Bamford behind.

At the door the cardinal stops; he does not turn.

'Lady Bamford, you delay?' he asks.

'Cardinal, I thought some prayers for the sinner would not be out of place,' she replies.

'You are indeed a woman of virtue whose generosity far exceeds its calling.' He turns to look at her, his gold ring catching the light and filling the room with a passing moment of golden glow. It feels more warning than comfort.

'Thank you, my lord, I am but a humble servant of the Almighty,' she says and bows her head just enough.

'Very well, but dally not, it has been a long journey and Stephen has spent considerable attention on this evening's festivities.'

'My lord,' she says and this time curtsies as he turns and sweeps away.

She waits till the door is shut and they have all left. Irrespective of the muck and straw, she kneels down next to me.

'I have brought your favourite,' she says and reaches inside her gown and pulls out a linen. She unwraps it to reveal a marchpane heart. The sweet smell reaches inside me, it jolts a memory but not enough. I simply stare at her. What does she want, to gloat at the depraved creature? Offer prayers to save me from a being that does not exist. She puts down the marchpane.

'For later,' she says, as if we are on a picnic. I would roll away, but I am still covered in bruises and naked. I shall not wear a dress.

She sighs and sits back on her heels.

'Raven, you must try. You must rise. This will not do, this being in pain.' With that I cannot help but meet her eyes. Who is she to say anything? What does she know of pain?

'Raven, you have the power. It is easy for you to be free. They are waiting, all is in place, so you must try.' Does she think I will shift when it is my gift that has cost the lives of so many? I shall not shift again. It is best that I die and the abomination that I am is lost forever.

'Raven, you have the strength. Just call upon your namesake and your spirit will be renewed.' I roll over, despite the pain. When shall she leave and take her prattle with her.

'Do you think your grandmother would want this?' she says, vexed. I turn back and stare at her, the blanket falls from me as I sit up, but I care little; everything has been stripped from me so why hide my flesh?

'Your grandmother raised a strong spirit, moulded a brave, courageous being. It is not their actions that shame you but this surrender. It is that that betrays your grandmother.' I cannot help it, my hand is raised, but she catches it before it hits her face. We stare at each other.

'I will go as far as needs be to save you,' she says, and I open my mouth for the first time since that night.

'Guard,' I shout but my lips and mouth are dry, almost stuck shut. I call again 'Guards.' This time loud enough. She drops my hand.

'Do not do this, Raven. It serves no one,' she says but the keys rattle and turn in the door. 'If you cannot do this for yourself then do it for your mother,' and the guard is in the room.

She crosses herself. 'May you repent, may you grow angel's wings, may you travel in peace.' She crosses herself and me.

She is helped to her feet by the guard and ushered from the room. My mother who abandoned me. Who chose wealth above her daughter. My mother who disowned her mistake. Why would I do anything for her? What does she know of her? I quickly retrace our meeting, the face at the window, the preferential treatment, and suddenly our twilight conversation in the garden makes a new sense, as do the new clothes. These are the actions of a mother, of my mother.

If I had imagined meeting my mother, and it is not a place I have visited often, this was not the reunion of my fancies. I had expected repentance, expected to be asked for forgiveness, expected recognition, that we would recognise each other. Yet there has been nothing. She has let me sup at her table and not felt the need to tell me. I laugh inside at her audacity. That she thinks she can present on the eve of my death and entreat me to action. What kind of fool is she?

I burrow deep under the blanket, convinced more than ever that the executioner's task is just. I find comfort in knowing that the end is but a few short hours away and I shall be released from the pain that has become my existence. Mary shall be better off, free to find a love that does not need to hide its face. Free to find the independence she craves. The "society" will find a new toy to do its bidding. The men that seek to claim the gifts of the earth for their own will have removed this contrary evidence and my mother lost all right to me, all privileges, when she cast me out, no matter her explanation. It is clear my death is the best solution for all. For I do not wish to live on the earth when there is no space for me. I fall into a deep, restful sleep, happy with my reasoning.

Yet it is not long before my dreams become a tangle of memory. Images flash and I cannot tell if they are remembrances of the future or of the past. Voices call to me in all manner of tone and entreaty, but I do not respond, cannot respond. I seek the still emptiness of the past few days, call for its numbness but it does not come.

Then I sense her, and it is more than I can bear. I sense Sabby and I feel my soul turn from my body all over again. Everything else ceases; there are no memories, no voices, no past and no future, just this singular place of pain and it engulfs me. I sink once more to its depths. If her spirit sought to soothe, it has been mistaken. I sit staring into nothingness, suspended as the light changes from light to dark to light again.

Chapter Thirty-Fve

I can hear the hammer falling as they erect the gallows, hear the tradesmen set up their stalls, hear the people as they begin to gather. The early arrivals set upon a stage side stance. There is merriment and jolity. Their lives will continue past this day whilst mine shall not. I cannot quite comprehend my infinity and somehow in my being is a belief in tomorrow. Yet I am still far away, observing all from a distance but I do not know where this distance is. I have lost all connection to feelings and the passions that have so consumed me have fallen into nothingness. Not resolved just free floating. I await my death with a certain sense of peace and calm. I think myself to have reached acceptance.

A good crowd has gathered by the time Ben and two guards burst into the room.

'Mistress Raven, you are not dressed,' says Ben.

I look at the linens and kirtle. They cannot send me to my death in these. I look at him and shrug. He signals to the guards, one grabs hold of me, forces me to my feet. I barely resist. The other guard takes hold of the linen, prepares to pass it over my head. I think I shall be sanguine, I think I shall not care what cloth is on my back. I think I am beyond all this but when the smock approaches I find I writhe, I squirm, I resist. The guard cannot hold me, and I flee to another corner of the cell. It is the most I have moved for the past five days and I am somewhat surprised to find I can.

The guards try again. Again I escape their grasp. Ben calls for more guards, three more join. I wriggle and squirm, become a dead weight. Soon I am biting and howling, a rabid, caged beast pursued by men of reason. They become aggrieved, they become scared, they become exasperated. More men are called. I have lost all sense. I know not why I am here, why I fight so, for what I am resisting. It is as if I am repelled by the cloth and have no choice in my actions.

Time is pressing, the crowd outside at once restless, at once their appetites piqued by the screams that come from my cell. I had planned to be sanguine, resigned and dignified. In the end it takes twelve full grown men to force me into the smock and kirtle. By the time they have finished I am exhausted and empty, I can hardly stand, and my body is awash with a fresh set of wounds and bruises. I have lost all sensation in my shoulder. I stand a shell of bones supporting a frock. Ben approaches, smiles at me and ties a ribbon in my hair and they laugh till they can hardly stand. He is the first to compose himself and walks to the door as the executioner's bell tolls.

I am marched through the castle and into the square. The roads are lined with people. They spit at me, jeer and laugh. Yet still everything is far away, and I comfort myself with the knowledge it will all soon be over. I stumble and trip, so unused to wearing a skirt I do not know how to move in it. My death shall be ridiculous, and I am glad my grandmother is not here to see it. I stumble up the steps to the platform. The guards hand me over to the executioner, their touch tender by comparison.

They stand me next to Philip and from deep within me is a stirring, a remembrance of feeling. My head is bowed but I turn towards him and he towards me. With all I have I try to say sorry with my eyes, to plead for his forgiveness. Yet I see the same look in his eyes and a sense of release spreads through my being. I feel my eyes melt as I watch his do the same and I know all is resolved between us.

Then they take him to his noose. With my head bowed I can only just make out the progress, but I sense the noose around his neck. There is a pause whilst the executioner asks forgiveness and Philip grants it. The crowd take up their thirsty chatter. Then silence and I am close enough to hear the bones snap in his neck and his last breath escape.

A soft breeze circles round the square, his spirit leaving his body. I feel a sense of joy and optimism, in moments I too shall be so free. It is as if I am awake for the first time since that night. I lift my head with certainty; in seconds I shall escape, be free of this world. They think they do me harm when in truth they set me free. The executioner approaches.

'Do you have any last words?' he asks.

I look round the crowd, slowly taking my time, searching for faces I know. The butcher stands by his shop, his expression a mix of shame and pain. Astral hides in the shadows, shielding his eyes from mine. Master Lovell has a front side spot and nervously eats pie and gulps ale. I find Mary buried amongst the crowd, tears flowing freely down her cheeks. I want to reach out to her, to reassure her, explain my acceptance, to share our love one last time with a smile, but I cannot, I cannot risk her life too. For a fleeting moment our eyes meet, and the love speaks. Then it is gone, for longer would rouse suspicion. Yet it gives me courage. The sun catches the Merkaba and it is as if I am held by Grace's and Mother Gray's embrace. I look into the executioner's eyes and shake my head.

'You are forgiven,' I say and clasp his hand.

Then I turn and walk towards my rope in honour of the girl that introduced me to the gallows back in the square just weeks ago. The crowd are uncertain, then they take my courage as an affront, a challenge to the proceedings and the shouts and jeers commence with such venom it would be hard to conceive of what I could have done to warrant such abuse.

The air is still, it is a warm, mild, cloudy day and as I look up to take one last look around me of the earth, I see the boy and his hawk from the bridge perched high above the crowd on one of the buildings. They stand when they see I have seen them. Silently taking up position is every raven, from miles around, perched on roofs and chimneys, unseen and unnoticed by the crowd. There is a stirring inside me, of something welling, brewing from the depths of my being. Something powerful is surging through me as the executioner places the noose around my neck and I hear her, her cries reach me through the crowd. I look - there is a slither of space between buildings and sitting proud and sure on the rubble of Grace's house is Sabby.

Then it explodes inside me. A volcano of remembrance erupts throughout my being as I remember who I am. As the wood is pulled from underneath me I feel my raven wings spread wide and sure. The contested clothes fall from me as I rise up above the crowd and as I rise, the ravens descend. They dive at the crowd, sweeping and attacking. Chaos ensues as a black cloud of raven conspiracy fills the air. The crowd scream and scatter, trampling those who fall, scrambling over anyone or anything in the way. I circle high above, enjoying the spectacle yet ready in case Mary should be in danger, but she is saved by the butcher who pulls her out of the sway of the crowd and into his shop.

Sabby has run from the rubble and the crowd and as she reaches the edge of the town I swoop down and join her. Our eyes meet, and I see myself reflected in hers and I know I have returned. I rise up into the sky, and whilst the ravens have their fun with the people of the town, we speed away into the distance together. The words of the recluse's poem, now lost in the destruction of my grandmother's home, echoing in my mind:

Sister so you seek what
Has always been within.

Rachel McJury

Rachel has worked for many years within the arts environment initiating, leading and managing a wide range of projects but with specific experience of cross-artform events that have brought together poetry, dance, theatre, music and film. To date, she has written, directed and produced ten theatre and musical productions. She has performed her poetry at a variety of locations across Britain and Europe from Brighton to Dundee to Dublin. Her poems and short stories have been published in: Chameleon, Nomad, Cutting Teeth, Citizen 32, Poetry Scotland, The Gay Read, Hidden City, Mookychick and her collection of poetry *Laughin' Lesbians Vol 1*. In 2006 she received the Jackie Forster Memorial Pride Award for outstanding contribution to culture in Scotland.

Printed in Great Britain
by Amazon

46099604R00136